NOTHING
IMPORTANT
HAPPENED
TODAY

By

Mark Davies

ISBN-13: 978-1540647887
ISBN-10: 1540647889

DEDICATION

To Joan.

CONTENTS

ACKNOWLEDGMENTS

Thank you to Bob Ashwood for all his insane encouragement. And to Colin Nimick, Matt Williams and Ross Keenleyside for all their sane encouragement.

1

Jack was bored. He wished he had been asleep when the alarm clock had started whining at him, but he wasn't. He'd been up for hours. Wandering around the flat. Reading a book. Making himself a sandwich. Anything to while away the empty sleepless hours before he had to go to work.

Neep, neep, neep, neep, neep, neep, neep.

The noise chipped away at his mind like a pick on packed ice. Slowly he was being drawn back to reality. All he could think was that the clock was being rude. He wasn't asleep but that wasn't the point, it was interrupting his peace and quiet.

Neep, neep, neep, neep, neep, neep, neep.

Phones were the same. They rang and demanded to be answered. You couldn't ignore them. You had to respond even if it meant throwing the damn thing against the wall then telling your insurance company 'you dropped it'.

Neep, neep, neep, neep, neep, neep, neep.

The sound continued, loosening the cobbles under his daydream and tilting him closer to reality. This was the sound that heralded the beginning of his day. A cacophony that seeped through the wax in his ears and played a bongo solo on his ear drums

Neep-neep, neep-neep, neep-neep neep-neep.

The alarm clock cried like a baby in its crib. Demanding attention and not getting it. This really wasn't on. If no one saw to it soon it would have to take things to the next level - and no one wanted that.

Neep-neep, neep-neep, neep-neep neep-neep.

Jack stood up bleary-eyed. His Sunday night-Monday morning insomnia was the worst of all his nights and left him incapable of reason. He could have stayed in bed and stared at the Artex ceiling but that would depress him more. He had to get up and do something, anything. Even if it was just doing laps of the flat.

Somewhere after his 20th lap he'd sat in the lounge and just stared at the television. It wasn't even on but there he was staring at it expecting it to entertain him. Or allow him to nod off again for a few precious minutes.

NEEP-NEEP- NEEP-NEEP- NEEP-NEEP- NEEP-NEEP- NEEP-NEEP.

The alarm clock, not one to be ignored, decided to escalate its assault. Jack finally spurred into action shuffled into the bedroom. In an almost fit-like lunge of desperation he managed to locate the alarm and slam it off with the palm of his hand.

On the weekends when this infernal device decided to play its tricks, he had always contemplated hitting the 'snooze' button. But that wasn't the way he was made. Going through the rigmarole of waking up again when his nerves were frayed already, was not something he wanted to experience.

Besides, he always felt anxious about the time limit of the 'snooze'. He'd always worry. No, he was awake. Or as awake as any human being could be at 6:30 am on a Monday morning after a night running around the walls. If he had built enough speed he was sure that he could perform a 'Wall of Death' without the motorbike.

Jack placed the now silent alarm clock back on the side-table and stared at it, grumpily. Why had he bought an alarm clock that was so annoying? Wouldn't he prefer one that gently elevated the levels of light so that he woke slowly and naturally rather than one that sounded like someone was strangling a fox? No, that wouldn't work. A gentle awakening wouldn't shock him out of sleep as well as the rude awakening that his insistent clock did.

Truth be told, he'd tried a number of clocks before he settled on the fox-strangler. The first one you could plug in and wake you with either radio or a CD. Unfortunately, a power cut in the middle of the night had wiped its settings. For some reason the battery backup had failed as well, so when the power came back on it just flashed '12:00' back at him.

By the time he'd struggled to a reasonable conscious state it was 10:15 by his watch and panic stations for the next hour as he worried himself to work.

The second clock therefore had to be battery operated. He'd taken a shine to one in *Robert Dyas*. This one looked like an alarm clock. Big white face, ornate hands and two bells standing proud on the top with a small hammer between them. It even ticked like a clock; an almost hypnotic gentle clunking of cogs and whatnots somewhere inside that gave the impression of clockmakers toiling away to create a real timepiece.

Romantic notions flew out the window the next morning when the hands hit 6:30 am. Rather than a musical chiming of bells, a machine gun-like rattle filled the room. Jack jumped out of bed and grabbed the offending article but had forgotten how to turn it off. For the next 10 seconds he'd wrestled with the clock before remembering the 'off' switch was on the back. After that, the silence was palpable.

His first reaction was to throw the damn thing in the recycling bin. But which bin should it go in? He had so many different bags of different kinds of rubbish now that his kitchen resembled a recycling plant. Instead, he had put the clock in the loft. Out of sight with the rest of the stuff he didn't know what to do with.

Finally, he'd settled on the *'Neeping'* thing. Battery operated. Small. He could take it anywhere with him without taking up too much space. And, more to the point, it was less frightening than any other alarm he'd ever had. It was annoying though. He'd reasoned that anything that wakes you is annoying. Even if a naked woman purring erotically woke him he was certain that it would make him grumpy.

Jack's brain rebooted slowly as he began to really wake up. For the last few hours he had been doing the walk of the dead. Not asleep and not awake. He'd been a shell of a man. Nothing had felt real until the alarm clock had started to make it real.

Fingers of realisation began to stretch their way through the lump of grey matter in his head. His particular re-boot sequence wasn't a pretty one. He went through denial, anger, bargaining, depression and finally acceptance of who he was. Each stage brought with it vast files of memories, some complete, some half-remembered and some unexplored for years - rarely did he open these in case an embarrassing memory floated to the front of his mind and made him wince.

Mentally whole, he surveyed his domain. By the bed was a battered table where an equally battered and dog-eared Post-It Note desperately clung to the side with all its might. Which really wasn't all that strong to begin with.

'Don't worry, it's just the drugs', was written on the Post-it in his own fair hand. Great. That made it all better.

Full realisation hit him in the stomach like a punch from a mailed hand: the one thing that had turned his life upside down. All the memories he didn't want to remember crashed into his brain. Each one slapped him around the face and walked away having accomplished their demeaning task.

Desperate for distraction, he looked around the room for some more clues to his existence and found nothing much. How bland must he be?

It struck him how plain his bedroom was. White walls. White ceiling. White-ish, beigey sort of carpet. White sheets. Even the duvet cover was white: Egyptian cotton no less.

This sea of white was broken up by a wooden bed and a wooden chest of drawers. He'd hung up guitars instead of pictures or paintings; a white Fender telecaster and a white Fender Stratocaster both with rosewood necks, hung majestically on the walls. People often asked why he did this - it was a little strange after all. He explained that he liked guitars, so why shouldn't he enjoy looking at them when he wasn't playing them? After all, to his eyes they were works of art.

At the end of the room, directly across from the foot of the bed, stood the wardrobe. A built-in wardrobe. Jack wondered what possessed a man (or woman) to make such a thing a permanent structure. It was white or had been at one stage of its miserable life, which sort of fitted with the décor, but it had a gold trim on the doors and drawers. Somehow it didn't work. Every time Jack looked in its direction he wanted to destroy it. To be fair it housed his clothes and what-nots perfectly. But that gold trim just offended him. He wanted to remove the doors of wardrobes and drawers and replace them with something more tolerable. But that didn't solve the other problem. There was just too much wardrobe for one man of his limited elegance. Something smaller maybe? Something more natural-looking would be ideal.

As it was, this wall of white and gold took up too much of the room for his liking. If he could knock it out and replace it with one of those wardrobes with a chest of drawers underneath he would have so much more room to play with. There would be room for his bench press. Or put his exercise bike in the bedroom. Work off some excess energy and frustration that way. Or he could move his bike into the bedroom instead of hanging it up in the hallway where there was precious little space as it was. But then…STOP!

He was doing it again. Getting himself wound up about nothing. His brain had rebooted, now it was time to slow it down before it set him off redecorating the room, rewiring the light fixtures and changing the curtain poles.

He lay on the bedroom floor and poked his feet under the bed. The first sit-up was always the worst. His body cracked and creaked. The second was easier, the third not bad, and then he drifted into a rhythm of movement and breathing that helped him through his routine.

180 sit-ups later he shifted into press-up position. The arms were always worse. He would have thought after the sit-ups the arms would have fresh blood to feed them and were ready for their morning onslaught. Again he struggled and again he managed to push through his body's sluggish and lazy behaviour. 180 press-ups later he let himself fall to the floor in a heap.

"Why do you do this to yourself?" he asked, his voice muffled by the carpet fibres that were now in his mouth. It wasn't as if he was training for a marathon or trying to stay fit for anyone special. There was Marianna but she wasn't special. She had a fantastic body. Aesthetically pleasing. But she was just someone he was seeing. Dating. Having sex with now and then. She wasn't even all that interested in him.

He stood up and walked down the hallway and into the living room. A quick left turn and he sat at his desk. He emptied the contents of Monday morning's pill tray into his hand and tipped them into his mouth. Opening the half-empty bottle of water on his desk he washed the anti-depressants, Vitamin B complex and chlorella and spirulina down. He should have put the bottle of water in the fridge last night but couldn't be arsed. Now it was probably crawling with bacteria, which had just found a lovely warm stomach in which to replicate. Hopefully, his stomach acid would kill them – it didn't seem to do him any other favours these days.

He then took a long draught of the water. He'd read somewhere that during the night your internal organs had been working overtime to clear the body of its detritus, putting in more clean water would help flush out the toxins and hopefully clean out anything that was thinking about sticking to the pipes.

He was just about to go into the kitchen to turn on the kettle when he heard it click off. Funny, he didn't remember going in to turn it on! Walking in he saw steam billowing out of the spout. He took a clean cup threw in a red tea bag and poured the water over it. How come he'd forgotten that he'd turned the kettle on? Was it one of those automatic reflex things? Muscle memory? Trouble was, he couldn't remember going into the kitchen at all. But he must have done. Shrugging his shoulders, he walked back to his desk and sipped at the red tea.

This was the bubble; the centre of operations. The remote controls were all lined up like soldiers eager to do his bidding. He stabbed at the TV remote and the small flat screen slowly blinked into life. He'd considered getting one of those mammoth things that he could hang on the wall but decided against it on the grounds that he would rather hang guitars there instead. He leant back and allowed BBC News to fill his head with the gobbets of information he would need to engage people in conversation today. Korea and Russia were at loggerheads again. Trouble brewing as always from that little pocket of insanity. He rolled the world around in his head. Then rolled those words around in his head, thinking how clever he was to come up with such a phrase.

After his 'cuppa' it was time for the inevitable trip to the bathroom. He stood in front of the toilet and let himself relax then stared into the face reflected in the mirror. The positioning of this mirror had always bothered him. Why would anyone put a mirror there? So men could watch themselves as they pissed? He thought, probably not for the first time, that he should remove the mirror but it was right next to the bathroom sink – handy if you were having a shit and were throwing up at the same time – so removing it would mean shaving would be problem. In all likelihood he would probably slash his own throat and die in a pool of shaving foam, and blood and the only way anyone would know was when the foamy blood seeped through the ceiling of the flat downstairs.

In the end he decided to leave the bathroom mirror where it was. It wasn't doing anyone any harm and if he started to remove things he would replace it with one of those mirrored medicine cabinets and that would cost money and take time and he would probably end up becoming frustrated when the do-it-yourself turned into a fiasco-in-the-making.

Mentally, he slapped himself on the wrist again. He was never satisfied. Everything could change but why did it have to? Besides, if he changed absolutely everything in his flat and sat down to survey his handiwork, then what would he do? He'd probably change something else and something else ad infinitum. Wouldn't it just be easier to move somewhere else? Somewhere nicer.

This time he didn't just mentally slap his own wrist he threw himself mentally to the floor and started pummelling himself about the face and neck while repeating the phrase, "You do not change shit for no good reason! You do not change shit for no good reason!"

He stared into the bathroom mirror. Squeezed some shaving foam and coated his cheeks and his head, then continued to shave himself smooth. Overnight the bristles on his cheek and scalp had decided it was safe to come out and had set up camp on the surface of his skin.

Every night they did this and it was his task to remove the invading forces before they gained a permanent foothold and overtook his face and smothered him. The goatee had already become permanent face furniture - or was it a Van Dyke he could never remember - the thing had exploded out of his chin and lip and now dangled like an overgrown hairbrush. He called it his 'ZZ Top' beard but it was far less impressive.

He'd shaved his head not because he was going bald. He didn't mind that idea. No, he removed his hair because he had gone prematurely grey. His worrying mind had sucked all the colour out of his hair and made him look more ancient than he was. The first time he took the razor to his pate, he thought he would feel self-conscious but when confronted with this strange, smooth person he actually liked the effect.

He saved money on shampoo but the cost of his razors went up. Until he bought the cut-throat. His first attempt at shaving was a frightening experience. He didn't trust his hand not to suddenly lose control and go on a murder spree about his face. It took a while to master the lethally sharp and unleashed blade but after a little time he was shwooshing it over his face like a samurai warrior deftly whittling his enemies to their grave.

He shaved over his head and around the beard leaving as many surfaces as smooth as possible. Then he stopped, he drew the line at 'manscaping'. He'd shaved 'down there' once before and the itching as it grew back was more annoying than toothache and far more embarrassing if you tried to attend to its irritations on public transport.

When he was finished with his face and head he undressed and climbed into the shower hearing his knees pop. Turning on the water he realised his next mistake. Yes, the water was set at the right temperature but it took a few seconds to get up to that temperature. A bolt of cold water hit him square on the chest and he jumped. There were no half-awake thoughts now, his eyes dinged open and he coughed a small expletive to the shower head.

Then everything went warm and fuzzy as the heat from the water massaged his poor aching body. If only he could stay in here all day. He couldn't of course, so he reached for the unscented 'kind to the skin' soap and got to work erasing the night's grime from his body.

2

Now he was disbelieving the bed. Not that disbelieving the bed was part of his normal morning routine in any way, the fact was, it was tidy. The duvet had been pulled taut, the pillows plumped, the fitted sheet had been battered back into shape. And, for the life of him, he couldn't remember doing any of it.

Normally his nocturnal twistings and turnings would turn the duvet into a twiglet, the bottom sheet would be as crumpled as a piece of bark and the pillows, if they were on the bed at all, looked as if someone had shot a rubber bullet into them. But no, everything was tidy. Jack even checked to see if the t-shirt he wore for bed was somehow screwed up and placed in a knot under the pillow. Nope, even that had been folded neatly. Well, as neatly as a single man could manage. Women had far more rigorous standards when it came to bed neatness. If you couldn't bounce a £1 coin off the taut bed sheet then it would have to be done again. The duvet had to be similarly crease-free and the pillows would have to be

13

as smooth as two giant marshmallows. This was close but not up to those standards.

'Elves,' he thought to himself. *'I'm infested with benevolent elves.'* Of course, there was no such thing. He knew he had done it. In his heart of hearts, he knew there was no other explanation. At some point he had walked back in, tidied everything up and then got in the shower. So why had it not registered. Was his poor, muddled mind now blocking out all the tedious tasks?

Could it be elves? Or Elvis? Is Elvis a singular of elves? His brain was racing again. It needed something to concentrate on or this constant stream of consciousness bleating would take over and before you know it he would be sitting in the corner drooling and singing Elves Presley's 40 Greatest Hits.

'Music.'

'Put some music on,' he thought, and that would occupy his mind so he could get ready for work before his brain ambushed him again. Turning on the CD player, he heard the slight whirr as the player searched for the first track. 'Reading' flashed up on the screen in a digitally sort of type that really could be so much better given today's advances in technology.

'No, not Reading,' he said out loud, 'I live in London.' Ba–dum tish went the imaginary drummer in his head as he pressed play. He composed himself, stood back, closed his eyes and pretended to start conducting as the mathematical metal sound of 'Animals as Leaders' swirled and juddered out of the speakers.

His mind started following the contours of the music, speeding and slowing as the music embraced him. Despite its frenetic mix of time signatures, it relaxed him. It seemed to be attuned to his mind's pulse and that seemed to calm the erratic firing of his neurons.

Strangely enough, some nights he put calm and serene music on to listen to while he waited for sleep and found that it agitated him.

No music at all and his brain would turn into a racehorse during the steeplechase; thundering along then leaping over explosions of thought.

Put on some heavy rock and he would relax. It was very strange. The next time he went to see his psychiatrist he would have to mention this to her. See what 'take' she had on that.

Chances are she would say having any music on while you were in bed made your mind too active. But what if you were one of those freaks that actually drop off to the sound of Iron Maiden playing the *Trooper* at breakneck pace?

Would you stop someone doing something beneficial for them just because it doesn't fit in with what you think is right? He was of the mind, such that it was, that anything that helped him reach the land of slumber was worth it.

For many years he had explored the many merits of alcohol to help him drift into a quiet repose. Drifting off was no longer a problem. Staying in there was impossible. It wasn't just the dehydration that sent him scuttling to the kitchen for a pint of water, the fact that he needed to pee at the same time was an anomaly his drunken brain couldn't quite fathom.

There he was at 2 o'clock in the morning, standing in the bathroom with the palm of the hand pressed against the wall, mouth like the Gobi Desert with Niagara Falls dropping out of him. At that time, all he wanted to do was sleep and his body wanted to urinate. So it was no surprise that he would return to the bathroom in the morning to a toilet mat that was a little damp underfoot.

Yes, the drink had helped him get to sleep, or beat him unconscious, as the case may be.

Before that he had tried exercise; cycling, running, swimming, anything to tire him out and make sure by the time it was bedtime he was thoroughly knackered.

Trouble was, he was up and down all night getting water, raiding the fridge, and in the morning he felt as though he had been in an accident.

There just wasn't any answer. He tried all the over the counter medicines and all the herbal stuff and he just wasn't drifting off. Once again his mind was trying to kill him, this time through sleep deprivation.

If anyone wanted to torture him or disorient him enough so that he would spill the secrets of the nation to terrorists, all they had to do was give him a cup of coffee before bedtime and then give him a problem to solve. By morning he would be giving away the secret locations of Britain's nuclear arsenal and every secret agent's name and address around the world.

Once, he had heard about someone being put into a chemically-induced coma for medical reasons. Wouldn't it be great if for one week he could be put out and then re-awakened later just so he could catch up on some sleep?

Music beat all of the pills and potions, exercises and stretchings for the most reliable method to get him to sleep and to keep him there.

The only trouble was, music stops; there are brief moments of quiet between the songs. If the stop was for a prolonged period his mind would ask, *What happened to the music?'* and would force him to wake up, get up and put something else on.

If he could time it right, the music would stop or soften while he was in a deep sleep and his mind wouldn't notice. Leaving him to rest for his regulation 7 hours.

Weekends were a different kettle of herbal tea bags altogether. If he managed 3 or 4 hours, that was okay. At 7 in the morning he would have a little breakfast, take his morning pills, and then it was lights out until lunchtime. Or until one of the neighbours buzzed him and dropped a parcel round that had gone to the wrong address.

On more than one occasion his Saturday morning lie-in had been ruined because of the postman. If it wasn't the fact that he had received a 'whilst you were out' message during the week that told him he had to collect an item of post – and the only time he could collect it was 7:00 am to 12 Noon at the local business centre, it was the fact that the postman for the flats occasionally miss-read the addresses.

His post had invariably landed on the doormat of someone who wasn't supposed to receive it. It was a regular occurrence and not isolated to his own mail.

There seemed to be a communal moment every morning where everyone crossed in the parking lot trying to deliver the right mail to the right door. It was the morning ballet of the miss-posted letter.

But, because most people were out at the time trying to deliver the right mail to the right door, they usually found that most people were out and couldn't get into the appropriate building. Which meant they would have to return later on.

This didn't encourage social harmony. Most people within this microcosm of habitation had already endured previous dealings with their neighbours and some were antagonistic.

The result? More upset, and more acrimonious behaviour. Letters wouldn't be pushed helpfully through doors, they would be crammed through in a fit of pique. Parcels, rather than propped up delicately against doorways would be flung haphazardly against entrances usually leaving scratches in paintwork and crumpling package corners – the contents shaken as if they had been handled by a British nanny looking after an American family's baby.

Sleep patterns and music aside, he'd started to calm himself. The bed was made, he was shitted, showered and shaved and the only thing left to do was dress himself.

Like most single men, he wasn't too concerned about his dress-sense. His job meant that he could put on jeans, a t-shirt, some clean trainers and cover himself in a coat of varying thickness, depending on weather, and he was good to go.

His entire wardrobe (and chest of drawers) were governed by the idea of ease: black t-shirts with varying designs, blue jeans, black socks and black trainers.

Some socks were a little charcoal grey after years of use and repair, some t-shirts were a little tighter around the arms and chest after his more recent training exercise and some jeans were worn in different ways after the way his body had changed over the last few years.

Despite these small, irrelevant changes, everything was much the same as it was for the last 20 years. Bob Marley t-shirts, Clash t-shirts, Motorhead t-shirts, were always mixed with jeans and trainers.

The only thing that had changed drastically was his jacket. He now wore a North Face jacket much like every other middle-aged Londoner.

It was just one small concession to his middle-age. Out goes the leather jacket, in comes the North Face.

The one big decision today was, *'what t-shirt should I wear to complete this ensemble?'*

Anything with a blatant logo seemed a little crass. Why show a picture of Bob Marley and then have the name 'Bob Marley' emblazoned above or below it in words? It just didn't compute. His favourite t-shirts were ones that just had a picture. His favourite was his Clash t-shirt. It didn't have the name 'The Clash' ripped across it in typefaces galore. It just had the picture from the cover of London Calling. Simple, beautiful and black and white. Economical in style and powerful in execution.

Today, he would have to be satisfied with his Bring Me The Horizon t-shirt from the cover of *Sempiternal*; a black t-shirt with a gold intricate circular design. Anyone who knew the album would know the t-shirt, anyone who didn't, well that was their problem.

He'd always remembered that if you wanted to advertise something on your chest make sure it was yourself, but seeing as how he didn't have a band and putting his own name on his chest felt arrogant, he decided to leave it until he had something better to advertise.

Since he had Bring Me The Horizon on his chest what better choice of music to play after 'Animals as Leaders' was *'Sempiternal'*? It was one of those CDs that lived in his most played pile, so it was easy to find.

Popping it into the CD player he did his 'Reading' joke again and stood back to ready himself for the heavy onslaught of drums and guitars. It arrived and he gave the room a heavy metal salute. His 'most played' pile looked at him forlornly. They'd had their turn, he thought. But every time he listened to a CD from here he glanced at the titles and wanted to play them all at once. It was impossible of course. Some days he just stared at the pile immobile unable to make a decision.

Or he would start one CD playing, stop it, then put another in the player. Sometimes he'd be three CDs down before he stopped himself.

The rest of his CD collection covered an entire wall of his bedroom. Every shelf was rammed with

CDs of every musical style, and shape. Some were immediately recognisable from a distance; PIL's *'Metal Box'* stood out like a sore thumb and the Pet Shop Boys' *'Very'* glowed fluorescent orange amidst the white and black. Collections stood out as well. Iron Maiden's albums stood out because the edges created an evil picture of Eddie the head from the illustration on the front cover of the first album.

Apart from his 'favourites' the CDs were filed in alphabetical order with a few exceptions. His Beatles collection, for example, had all the Beatles albums but also the solo albums of John Lennon, George Harrison and Ringo Starr. Paul McCartney's efforts with Wings were under 'M' – he just couldn't bring himself to put Paul McCartney back with the Beatles for any reason.

It may be the fact that after John Lennon's death, Paul McCartney contested the order of song writing credits on their songs or it just may have been the fact that without Lennon, McCartney had written *'The Frog Chorus'*. Either way Mr McCartney was forever banished to his own section of Jack's CD collection.

Harsh it may be, but that is not to take anything away from Mr McCartney. The only reason he had got into the Beatles in the first place was because he had heard Wings' *'Band on the Run'* and wanted to know more about the group and whatever else they had been involved in. McCartney may have started Jack's enthusiasm for music, but *'The Frog Chorus'* had certainly ended his appreciation of Paul McCartney.

With this little thought rebounding around his brain, he pulled on the t-shirt, slipped on his North Face jacket and popped his *Kindle Fire* into his pocket.

He took the big *Sony* earphones and put them over his head. He hit his 'favourites' collection on Spotify then hit 'shuffle'. Before he opened the door to his flat, the music was smashing into both sides of his skull attempting to meet in the middle.

As always he gave an appreciative glance to the Motorhead poster on the back of the door. The warpig logo sat in the middle but underneath in Germanic type were the words 'The World is Yours'. He thought about it for a few seconds. He thought about 'the meek shall inherit the earth' and 'life's what you make it' sort of statements.

'Bollocks it is,' he said as he opened the door and allowed it to slam shut behind him.

3

On the landing he locked the door and put his keys away. He patted his pockets to make sure he had all his accessories; *Kindle Fire*, phone, wallet, *Oyster* card, security pass for work. Everything appeared to be in place, so he set off.

He was only 3 steps down the stairs when a thought struck him. *'Have I left anything on that I shouldn't?'* He was instantly paralysed; one foot on the 3rd step, the other firmly planted on the 2nd. Growling to himself he searched his memory banks. Telly off and unplugged, cooker off and turned off at the wall. Boiler off. Stereo? Doesn't really matter, he supposed, the CD hadn't finished and was still plugged in at the wall.

Ah but what about the display burning through electricity like wildfire? As a kid he'd watched the electric meter at home. The disc on the inside always seemed to be travelling like a buzz saw. He'd turned things off around the house until he'd got it down to a reasonable speed, which was everything except the fridge and the freezer, but even then it was still travelling at some speed.

His dad was always moaning about bills, electric, gas, the mortgage, so thinking he'd help save a few pennies he'd turned the power off for the fridge and the freezer. He thought he'd done a good thing. And it was satisfying to see the little wheel stop twirling and eating his dad's money. He wasn't made of it, after all.

Happy with his day's work he went and read his book. The next day his mother and father had found out what he'd done when a pool of water had gathered on the floor in the pantry. Mum had found the fridge turned off and turned it back on the night before thinking that for some reason, in one of her more scatty moment, she'd turned it off. But what she didn't realise the freezer was still left off.

The freezer was choc-a-bloc with food and rather than see it go to waste they had cooked and eaten as much as possible. The day after, the bin ate the rest. Jack had been given an extremely stern talking to and a slap on the bare legs from his mother to make sure the lesson stuck in his mind.

His dad was always turning things off. If he went to the toilet and left the TV on by the time he came back it would be turned off. Even at a young age Jack had a firm notion of revenge. Every time his father left the room and left something turned on he would turn it off 'because his dad wasn't made of money/money doesn't grow on trees/do I look like the Sultan of Brunei?'

When his dad discovered Jack's 'power down' theory he couldn't really say anything because it was the practice he was preaching. His mother was a different kettle of fish. He turned the iron off while she was ironing and couldn't quite fathom why the creases weren't coming out of the clothes. Realising that Jack had done his 'power down' on her, she swiftly slapped his legs with a dangerous flick of her whip-like arm – it was shortly after this that Jack specified he was too grown-up for short trousers anymore in the hope that long trousers would offer some protection from her vicious arm. He swore one day that she had flicked her long arm and had broken the sound barrier.

Jack gave in. He walked back up the few stairs he had descended and unlocked the flat door, he walked to the bedroom and flicked the wall switch off, then set off again, casting his 'is everything ok?' look around the flat before relocking the door. This time he bounded down the stairs. Funnily enough, he felt good. His knees popped a little, his ankle creaked a bit and he felt a twinge from his hip but after a bit of a walk he was sure even those nagging little aches and pains would disappear. As he reached the front door things were beginning to move fluidly, if only his mind was such wonderfully functioning machine!

He'd read that depressive people like him were better at solving problems. *'Interesting piece of information,'* he thought. *'It would explain a lot.'*

Because their brains were wired to dwell on every little problem, they were great people to put in front of a puzzle. Given enough time these people would fathom out the most convoluted situation and provide an answer. Given an infinite number of depressive people, he reasoned they could solve the mysteries of the Universe and the meaning of life.

This wasn't a new theory of course. It had been floating around for a while. Especially since they saw depressive behaviour and problem-solving abilities seemed to be linked in some inexplicable way.

They had said the same thing about autism at one stage. Parts of their behavioural mechanisms are restricted while other brain functions work at 210%. It was all very fascinating to Jack because he was interested in that sort of thing. It gave him a reason for why he was the way he was. But try and bring it up in conversation and other people looked at him as if he was an alien.

Then his gaze caught the front door of the block he lived in and he felt that familiar feeling of dismay. The front door was a glass-fronted thing. But it seemed that every time he opened it there was a new sticker. There was a 'No Smoking in the hallways'. A 'Property is DNA protected for your safety'. Then a 'This is a Fire Exit' (no it isn't it is a front door!) and a 'No junk mail'. There was another new sticker saying 'Anything left in the hallways will be removed'. *'Great,'* he thought, *'if I leave my rubbish bags in the hallway someone will remove them for me.'*

It didn't mean that of course but if he did do that and someone questioned him about it, that would be his defence. There were signs all over the place explaining you were on CCTV and you must place all bags in the bins, and make sure your recycling goes in the **'Propper** bins provided'. Finally there was another sign saying: 'This is where you live, please keep it tidy.'

How had he resisted the temptation to put up a sign that 'forbade anyone to put up signs as it was making the place look untidy'? He wouldn't, of course. Far too many times he had pointed out the stupidity of something and then been told he was being facetious. The sign thing would just be another nail in his coffin at the residents meeting. These people had no sense of humour.

Come to think about it, he couldn't be bothered with all the aggravation anymore. He remembered being an angry young man and had fought against everything and anything. Stupid signs, stupid people, all the stupid that ever came into being anywhere and it was all for nothing. Stupid, it seemed, was eternal. It never died or rested. It carried on and on, ad infinitum. Long ago, he wouldn't just question the signs, he'd take them down, he'd write to the tenants' association, he'd turn up at meetings and argue the toss. But after years of dealing with jobsworths and naysayers and rulemakers, he was tired. There was just far too much idiocy in the world for one man to combat.

He walked on ignoring the sign on the bin shed that said 'do not leave rubbish bags on the floor as it encourages mice – this means you!!!!!'. He hoped whoever had pinned up that last note had broken their exclamation key on their computer. He also wondered if the sign was insulting. Did the 'this means you!!!!!' mean he was one of the mice. Or equally funny, was the sign meant for the mice and they should consider themselves suitably chastised.

The sign was ill-conceived and threatening and probably put there by someone who didn't understand the tone of voice of these things - like a grandad texting in block capitals all the time because he couldn't figure out the caps lock.

As he walked through the car park he noticed that someone had parked in his spot again. He didn't know how to feel about that. On the one hand, they should park in their own spot because each flat had a designated parking place. On the other hand he didn't have a car anymore so someone using his spot was irrelevant. On the other hand, (his third, by his reckoning) the rules said you can't park in someone else's spot, so he had much admiration for the man who did it. And on the other hand (the fourth, if you're keeping count) if burglars were to see that his parking spot was occupied they'd think twice before kicking his door down again, believing that if the parking spot was occupied, the flat must be too.

Walking on, he keyed the exit code into the gate and pulled, he was out, time to put on his game face. He smiled and then *'Perfectly Imperfect'* by Stone Sour started to play in his ears. *'Nice,'* he thought.

The gate squeaked open and Jack made a mental note to get some WD40 on it tonight when he got home. As he stepped out onto the street he noticed something odd. OK the signs were odd and the man who always parked in his space was odd, but they were 'usual odd'. What was unusual was the absence of the birds.

Jack looked back at his roof and the roof of the sheds where the rubbish bins were kept. No birds. On a morning like this there should be two magpies chasing one another playfully in the courtyard. They were nowhere to be seen. He would always see one then stand around waiting for the other one to pop into view. He couldn't very well go to work without saying his morning rhyme:

One for sorrow, two for joy
Three for a girl and four for a boy,
Five for silver, six for gold,
Seven for a secret never to be told.

What's the significance of no magpies? He looked at the roof of his flats and the foreboding bird that sat there was nowhere in sight. He always thought this was the Raven from the Edgar Allen Poe poem *'Nevermore'*, but even he wasn't there.

Come to think of it, as he looked at the skies there were no birds at all. Not a twitter. *'Never mind,'* he thought, they were probably having an early morning conference somewhere about national 'tweet' volumes or something. He closed the squeaky gate and set off down the road. Maybe the squeaky gate sounded like a hawk or something, so they had scarpered pretty sharpish not wanting to be breakfast for some bird of prey.

People whizzed by on the pavements, cars waited patiently on the roads, and cyclists wove in and out of the stationary vehicles. Jack sauntered on. He didn't want to race the people who were walking; they seemed to have some kind of urgent need to get where they were going. Their lives must have depended on it.

He remembered a quote from a film with Robert Duvall and Sean Penn, Robert Duvall was telling the story of the young bull and the old bull.

The young bull says, 'Let's run down there and fuck us a cow.'

The old bull said, 'Let's walk down there and fuck them all.'

Jack wasn't sure if that story applied here. He wasn't going to fuck anything, but he was damn sure he wasn't going to rush to the tube station so he could be crammed into a train in the sweltering heat for half an hour. Walking fast would only exacerbate the situation, he'd arrive hot and bothered and then the heat of the tube would make things worse. No, thank you. He'd spent many years doing the 'torpedo walk'. He'd arrive at the tube station and wait on the platform, and see all the people he'd passed on the pavement walk onto the platform and just step on a train. Somehow it just didn't seem fair. So he'd given up on the race into work. To compensate he had set off half an hour earlier, walked at a normal pace and found that this calmer, earlier walk delivered him to the office an hour before he normally arrived. Somewhere within his urgent need to get into work he had managed to lose more time and arrive more vexed. Not anymore.

As he walked, he could see the bus stop in the distance, There were people waiting and he asked himself the question, as he always did, should I catch the bus? It would take him 2,325 steps to get to the tube station, give or take. But if he could see a bus coming wouldn't it be quicker to catch the bus than to walk? *'Ah but,'* he reasoned, *'the bus usually got stuck in the jam and he had seen people walk leisurely to the station while he fumed on-board.'* On other occasions he had walked past the bus stop thinking that the damned thing would get fouled up in traffic, minutes later the bus had roared past mocking him in a 'eat my exhaust, motherfucker' way.

'Tell you what,' he decided, *'if I turn around and see the bus in the distance I shall try and catch it at the stop.'* He turned and saw nothing but a long line of traffic; cars, trucks and a minibus but no red bus. Turning back he carried on. He looked over at the bus stop queue and 'Old Gus' was there smiling and waving at him. He waved back then pointed his nose resolutely towards the tube station in the distance. Gus was a lovely old bloke who always liked a natter. Trouble was he liked a natter too much and you could never get away from him. He'd seen people who he talked to slowly but inevitably turn away from him, their eyes rolling up into their skulls and their mouths trying to stifle yawns as he continued to talk oblivious of his effect.

It was a good call to keep walking but then he felt guilty for not going over and having a chat. Gus was harmless but you can bet your bottom dollar that he had nothing new to say. It may have been early in the morning but he would talk about going to the Wetherspoon's in Wimbledon and how much it had gone up in price since he'd been going there. The Wetherspoon's was called the Wibbas Down and was probably the cheapest pub in the area. Jack had never been there but he knew what cheap beer meant. The bargain hunters would be there. And there was no way he was getting involved with that clan of drinker again. It wasn't because he was snobbish, it was just that he had spent the best part of his teens and his twenties with a drink in his hand. Somehow he had survived but he wasn't quite sure how. Some terrible things had happened to him, but then again some amazing things had happened too. It balanced out in a sort of cataclysmic, cosmic benevolent way, but these days he couldn't face the excitement. He also didn't want the hangover - not that he really suffered from them. Early on in life he knew that drinking water after a night of drunken revelry would leave him relatively unmolested by the hangover fairy. But sometimes if you woke up on a ferry to Calais you sometimes forgot the pint of water before bedtime and concentrated more on how you were going to deal with France's passport control when you didn't have a passport with you. More to the point, how did you get on the ferry without a passport anyway?

Jack soldiered on admiring the day, trees lined his path and the green leaves filled him with hope. Even on this road stacked with metal machines and surrounded by brick and concrete boxes there was a bit of green to lift the spirits. In one place a tree was absent and he remembered that a woman had tripped on the raised tarmac caused by a growing root. She had tripped, spilled her shopping and proceeded to sue the council for not maintaining the pavements. The council had uprooted the tree and carted it off to where naughty trees are taken, leaving just a sad little raked patch of soil and a freshly tarmacked piece of pavement.

Never mind that the tree had endeavoured to grow and survive despite being planted by a roadside and left to battle the 20th Century alone. Somehow it had flourished, grown strong and managed to shift a man-made pavement. Then some gormless twat had walked along not paying attention to where she was putting her feet and put an end to its efforts. The woman had won damages of £2,000 because she had hurt her ankle and was laid up for a couple of weeks. In his mind, the tree should have been given damages, relocated to a nice forest somewhere and the woman should have been taken away and destroyed for being stupid. But hey, that was his opinion. Shame the council didn't agree.

Someone blurred past him as he walked and for an instant his speed increased. He stopped himself almost immediately, it was almost as if he had been sucked into the slipstream of the passing man. If he hadn't stopped himself he would be chasing after him now, thinking that if he fell behind the rest of the rat race he was somehow inferior.

It was 7:18am. If everything went to plan he would be in work by 8:30. At that time receptionists, security and despatch would be there but hardly anyone else. He told himself to chill his boots again and regulated his pace back to a regular amble.

Somewhere during his walk, he drifted from a Croydon postcode to a London one. He wasn't quite sure where the divide was but some people regularly shifted it during their conversations. The London postcode he'd walked into was SW19 and although it was Colliers Wood some people still called it South Wimbledon, or Wimbledon Reach an element of snobbishness that amused him immensely.

In truth it should really have been called Wimbledon Stretch because it was only by a phenomenal stretch of the imagination that you could call it Wimbledon 'anything'.

He'd heard that the people of SW19 wouldn't dare darken their moccasins by crossing the great divide into Croydon. Similarly, the Croydonites weren't happy when they crossed into Colliers Wood.

It was all taken to another level by the Croydon postcode brigade. Some were said to live 'the wrong side of the barriers'.

As soon as you headed south from Colliers Wood tube station the road divided into Great Western Road and Church Road. Further south, these diverging roads were connected by smaller ones - or so it seemed if you were to look at the map.

To stop people driving down these roads, metal barriers had been erected halfway. Henceforth no through traffic, only access for residents. But what this had also done had created another demarcation line for the people who wanted to be as posh as the SW19 crowd. You were either the wrong side of the barriers or the right side of the barriers.

Personally, Jack couldn't give a stuff if he was right side, wrong side or upside down of the barriers. His mortgage was a darn sight smaller than most people's, his flat was pretty cool and from what he'd seen of the neighbours over the years they were a relatively good bunch of people. Despite their mutual distrust of the postman's ability to read a flat number correctly.

Decades previously the whole area around Phipps Bridge was seen as a rough place but when Jack had moved in, he saw no more trouble than you would see in Wimbledon, Clapham or Streatham. When Jack had moved in, he had walked into the local pub and everyone had kept their distance.

He understood the fact that he was a new face but couldn't quite understand why everyone was stand-offish. Then one of the locals had approached him and asked if he was a copper.

"No, of course not," Jack replied.

"You look like a copper."

"Well, I'm not. I work in advertising."

"Advertising for coppers?"

"No, just plain old advertising as in press TV and online."

"Okay," the man replied. "But you do look like a copper." And then he walked away.

To make them feel at ease, he had shared a joint with a couple of the locals and played a game of pool with them. Then shortly after that the council had demolished every pub within staggering distance of his home and built flats in their places.

It seemed to him that there were more flats than ever springing up in the area. On the outskirts of Wimbledon, a stone's throw from Colliers Wood and just out of London postcodes. When he had moved in, there was very little in the area. In the last 10 years they had built a *Boots, WH Smith, Starbucks, Argos, Next, JD Sports, TK Maxx* and an assortment of low end restaurants there. Civilisation was slowly creeping up to his doorstep and he wasn't sure he liked it.

Walking by them now seemed wrong. What had happened to the little greasy spoon café that he loved? Where was the 'salt of the earth' pub? Shockingly, they had all gone. Pleasant little shops with balconied apartments had suddenly appeared. Even the quaint Abbey Mills market was now surrounded by expensive flats, a *Pizza Hut* and a *Virgin Active* sports centre. All the charm of the place was slowly being siphoned off. Even the old roundabout had been plucked out of the road to be replaced by a crossroad junction controlled by traffic lights. A lot had changed in the 10 years he had lived here. And there were probably more plans afoot. The latest upgrade dominated the skyline.

Rising above Colliers Wood station stood 'The Tower'; it had been a huge monolithic grey thing that had fallen into rack and ruin. The thing had been an eyesore of epic proportions. Then they had clad it in metal and glass and decided it was going to be 'luxury flats'. Which meant they were going to be beyond reach of the first time buyers who really needed somewhere to live.

They were probably going to be sold to rich people who needed somewhere to stay when the Wimbledon Tennis tournament was on.

At the moment it was just a shell of a building but its effects were felt all around. Every wind that blew would be magnified by its presence. A simple gust would grow into a whirlwind. If there was any litter left in the street, it would form a cyclone of paper that would rise up and then smash down throwing remnants of fish and chips onto the pavements. Umbrellas would take off. Skirts would fly, embarrassing their wearers and occasionally a pair of glasses would be ripped from a head then deposited unceremoniously on the ground.

Jack had experienced this last one himself. Late one night after a merry beer or 7 with friends, he had walked out of the tube only to have his glasses removed and thrown to the pavement by the wind. Luckily, they didn't break so he set off after them. That was until another gust of wind blew them from the pavement into the middle of the road.

Looking around Jack saw that the road was empty except for one car approaching. He believed wholeheartedly that his glasses would survive, especially knowing how little of a car actually touched the road. Sadly, that one car, drove straight over his glasses and smashed them to smithereens. He couldn't believe it. There was no other car in sight – well, that he could see now. In a fit of disbelief he sat down on the edge of the pavement holding his crumpled glasses frames and laughed out loud.

It cost him a pretty penny to have them replaced but even now the memory of that incident still brought a wry smile to his face. If the car had just been a few inches away from the centre of the road, his glasses would have survived. But no, fate had decided he should lose his glasses that night and pay a hefty bill to have them replaced. After that he'd contemplated having laser surgery to correct his vision but knowing his luck, the Colliers Wood Whirlwind would blow him into the middle of the road and a car would run over his head, the day after he'd had it done.

Looking up at the monolithic building he couldn't imagine these being luxury apartments. Dreary dull flats maybe. In his opinion the building was just 16 floors of plain ugly. Even with the refurbishment work, it just looked 'wrong' to him.

Anyway it wasn't his problem or concern, there was no way he would want to live there and by the time it had been fully converted he guessed there was no way he could afford it. Well, he could, but why on earth would he want to? He was happy where he was, as he had thought before, why go changing anything if you're happy where you are?

Years ago, when he was married he had just got their first one-bedroomed flat looking the way they wanted, only to have his wife announce that they should move to a house. As he recalled, he had done a lot of work building in cabinets, tiling, installing or removing things etc. He'd spent an inordinate amount of free time on the place. It was nice, it was liveable and he'd looked forward to sitting in the garden sipping margaritas and just relaxing a bit before they took another step up the property ladder.

The only thing that had persuaded him to move was a property evaluation. This was the time when property was on the rise and with all the work done, they had doubled the price of the flat. In less than two years. They could easily afford another 'doer-upper' just a bit further away. For an extra 15 minutes on the tube they could afford a house. A place where grown-ups lived.

They had moved eventually to a 2 and a half bedroom house in Colliers Wood and his wife had immediately rolled out her plans on what they (he) was going to do to the place to make it the way they (she) wanted it. Perplexed and half-heartedly he had started measuring and planning. It was not long after that, that they had split and inevitably divorced. They sold the place, split the profits 50:50 and he had moved to his little flat with no one telling him what to do - except the little voices in his head.

She'd left him in Colliers Wood. Sitting in the house they were going to start a family in. When she left he'd done the place up a bit to get a better price, but then he'd moved to his one-bedroom flat just down the road. And there he'd stayed.

4

Jack had liked Colliers Wood and Mitcham the minute he'd wandered around the area. Mitcham had a small village feel to it with a centre or green to it, a cricket pitch, a little market and some small shops filled with bric-a-brac, pet supplies and small pound shops. It felt quaint. Whereas Colliers Wood was more a point where Tooting Broadway and Wimbledon had both spread and collided. But it did have a park and a rather imposing *Sainsbury's*.

He liked the area, he liked the people. It wasn't a leafy suburb, but there was enough green and trees around to make you feel like you weren't part of some sprawling metropolis. The illusion fell apart as soon as you saw the monolith because underneath lay the maw of Colliers Wood tube station, swallowing London's workforce as they unquestioningly threw themselves inside listening to their *iPods*, reading their *iPads* and fingering their *iPhones*.

It always seemed unnatural travelling underground. Like flying it was one of the few things that just seemed plain wrong to him. Yet everyone else let themselves be conveyed on metal stairways into the bowels of the earth to be crammed into a metal box and propelled at questionable speeds along a tunnel lined with various electrical devices, below rivers and roadworks.

The whole idea was preposterous – as mad as sending an 180,000kg metal vehicle roaring into the sky with 104,000lbs of highly combustible fuel and 4 dirty great engines to ignite it in controlled quantities.

Another great mystery to him was why did they pack as many people as possible into a finite angry, little space and believe that none of them will go into a mad killing spree.

Worse, what if the whole lot of them went on a rampage trampling everything in sight? All it would take is one spark in the tinderbox and they could all turn into lumbering, unstoppable animals.

Madness! Absolute madness, but every day they did it. Without thinking. As Jack walked into the tube station he could feel the claws of terror scratching at his heart again. Anything could go wrong down there and he would be trapped.

'Breathe normally,' he told himself. *'There's nothing to worry about.'*

'Yes there was,' his brain told him. *'You're going to send me down there with those madmen, in a hot, confined space? They could be carrying guns, knives, body odour…anything.'*

The stress started as soon as he walked into the tube station. Rather than pick up a copy of *Metro* in an orderly fashion, people were pushing and pulling to pick up a copy that wasn't creased and get to the barriers. For some reason they wanted a pristine edition that was as flat and smooth as a white woman's bottom.

He felt like shouting 'They are all the same.' But that was a bad idea. Don't draw attention to yourself. At least try to go with the flow a little.

Buffeted from side to side by this wave of humanity, he eventually reached the front and got his paper. Then he tried to walk away to get to the barriers but the people had trapped him. He was well and truly circled by grasping hands. If starvation was rife and this was a food truck he could understand the fervour to get to it, but this was the *Metro* newspaper. A free newspaper, granted. But there were hundreds of copies all stacked up with the promise of more on the way. It wasn't as if they were going to run out in the next few minutes. Maybe they had been intellectually deprived of stimulus over the weekend and their brains were going to expire if they didn't start reading some printed material within the next few minutes.

'Doubtful,' he thought, they had their *iPads* to nourish their poorly informed brains. So, why this surge of humanity? He walked on pushing through the throng. This was not a place for an 'excuse me' and wait for the crowd to part. This was the time for an 'excuse me' and barge your way through. When you left them trampled and bloody, was the time for a courteous 'thank you' then prepare yourself for the automatic gates.

After years of dealing with these particularly awkward objects, Jack developed a sense of distance. He never walked too close to the person in front as they went through the gates just in case their card was faulty. If their card failed them and then he planted his card on the reader, he inadvertently let them through. Leaving him stuck behind trying to 'seek assistance'.

Now Jack always left a gap between him and the person in front. So, when they put their faulty card on the reader, the gates would close with a severe 'clang'. They were the ones who ran stomach-high into a pair of metallic pincers that could wind a buffalo.

Jack gave the person in front a good 3 seconds of space. Luckily they got through unmolested and even his card let him through with the minimum of groaning and whirring. So far, so good. A few minutes into his tube journey and he had navigated two of its major hurdles.

He walked purposefully towards the down escalator but even with his no-nonsense stride, people still jumped in front of him. Undeterred, he carried on. One man had to stop himself or he would have walked into the side of him. Jack gave him a withering stare and watched as he stepped back into someone else who was trying to rush down the same escalator without paying attention to where they were going.

All these people seemed to be on auto-pilot. They never picked their path. They just walked and expected other people to get out of their way.

Jack walked slowly down the right hand side of the escalator as people sped past on the left. Their feet flew as they raced downwards. The reason for this 'feet of fury' move was equally unfathomable. If they just checked the dot matrix screen above the ticket office they would know there wasn't another north bound train for 3 minutes. There wasn't another southbound train for 4 minutes. Were they going to arrive on the platform jump down on to the tracks and rush down the tunnel screaming whoooo whoooo? Or were they going to get on the platform and try and push people out of the way so they could get to their favourite seat on the train?

That was another thing. People had their favourite seats. If there was a way they could have reserved them, these people would pay extra just for that privilege. They would also be the people to rigidly enforce their right to own a seat for the whole of their journey, righteously indignant if people had the effrontery to park their cheeks where they were not wanted.

On this one point, the tube was a great leveller. The privileged few had to mix with the great unwashed, sometimes literally. They objected, they squirmed, they shouted in voices used to being obeyed that people should 'move down the train'. These voices were lost in a carriage full of people who really didn't care for people telling them what to do.

God help anyone who tried to wrest them from their seats once they were super-glued there. You could be an aged one-legged pregnant mother standing in front of them pleading for a seat and they wouldn't bat an eyelid. They were suddenly blind and deaf to everything except the functions of their *iPads* or the next level of *Angry Birds*.

Arriving on the platform, he saw one of the guys who had rushed past him almost frothing at the mouth with impatience. As usual people stood in little clusters where the train doors would stop and they could get on easily. Unfortunately for the frothing man, the clusters of people were quite large and there was no way he was going to get to the front. You could visibly see his brain trying to work out where was the best place to stand so that he could not only get on the next train, but also get a seat. The puzzle was completely unsolvable. He danced from one foot to the other. He moved from one side of the cluster to the other desperately trying to find a chink or thoroughfare he could exploit.

Wise to his train-boarding dance the cluster visibly spread themselves out. They didn't increase the spaces between themselves but shoulder bags were taken off shoulders and dangled nonchalantly at their sides. Men spread their shoulders and women altered their stance so as to take up more room than they normally would have done.

Witnessing this sudden expansion was a joy for Jack. For the frothing youth it was mental torture. If he couldn't get on the next train, could he get to the front so that he would be first on the next train?

The seat was the golden fleece, the panacea, the goal for which all men aimed. He knew he was about to fail or have to stand up on the way into work.

Jack surveyed the little groups of people. He assessed their demeanour and the way they stood. He spied a group further up the platform that looked uncertain, tourists probably, prime candidates to walk up behind and they would allow him to integrate their group without any fuss. He knew for a fact that he wouldn't get on the next train, but it was early, so

45

even if he didn't get on the next train, he knew he'd be on the one after.

Once these people had cleared, he'd have prime door position. Then he could just waltz onto the train and into a seat unmolested and untroubled. But the Law of Uncertainty that governed the Underground would kick in at some point. Trains would disappear from the arrivals board. Doors which had opened and closed a million times before would refuse to do anything and the train would be removed from service dumping all its passengers unceremoniously on the nearest platform.

Signals could fail and did with alarming regularity. Whole sections of tube line would be plunged – if they could go any further down – into inactivity for the remainder of the day.

There was one announcement which made him go white; 'service has been suspended due to a passenger under a train'. Jack was always horrified, not by the fact that someone had taken their own life by jumping in front of a train. He'd always felt sympathy for the person and the poor driver who had witnessed this moment of desperation, what horrified him were the reactions of the people around him.

All they were concerned about was getting into work. They were upset about the delay not the fact that a human being so low and so mentally desperate had decided to end their own life rather than suffer the anguish of their own tormented minds.

He heard phrases like 'they should have more consideration for other people,' or 'why don't they do it when it isn't rush hour?'

Clearly these people had never been depressed. Jack had a case of depression a few years ago. He was now on anti-depressants and some other pills to help him sleep. He was actually diagnosed with a mild case of depression and at the time he thought, *'God help the people who have it bad.'* The simple task of getting on the tube was gut-wrenchingly terrifying. Being surrounded, the feeling that the walls were too close and the people were closer still. When the doors closed it was like they were closing the doors on his coffin. He couldn't breathe. Panic gripped his chest and a number of times he thought he was having a heart attack, the symptoms were so severe. Every day was filled with panics. It was like he was drowning in the fresh air and only he was experiencing it.

He shrugged the thoughts off as he stood on the platform. The last thing he should be doing was thinking about panicking. That's one sure way to start panicking. The frothing man was now looking even more perplexed. At first, Jack had relished his frustrated impotence to get into work, now he almost felt sorry for him. *'What was so important that he had to rush into work, it was barely 7:30am?'*

Looking back at his own mental fallout period he remembered he had to get the earlier trains because the later ones were always too full. He physically and mentally couldn't force himself onto a crowded train. The smaller people seemed to be able to squeeze into any space. Being 6 feet tall, he had trouble unless he could stand upright in the centre of the train. There was no way he could put up with being pushed into the curve by the doorway where people of his size weren't just cramped width-wise but also height-wise as well.

A cool column of air touched his cheek and he turned to face the tunnel as the train poked its head out of the tunnel. Feet shuffled around him. Bodies edged closer to one another but their electronic devices remained fully plugged into eyes and ears. God forbid they should miss an instant of entertainment to do something as mundane as acknowledge the arrival of their carriage.

Jack watched the train chug ever so slowly up the platform. He wasn't sure how old these trains were but the cold grey of their exterior always made them look ancient. There was a splash of daring red along the sides and the interiors were an honest blue with flecks of other colour.

In the cabin the driver's face was unreadable. Flat. Just an ordinary man going about his work.

What would be the effect on passengers if drivers were laughing maniacally as they approached or weeping uncontrollably onto the dead man's handle? He had no idea what was going through their minds as they approached. Were they watching for jumpers or just looking at the mass of human flotsam and jetsam waiting for their arrival and thinking 'I am your King, without me, you're going nowhere'.

It wasn't hard to imagine the drivers thinking those things because that's what he would be thinking. *Where would all those besuited and bespectacled businessman and woman all plugged into their iPads and iPods, be without me getting up at God knows what o'clock to ferry them back and forth from their companies?'*

The press however, branded them dissenters and implied they were 'terrorists' whenever there was a whiff of strike action in the air. It didn't matter that they were being screwed by their employers – demanding fair wages, benefits and pensions was like joining the Taliban, according to the newspapers.

Slowly getting on to the train and sitting down, Jack watched as this game of musical chairs flapped and squeaked around him. Unlike 10 year olds they huffed and puffed as other passengers got to seats before them. When the seats were full, a few passengers resigned themselves to stand. Others leapt off the train before the doors could close in the vain hope that the next one would allow them to get a seat.

A few pairs of eyes settled on Jack, he had slowly but surely walked to the first empty seat and sat down – not the seats for elderly and pregnant passengers but the next ones. There was no way he was going to sit in the 'ungentlemanly' seats. Those were the seats for cads and bounders who refused to stand for the people who really needed them.

The reason for the hard stare was that Jack had plonked his behind on one of the more comfortable seats and left the flip-up ones alone. No one seemed to find any comfort on these poor excuses for seats. At some point in their lives someone over 25 stone had decided to bounce up and down on them and they'd never been the same since.

Broken and bent, if anyone planted their buttocks on them they would slide to the floor. Even leaning back slightly could dump an unsuspecting passenger unceremoniously on the floor.

No, those seats should be left alone. Especially if you wanted to slouch down a bit and catch a few winks of sleep before work.

Which, come to think of it, was a good idea.

5

It was a good idea until the train pulled into Tooting Broadway station and the next kerfuffle of passengers threw themselves onto the train. Not content with barging on like a horde of elephants, the lead elephant decided to kick his foot out of the way. Looking down Jack tried to shuffle his trainers to the side but there was no room. The people on either side of him had spread out to take up the armrests and the foot space 'and to hell with everyone else'.

'*Right,*' he thought.

Jack had played this game before. Two spreaders at either side and standing in front was the worst 'space invader' of all – a man with a backpack and no regard for the people behind him.

He had to exert his authority or he would be scrunched into a little ball by the time he got to Goodge Street.

Tugging forcefully on the backpack Jack gave his best, completely unapologetic 'excuse me'. Even if Mr

Backpack had ear phones in which was extremely likely there was no way he could ignore the insistent pull.

Turning almost indignantly to face Jack with eyes blazing, he assessed the unwanted intrusion to his day. At first there was an angry look of surprise on the man's face but that was no match for Jack's blank, humourless and cold eyes. A little taken aback, Mr Backpack removed the earbuds and cocked his head to one side.

"Yes?" he enquired with all the warmth and helpfulness of a polar bear with piles sitting on a glacier.

"Your backpack is in the way," Jack replied pointing to the offending article. "Either take it off or move up the carriage."

There was no point in saying please or thank you to these people. Please or thank you were weaknesses to be exploited.

"There's nowhere to put it," He chimed up as if he was expecting luggage racks on London Underground's finest carriages.

"There's the floor," Jack replied matter-of-factly without breaking eye contact. "If you would just be so kind to move it out of the way, I'd be very grateful."

Jack couldn't show any weakness at this point. He was making an example of this guy so that the two guys on either side of him would know he wasn't to be trifled with. Especially, since his next action involved them, directly.

With a shrug of his shoulders he shucked the backpack off and put it at his feet. He turned away from Jack and replaced his earbuds. The matter was over. He toyed with the idea of tugging on the back of his shirt and when he turned round he would thank the man. But that would be rubbing salt into the embarrassment of the moment. There was a limit to which you could push someone on the tube before they became a berserker and started clubbing you to death with their tablet. Jack had a feeling he was already uncomfortably close to that point and any gentle nudge would send the man into a blitzkrieg of abuse that wouldn't stop. No, that little conflict was over. It was time to turn his attention elsewhere.

The men at either side had uncomfortably lifted their newspapers when Jack had begun talking to Mr Backpack. They had spread a little too far into Jack's personal seat space for comfort. The one on his left had pulled his arm back a little and closed his legs a little so that he wasn't displaying as much of his crotch as before. But the man on his right had planted his arm and his feet with more determination. He was the one who was going to give battle.

Mr Right was a man in his late forties, early fifties and was marshalling his defences. His thoughts were almost palpable – 'if that bleeping bleep-head thinks I'm bleeping moving a bleeping inch he's got another bleeping think coming'.

There was only one thing to do – Jack let his knee slide ever so gently next to Mr Right's. It was time for a game of gay chicken. There was nothing sexual in the action, it was just Jack spreading his legs slightly so that he didn't crush his genitals in the folds of his jeans.

The reaction as soon as Jack's knee touched his was an almost defiant fixing of his leg position and another almost visible bleeping bleep sent into the carriage.

Jack unfolded his *Metro* and started to read, his knee still touching Mr. Right's. As the tube accelerated and slowed with the strange accelerating and decelerating jerky motion that only a tube driver could manage to recreate, their knees met.

Each slight push caused Mr Right to push back slightly harder, while Jack ignored every motion. Jack had christened this game 'gay chicken' because at some point one of the combatants would pull away from this man-on-man confrontation.

Both men had an equal stake in the territory their legs occupied. If one were to relinquish ground, then the other would have won. Jack had played this particular game many times before and had never given an inch. On his best day he had kept his knee pressed against another man's for his entire journey.

At Tooting Bec another onslaught of humanity filled the nooks and crannies left by the previous horde and that was then Jack knew the real 'fun' would start. It was only 7:46 in the morning, the tube train was only 4 stops into its journey and it was already full. It was time to wish the rest of the Northern Line ahead 'good luck on getting into work, this baby is full!'

Creaking and groaning under the weight of human beings, the train lurched into action. A few people swayed from the monkey bars of the train and wrestled with inertia to regain their feet. Jack's knee glanced against Mr Right's with a very unwelcome tenderness and he pulled away. Jack had won. He had regained his territory. He didn't want to invade anyone's space but he certainly wasn't going to give ground to the people who called the 'Here-is-my-cock-I-will-spread-my   –legs-as-wide-as-possible-so-you-can-see-it' men. Every day he saw these people wide-legged and surly. If you asked them to move up they invariably started an argument. Touch them and eventually they shrank away from you.

They were almost as annoying as the women who put makeup on during their journey. It wasn't the fact that they were effectively still getting dressed on the tube that annoyed him, it was the mascara brush and the eyeliner pencil that made his toes curl. One sudden judder of the train and they would colour their eyeball in. Stab themselves. Worse, they could stab him. And he didn't want to report to Accident & Emergency with a mascara brush related puncture wound.

He wondered who was the first woman to start this trend of making-up on the tube. He knew how self-conscious some women could be about appearing without makeup. So turning up at the tube and applying on the journey must have taken a supreme amount of self-confidence.

Either that or a tremendous amount of fear because they didn't have time to apply at home and didn't want to turn up at a function or meeting without their perfect skin tone, polished lips and alluring eyes.

How on earth did this practice catch on? Did other women watching this transformation think 'I'll have a bit of that' and start decorating themselves en route. Or was it because someone had told them not to do it and the whole of womanhood stood up and said 'how dare they tell us what to do, tomorrow I shall put on Goth make-up on the Central Line, that'll show 'em.'

Jack was still waiting for all those men who said they would shave on their way to work to get on and do it. It may have happened but he hadn't seen a portable shaver appear anywhere on the Northern Line to date. He could bring his little cut-throat razor and sit there chopping away at his head but that would probably bring about screams of horror.

Jack believed men were just a little less adventurous. Women changed their outfits in backs of taxis, men would opt to change in bathrooms and locked stalls in public conveniences.

Of course some men would say that they left themselves ample time to get ready washed shaved etc, while women tended to do everything last minute. (Those are the cheeky chappies who seem to get away with murder whenever there's a woman around.)

It was all an alien concept to him this difference between the sexes anyway. He'd read the book Men are from Mars and Women are from Venus and was completely baffled by their behaviour.

His only view point after reading it was 'if they are from those planets just fuck off back there and get off his planet'. How many earthlings had had their culture and their way of life destroyed by these unwelcome immigrants from Mars and Venus? Who invited them in the first place? Certainly not him!

Come to think of it, who would understand him? All this talk of relationships was wrong. Yes, he understood the biological imperative to reproduce and look after the young until they were of age to make their way in the world but everything else just seemed like hokum.

While his mind had gone on its meanderings, he realised the train was approaching Clapham Common. It was floor-to-ceiling and door-to-door and end-to-end full of sweating, slightly agitated people. If anything were to happen it would be here. This was the place where you could ignite the blue touch paper and take cover. Taking care not to return to the incendiary situation at any time lest you get a good ear-bashing.

The train slid slowly into the platform like a nervous lover entering his partner for the first time. The doors slid back and the sound of scuffling feet drew his attention to the double doors. Sure enough, a square of people were trying to squeeze themselves into a round tube with no possible chance of fitting.

Then it happened. That one voice, eloquent and indignant was carried across the carriage.

"Can you move down, please?"

Jack bit his tongue, he so wanted to shout back 'no'. He'd said it before and was greeted with all manner of replies. It was obvious to everyone except the person trying to finagle a little standing space in which to fit their £1,000 suit that there was no more room. Even if it was Joseph and Mary begging for a small area to stand the answer would be the same. 'No room'. 'Zilch space'.

"Can you move down, please?" The man repeated more agitated than before.

From where he was sitting, he could see the man standing at the doorway. He knew this trick. Jack had seen men do it all the time. Sure enough, as the doors closed he pushed his way into the train. Once in, there was nowhere to shove him back. The whole mass of people just accepted the fact that the doors were closing and this man had through sheer brute force pushed everyone more claustrophobically together Couldn't he have waited for an emptier train? What was so special that he had to get on this one?

In the height of his 'panic attacks', Clapham Common was where he had to get off. He'd stressed about the overcrowding even from his seat. Figures looming over him. Feet moving closer. Bodies restricting him. Taking his air. The panic would build. What made it more unbearable was the train not moving. When the train was chugging through the tunnels he always felt like he was closer to his destination and freedom. But when the train was stationary, that was when the real fear gripped him.

This one man forcing his way on had rekindled a part of that fear. Jack knew that he was leaning or being squashed against the doors.

'Oh God, the doors,' Jack thought. *'He's pushing against the doors.'*

When anyone put their weight against the doors they would open slightly. Not much. But just enough to break a connection. Then a safety cut-off would slam on the emergency brakes. All the people crammed in would be thrown forward crushing one another. Worse still, the train could be stuck in the tunnel while the doors were unable to close and he wouldn't be able to get off. He'd be stuck under a pile of people scrabbling to get up. Unable to breathe, unable to move. Trapped in a metal coffin under the ground.

Jack's hands began to sweat just imagining this scenario. The fear was taking hold of him. He was holding his breath. He was forgetting to breath. Forcing out a long gust of air from his lungs he took in a good lungful of warm stale air from the carriage. This was supposed to make him feel better but instead all he could think of was all the germs and bacteria he was breathing in from other people. Tilting his head back he took a breath of the cool, recycled air that was blowing from the vents behind him. The effect was twofold; firstly he felt the cool air massage his poor, tense lungs back into life, secondly the cool air against his scalp seemed to ease his tensions a little.

In his view, forcing yourself onto a packed train was the ultimate in bad manners, it was worse than putting your feet on the seats. Even more loathsome than frotaging. There was something about personal space that was sacred. Admittedly, there's not a lot of personal space on a tube but forcing people together cock to arse and nose to breast was just inviting trouble. Especially if one arsehole wants to shove people even closer together.

'What is wrong with these people?' he thought to himself. Every time the train arrived at Clapham

Common he became agitated. Some instances were amusing but most of them just left him stressed and worried.

It didn't matter that by Clapham North the problem had been resolved one way or another, in his mind the damage had been done.

By Stockwell a great number of people got off the train to try their luck on the Victoria Line. The crowd thinned out enormously but that just made the carriage crowded rather than overcrowded. There was a little shuffling, a welcome blast of cool air from a train on another platform and then the doors slid closed again.

He physically felt himself unclenching. Mentally his brain calmed by 10%. It was enough for Jack to realise he had been clenching his *Metro* so tight the paper had ripped. Folding it up neatly and putting it in his pocket he pulled out his *Kindle Fire*. The paper felt bulky in his pocket but there was no way he was going to take it out and put it on the floor or the ventilation duct behind him.

People had already started littering up the train. There was a sweet wrapper on the floor and at least 3 abandoned *Metro* newspapers either on the floor or on the shelf behind the seats. Some passengers, when getting off the train, just stood up and left the paper on the seat. This made it someone else's problem to deal with. If they wanted the seat they had to have the newspaper, as well. If they wanted to read it, all well and good, if they didn't, they had dispose of it.

Jack saw in this one action people's attitude to their planet. They used and cast aside things they didn't want anymore. It was left to the next person to deal with their mess. Their attitude was 'leave it for someone else, they'll handle it and if they don't well it's not my problem anymore'.

He felt sick. Tears began to well up in his eyes, but then he stopped. It didn't really matter. None of it did. All these irresponsible people, himself included, would be dust in the next 75 years. Tops! The planet would be around until the sun expanded and consumed it. People were an infestation that would be removed long before the planet died. They were a minor inconvenience.

Long ago, he'd heard someone say that the dinosaurs 'ruled' the Earth for millions of years. Bollocks. They'd roamed the surface of Earth for millions of years and over 100 million years ago they'd been wiped out. They never ruled it.

Now they were saying the same thing about human beings ruling the Earth. Admittedly, humans had made a few advances, invented a few things, gone to the moon and back, put a few probes on Mars, but the end result would be the same. The Earth would dispense with them.

In another 100 million years the next dominant species on the planet would be digging up human bones and wondering what their lives were like. Their views of humans would probably be similar to humans' views of the dinosaurs: tiny minds, aggressive, always fighting one another, washed away or blown away to make room for something better.

Damn. He was only 30 minutes into his journey and he'd wiped out the human race and moved on.

To be fair, he'd usually killed off the human race in a million different ways, before breakfast. Today, just felt different somehow.

6

Shaking himself from his morosity, he realised he hadn't been listening to his music. His mind had been so preoccupied with the comings and goings of the passengers that most of his favourite tunes had been and gone without so much as a moment's appreciation.

Tempted as he was to go back through some of the tracks he missed, he decided to just let the track list play through. ZZ Top's *'Mescalero'* was playing now and the biggest crime was not listening to it.

The passengers had stolen his moments of enjoyment. He wished he could ignore them but their strange ways of behaving always drew his attention. He wondered what percentage of his life was taken up by being unwittingly manoeuvred down these strange and twisting avenues.

There were fountains of statistics spewing out of every area of life now. You couldn't go a day without hearing how many people couldn't go a day without hearing a statistic. You couldn't even brush your teeth without someone bemoaning the fact that you spend 5% of your life doing it.

Everything had to be measured quantified and regurgitated in huge reports that 90% of people never read, 67% of the time.

Christ, they were even measuring the speed of sneezes and farts. What possible use was that? Unless of course the fate of the planet depended on some person, in some cataclysmic situation, knowing that a fart travelled at x miles an hour.

The Venutians were about to destroy the Earth in 30 seconds. Their only weakness, methane gas. Jack Walker tied and bound, is helpless until he remembers a fart contains methane gas and travels at a steady 5 mph.

Jack squeezes one out and the Venutians, their fingers poised over the destruct button suddenly smelt what he dealt. Clawing at their throats and collapsing into helpless heaps of bubbling protoplasm the Earth is saved.

Wouldn't happen.

Emerging from this little daydream he realised he had now missed 'Mescalero' and Ozzy Osbourne's 'Shot in the Dark' wailed into his ears. Closing his eyes, he tried to settle himself into it. His mind wasn't just wandering it was running off in all directions like a hyperactive child at a birthday party who had just filled up on cake.

For a few moments he tried to concentrate on the lyrics, the guitar sound and the bass and then the drums. He selected the thump of the bass and turned down the rest of the sounds of the music on the control board in his head.

It thumped along filling the gaps and taking the tune into holes left by the other instruments. He revelled in its unusual rhythms and sounds. The guitarists and the singers were centre stage but he knew that the real mastery was with those bass players and drummers who gave them a solid platform on which to play. Without those guys they were just buskers.

The persistent pounding was quite soothing in some ways. Regular, yet musical in its deep and thunderous tones. He'd played bass on a number of occasions and loved the feel of the notes beneath his fingers and the way the vibrations coursed through the room. the runs and fills that accentuated the music took his mind off in other directions to the melody and he loved their little adventures.

He had really started to relax now. His folded arms dropped: his protective wall dropped brick by brick.

He began to think of the *Ballad of Halo Jones*. A story written by Alan Moore for the comic 2000AD. Besides the heroine there were some characters called 'Drummers'. They seemed like fanatics but were the calmest people around. These people dressed in white robes and had a chip implanted in their brain that played a steady thump-thump-thump beat straight into their brains. Because of this they gave up all the rush and fluster of their existence and became calm. All they listened to was the beat of their internal drum and were content. Vacant, but content.

Looking around the carriage again he saw the same vacant look on everyone. They were playing games on their phones. Reading and preparing texts for the next time they got a signal. Or like him, listening to music.

No one seemed to look up anymore. The only time any eye-contact was made with someone was when they were looking down at you with 'seat-envy'. And they quickly looked away when you caught them.

Jack scanned the standing passengers. He was especially on the lookout for "Baby on board!" badges. Every time he saw one he was compelled to give up his seat. He grumbled and moaned to himself but he couldn't let someone in greater need suffer. Even though he usually felt the pain in his hip began to prick at his bones.

Thankfully, no one was wearing 'the badge'. The badge that really said 'if you don't offer me a seat then you are a cunt'. That's what it meant. Forget all this gentlemen give up seats and 'baby on board' business.

You knew as soon as that lady got on the tube or you spied it from the corner of your eye there were only two things you could do: become overly interested in what you were doing, or offer your seat. Most chose the former. Their gaze became riveted to what they were doing. Or if they weren't doing anything, they pretended to be asleep. Anything so they wouldn't have to give up their tasteless nylon throne.

There could be another alternative but he couldn't think of one. It all boiled down to pretend or stand.

Were there really people who had no consideration for other people around them? Surely not. But looking around Jack spotted them. Wrapped up in their own little worlds. Cutting themselves off from the rest of humanity using earphones, *iPhones* and every other phone you could possibly imagine.

So this was it. The full and dreaded realisation hit him. This was the end of the human race. He'd physically killed them off only a few minutes before but there was something quite terrifying about these soulless zombies wandering the earth with their metal devices distracting them from the rest of humanity.

He wondered if there was a game where you could kill these techno-philic zombies. Oh the irony of someone being knocked down by a car and killed as they were playing a game where you earned points by killing zombies with a car.

Looking out the window he saw the sign for Leicester Square. Next stop and he would have to fight his way off. He'd rather not push his way through the people that were standing in the tube aisles but he knew they were statues. They wouldn't move unless coaxed into action.

You would have thought that approaching a station that they knew there were people who would want to get off. You would think they would have the good sense to look around to see if someone wanted to get past, but they were always oblivious and genuinely surprised when someone crept up behind them and asked them to move.

They stood like walls of flesh not looking, not listening, not responding until they were pushed out of the way. He hated to use the word 'sheep' or 'cattle' but that's how they responded. He wondered to himself if a cattle-prod would be deemed an offensive weapon if he used it on the passengers.

Probably. He'd heard stories of people being 'hit' with umbrellas and then they were regarded as offensive weapons. If that were true, the bastards who hit him in the eye whenever he walked down the street in the rain should really feel his litigious ire.

Standing up and moving into the centre of the aisle he got the kind of looks that said 'who are you?' He was 6 feet 2. Not a great height these days, but when it was packed with 15 stone of flesh that barely wobbled, people took notice.

When he was sitting, people just thought he was a broad shouldered fellow. But when you add broad shoulders to his height a few realised that the beast was rising and he needed space.

They parted, a little. Enough to give Jack the space he needed to orient himself towards the door and utter in his gravelly whisper, "Excuse me."

It wasn't loud, it just held enough gravitas for people to look around and realise he was heading their way and he expected them to move. Some didn't and that meant he would have to give them an extra, deeper, harsher 'excuse me.'

There was a third 'excuse me.' But that was reserved for people wearing earphones. It usually meant that he pulled their earphones from their head and sarcastically shouted 'excuse me,' into their exposed ears.

They wanted to object but the look in his eye said it all. *Don't even think about it.'*

When the doors slid open he found the widest gap and eased himself through and stepped down onto the platform. *'Free at last,'* he breathed, then set off towards the exit as people bobbled and bumped into him.

His next obstacle was the 'shuffling walk' he was caught right in the middle of a pack of humans and could do nothing about it. If by some stroke of luck he managed to get off the tube quickly, he could walk at his own pace, unhindered by the people in front of him.

Most days that was not an option. Everywhere he looked there were human beings. It took just one slow moving individual and the entire horde was reduced to an ambling, shuffling mess that stopped everyone.

In the midst of this maddening crowd he moved forward one miserable half-step at a time.

He wasn't free at all. He was in another prison where the bars were bankers, receptionists, business people, and baristas. In the distance he saw the escalators dragging these people from their subterranean journey back into the morning light.

No one was walking up them. Instead they crowded around the mouth of the device and waited to be transported upwards. The left hand side was completely empty. Why didn't they walk up? Why? Why? Why?

He was getting annoyed again. He wanted to be outside. Fresh air on his face and in his lungs. Away from the stifled farts and expensive colognes and scents that surrounded his body and invaded his lungs.

Some day in the future, he hoped that perfumes would be banned. Not because they didn't smell pleasant. It was more about the people who decided it was better to put on too much than too little. They reeked of an expensive designer cloud that followed them everywhere.

He was reminded of 'Pigpen' from the Snoopy or Peanuts cartoons who had his own cloud of dust and dirt that surrounded him. These people were the opposite. Shrouded in their sickly-sweet, smelling fragrance that could have masked their human scent from a bloodhound.

Maybe that's why they did it. They were on the run so they had bathed in *Chanel No. 5* so the dogs when they did get a whiff of them would go into some sneezing fit that would throw them off the trail.

Even in his human 'cell' wafts of smells attacked his nostrils. He couldn't identify the culprit or the offending fragrance but it punched him squarely in the nose.

'Just wash,' he thought to himself. *'Why must you spend your cash on how you smell when it could be used for something else?'*

He didn't expect an answer of course. People put on perfumes to smell better. It didn't matter that they smelled okay. This is the consumer age. Some people wanted to smell of success, so they bought it.

Some wanted to smell good for their lover, but surely just someone being clean was more alluring than covering up natural smells and pheromones with unctions and ointments?

He couldn't work it out really. There were so many more worthwhile things to spend money on than smelly water.

But then what would you buy someone for Valentine's Day, Mother's Day, Father's Day or Christmas?

Jack stopped himself thinking again. Wasn't this a similar train of thought John Doe was taking in the film *'Se7en'*? Was he beginning to despise his fellow man just because they behaved differently to him? Because he thought he was superior?

Thinking about it, he was no angel. His life was as self-absorbed as anyone else's. What right did he have to judge anyone?

His mind fell silent as he trudged to the foot of the escalator and rather than stand on the right and be whisked to the top by machinery, he walked up on the left. In the distance he saw a few young people braving the walk but as a whole the rest of the people stood in their silent disregard for anything and everyone.

Again their only focus was on the electronic device in their hands which were suddenly reconnecting to wi-fi networks. Emails pinged and *Facebook* notifications buzzed. An electronic symphony without order or timing. Bill Gates and Mark Zuckerberg would be rubbing their hands with glee as every cent rolled into their bank accounts.

His own phone pinged a message to him. *Argos* was having another sale - last week's must have been more successful than he thought. Someone else was asking him if he had checked to see if he was due reimbursement for a mis-sold PPI. And *Pinterest* was telling him that someone he had never met and probably never will, had repinned one of his pictures.

Where was the 'I don't give a fuck' button when you needed it?

Fascinating as all this was, he replaced the phone in his pocket and carried on walking. Everyone else was immersed in their devices and behaving like Pavlov's Dogs: one sound of a bell and they followed conditioned responses.

As he reached the ticket hall, he queued again for the privilege of leaving the station and made sure he kept his distance from the person in front. The anticipation to get outside was all that was on his mind but still he seemed to be caught behind a wall of people.

These were even worse. There was no escalator to get to street level so the ambling shuffling masses became a wheezing struggling mess as they tried to haul their bodies to street level under their own steam.

He emerged into the fresh air like a man surfacing from the depths of the ocean. The stress of actually making it this far had already taken its toll. It always surprised him how he managed to do this every day. It also surprised him how he managed to do this every day without killing someone.

But this was only the first leg of the day. He wasn't even at work yet. There was still Tottenham Court Road to negotiate. Bodies still huddled around him. At least the people were going in the same direction as him.

There were worse dangers ahead. People were walking straight towards him like kamikaze pilots. Heads down in their phones with no idea of where they were going or who they were walking into.

There was only one way through this melee; head down, walk straight forwards, and to hell with the consequences. Do what they did and if they collided with him well, that was their fault. He'd spent too many mornings dodging oncoming pedestrians and apologising for being in their way when they were the ones who weren't looking where they were going.

A woman bounced off of him and tutted as if it was his fault he was in her path. Jack stared at her and said nothing waiting for some words of regret from her. It just wasn't going to happen. Ignoring Jack's presence, she quickly recovered without an apology and re-set her course. She was gone. These people were like bumper cars. A quick collision and then they were off again to bounce off someone else.

Why should he care? He would probably never see this woman again. But his anger was growing again. No courtesy, no manners, fuck you and keep walking. This was the modern day. This was London. Other people were obstacles to be ignored. He wondered if anyone else was as annoyed about this as he was.

Looking around, it didn't appear so. They wove in and out of one another's paths and collided. Moved apart then set off again. They really didn't seem to share anything anymore. Not a smile, a wave, an excuse me, or a 'I'm very sorry'.

Jack felt sad for the human race again. They ignored one another more and more each day. Unless it was *Facebook*, *Twitter* or *Snapchat*. 'Love' and 'like' had been replaced by icons and other emotions had been replaced with emoticons and emojis.

Would the day come when people would wear an emotion sensor t-shirt that would guess their moods and then display it for all to see?

The human race was losing its humanity. All those films he'd seen growing up were lies. They showed that good triumphed. Out here in the real world there was only disregard, self-interest and self-preservation. Real life sucked. This was not what he had signed up for.

If you wanted to progress in this world you didn't work hard and help others, you sucked up, talked shit and backstabbed your way up the ladder until you were safely out of reach and then you shat upon everyone below you.

People were an inconvenience. Far too many of them. The beggars were moved out of sight as they reflected the shame of a society that had failed them.

And he felt ashamed too. He was part of it. What happened to him? He had visions of changing the world. Ending world hunger. Abolishing poverty. Destroying greed wherever it reared its ugly head.

'It's a good job I'm on anti-depressants,' he thought to himself, *'or I would really be in trouble.'*

Wrapped in his despair he arrived at the advertising agency's doors and he could barely look at his reflection in the glass doors.

What had he done? He helped sell stuff to people who probably didn't want it and couldn't afford it. He was fuelling this consumer monster that chewed people up and spat them out when they were milked of their usefulness.

He'd started off wanting to change the world with his ideas and now his ideas were being used by corporations and service companies to line shareholders' pockets.

Pushing the door open he walked inside. How many people could he get to part with their hard-earned cash today?

7

"Morning, good weekend?" John asked.

"Quiet one," Jack replied through his fake smile. "How about you?"

"Usual. Bit of football, bit of cinema, down the pub Sunday for lunch, then back here," John muttered fatalistically.

"It sounds like you're living the dream," Jack grinned.

"Fucking nightmare, more like," John answered. "If the car wasn't new I'd have driven it into a lamppost at full speed and hoped for death."

"You scratch that car and you won't have to take your own life, you know the missus will surely kill you."

"It would be a long slow death. I want it to be quick. Maybe sniffing cocaine off a stripper's tits."

"Ah the John Entwhistle way to go," Jack said thoughtfully. "That is but a far-off dream."

"But a lovely one. Mind how you go."

"And you," he replied.

Jack trudged forward to the lifts. John was part of the security firm that protected the building and he was a darn fine security man at that. But that didn't stop him having a bit of banter. In real life he had a heart of gold but in the middle of a crisis John could switch instantly from jovial bloke to menacing monster without breaking stride.

He'd seen it happen many a time. They'd be in the middle of a conversation about nothing then someone would catch his eye. Then he was off. All business and no pleasure. Removing some oik from the building or just standing outside like a robot sentry: cold and menacing and ready to kill.

When the riots hit London, the security firm didn't lock the doors and cower behind their desks. They just sent John outside with his shirt sleeves rolled up. The sight of him, bald head, bulging neck and arms that looked like he was cradling rugby balls in the crook of his arm, was enough to scare the tar out of a pasty-white protester at 50 paces.

He was so frightening that they didn't even dare throw anything at him and try to run for their lives. Their obvious thought was 'what if he catches me?'

Jack jabbed '4th floor' on the lifts and slumped against the mirrored back of it. Today was going to be another one of those days. Monday's were always strange. They just took too long to get going.

If he came in early to get some work done, he knew he would come to a dead stop in half an hour. He needed information from other people and they were too busy nestling into their desks and chatting to get on with anything. They were infuriating. They couldn't get started before 10:30am but were happy to stay late.

He wasn't exactly a morning person as they called it. But staying after 6 o'clock after work just seemed like a waste of time. If you weren't fried by 6 you hadn't been working hard enough.

Others would sit at their desks pretending to work so they could be seen to be there. But surely that was old hat. Anyone could see through that old trick.

Or maybe they didn't. People used 'tricks' to get ahead all the time and no one else appeared to see through the charade. Sucking up to the boss. Talking non-stop when they didn't have an idea in their head. They even used 'mirroring'. Whatever the boss did with his hands or his body, they would copy. It was supposed to have the effect of the boss feeling like they were in tune with that person.

After decades of watching all these tricks he was fed-up with their 'obviousness'. They would rather read a book on the shortcut to success than learn how to do their jobs properly. Some would spend half the day complaining they had too much work to do when they could be getting on with it and getting it done.

There were a few of course who worked and worked hard. But it always seemed like the charlatans knew how to deceive convincingly. And it was these people that more often than not got ahead in life.

He'd heard a saying once, 'shit and cream rise to the top'. He had to admit there were piles of shit everywhere he looked at the moment and the only cream was in the coffee machine.

The lift pinged and the doors slid back to reveal the 4th floor in all its drab majesty. It always amused him how a creative department looked. No matter how many posters covered the walls or how each individual had tried to spruce up their own little areas with pieces of their personality, the place always looked like an office.

Looking around there were small explosions of brilliance but underneath that there still dwelled the drab and malodorous tones of an office environment. Brown carpet was underfoot, a feeble attempt to the make the ground look like earth. But with a sea of designer formica tables nestled on his faux earth there was no fooling the senses.

It was as if every part was designed to suck the life out of the inhabitants. Truth was, it was cheaper to leave everything bland and uniform than to even attempt to disguise what it was; a place of business.

It was early but he could see a few people dotted around. Some bright spark had come up with the idea of ripping out the offices and leaving everything open plan. They called it 'agile working' now. It used to be called 'hot desking' but that had failed. It was an attempt to encourage 'co-operation' but in a place where everyone was out for themselves all it did was allow other people to eavesdrop on important conversations. Not that there was any need to hide in the eaves and listen intently, everyone could hear everything that was going on. The only way to get some peace and quiet was to leave the agency and find a quiet coffee shop where you could get down to some solid graft.

Unfortunately, if you weren't at your desk, they assumed you weren't working, so you would get angry phone calls asking you to return to the office, immediately.

There was a time when you could go to a pub, have a few pints, grease the imagination gears and you would be off writing a campaign within minutes. But nowadays, drinking was as frowned upon as injecting heroin between your toes at The Priory.

The powers that be didn't like drinking because it made the creatives argumentative. Or sometimes abusive when the account people were being particularly dim.

"What's to understand?" the creatives would bellow. "It says exactly what the brief says it should."

"Ah but we inferred that there should be something else."

"But it doesn't say it in the brief. If it isn't in the brief, it isn't in the work. I'm not a fucking mind reader."

As soon as you swore, you knew you had lost but the account team would invariably say something which was worse than an expletive.

"You're not really a team player are you?" they would say when they were at a loss for words.

"I am, I just don't work on Team Fuck-up," was usually Jack's reply.

Jack remembered some of these conversations. Most he consigned to the trash bin in his memory. Stupid comments that he hoped wouldn't see the light of day again. Sadly, they appeared again and again.

He had to feel sorry for them. The account handlers were just doing what the client told them. They should have interrogated the client a bit more thoroughly but when a paying client starts saying that they are the client and they want things doing their way, the account handlers lost every time.

As he walked to his locker he saw the TV screen in the distance. The sound was turned down or off but the ticker at the bottom revealed how Russian tanks were poised to enter Korea.

World leaders were condemning the action and Russian diplomats were assuring everyone that this was just a peacekeeping initiative to protect Russian citizens within Korea's borders.

He turned away from the world crisis. If he ignored it maybe it would go away. Instead he focussed his attention on the combination lock on the padlock and thought for a second. He was hopeless with numbers so he had tried the trick of creating a 'memory palace'. In his case it turned out to be a 'memory sand castle' with very little to it, so he had left it to fall to ruin.

His locker was number 27 so in a piece of ingenuity he had separated the number into 4 digits for the combination lock.

"1+1 = 2 and 2+5 =7." He recited to himself then turned the lock to 1125. It fell open in his hand and he opened the metal door.

He threw in his jacket and took out his laptop ready to start his working day when he spied his bag at the bottom of the locker.

"I must take that home," he said to no one in particular then felt a sudden tiredness that made him close his eyes for a moment. "Shit."

The bag wasn't the problem, it was what was inside that made his knees buckle. Years ago, he had loaded the bag with weights. Only a few to start off with but as he had gotten stronger he added more.

Now, the bag weighed over 40kg. Not a great deal for a strapping lad but walk with it for a mile or two on your back and you certainly felt it. The idea came to him from watching a programme about basic training for the army. They would frequently 'yomp' with 40lb packs and still have energy to fight. Jack thought that if these guys can do it, then he certainly could.

After a few years of adding to the weights, he was fitter and stronger than he had ever been. But that still didn't stop him from wincing at the very sight of the thing that had caused him so much sweat, and aches and pains.

He would take it home today, he could take it on the tube so that the torture was cut short. He should really carry it with him all the time bearing in mind what was in it. But sometimes the weight of it was just too tiring just to contemplate moving it.

One similar memory came back to him. He had to carry his guitar amplifier from his Sixth Form College back home, a distance of 2 miles up and down hills. It was a hot day and every hundred yards or so he had to stop for a breather. He had no idea how much the damn thing weighed but on that hot, sunny afternoon it had almost finished him. He'd done it. Collapsing in a heap when he got home and drinking the best part of 2 pints of water.

His father, who had refused to give him a lift, had told him that he was 'useless' and that when he was his age he was curling 40lb weights in one hand. Jack thought that, that wasn't much and he didn't carry it two miles. If his father was such a strong fellow why hadn't he helped him? He was at that age now where he questioned all the bluster that came from his father's mouth. It was all talk as far as he could see. Anyway, he didn't want to think about that now. Clanging the locker and his memory shut, he turned to the desk where he plugged the laptop in.

He wasn't all that concerned about where he sat, he just picked the nearest space. After all, this was agile working. He didn't want to circle the office like a dog settling in front of a fire. No, here would do fine. When his art director came in he could find a seat nearby. It wasn't as if they were short of space. There was 'oodles' of space. It's just that no one wanted to sit too close to another team who also wanted a bit of privacy to do some work.

Before he did anything else, he plugged in the laptop and hit the start button. It may as well try and get its act in gear while he was making himself comfortable.

By all account this was one of the fastest *MacBooks* there was. It was such a shame that whenever they upgraded anything it slowed down.

The operating system was fine to begin with. Solid. Fast. Effective. But they kept adding bits of software on, higgledy-piggeldy. The result was a mess of bits and pieces sticking here and there which took time to recognise everything it needed to come to life.

Of course it looked like a normal laptop on the outside. Inside was a shambles.

In the end the *MacBook* would try starting then have to go looking for another new bit of software to complete the task. If it didn't find it the machine would stall and freeze.

It was like the human brain. As we'd evolved from our humble reptilian brain to our simian brain and then human brain they'd all been piled one on top of the other without removing all the nasty shit in there.

Our baser instincts were still somewhere deep inside but we'd had our more civilised brains built on top of them. No wonder we were screwed.

Our old brains told us to feed, fuck and flee. While our human brains told us to snack, build a relationship and stick with it. They contradicted one another all the time which meant people were generally in a state of confusion whenever any situation presented itself.

Our brains just like computers were fed conflicting information. We could only be turned off and then on again overnight, so if a fatal error occurred we'd have to wait till bedtime to sort out the operating system.

The machine stared at Jack blankly. He stared back daring it to do something but nothing much happened.

Symbols whirred and strange noises emanated from the device but still nothing happened. He wanted to at least get the login screen then he could tap in his identity and password and then go to the toilet and get a coffee while the damn machine thought about its next step.

He tapped his fingers impatiently. Nothing happened. And then nothing happened again. Then again. The symbols stopped spinning for a second. Then started spinning again.

After what seemed like an eternity the login screen blinked painfully into existence. Jack hit the trackpad hoping that the cursor would appear on his screen. No such luck. It was still thinking.

Finally, the cursor appeared and he clicked on the empty fields on the screen. Again, the machine laboured to understand what was going on. It was early. It hadn't had its coffee and was going to remain sluggish until it was good and ready.

Then it understood. The flashing vertical bar appeared in the identity field and Jack tapped in his name. He was now bursting to go and piss and was contorting his body to try and keep the urine in. But he couldn't go until his log-in was sorted.

The bar appeared in his password field and he hastily tapped in his password. Hitting return was to be his cue to leg it to the toilet but the machine had better ideas. 'Login or password incorrect'. It taunted.

"Why are you doing this?" he asked the machine.

If it could reply, it would probably say "It's not me, you entered the wrong information."

He tapped the information in again slowly and then hit 'enter'.

'Login or password incorrect'. It said again.

"Which one?" he pleaded.

'Not saying.'

"Oh come on!" he yelled, doing the dance of the imminent pissed pants.

At these moments he wanted to rip the computer apart like Dave Bowman did in *2001: A Space Odyssey* but he knew he had to get in or be locked out on his 3rd try.

Obviously, not a major problem except that he would have to go through the rigmarole of talking to IT to get it unlocked. And he wasn't sure he could put up with their tired and patronising questions.

This time he sat on the chair and hit every key extremely slowly and deliberately. Finally, the login screen disappeared and his computer began to download all the rubbish he'd written in the last 5 years.

"Thank God!" he exclaimed and stood up carefully so as not to jog his protesting bladder.

He walked to the toilet in a quick desperation, biting his lip as he went. The grey corridors seemed to move slowly as he stumbled through them desperately trying to control his bladder.

The toilet door was now in front of him. This was the moment he had to concentrate harder. His bladder would be starting to relax with the promise of release but he knew better.

There were zips and underpants to navigate before the moment of blessed relief. "Stay strong," he muttered as he cross-legged-walked through the door and up to the urinals.

It was too late, he could feel himself letting go. With a flourish of panicked fingers, he ripped open his flies, wrestled his boxers aside and relaxed. A stream of urine burst into the urinal violently. He couldn't believe the cup of red tea he had for breakfast was entirely responsible for this much liquid, but where else could it have come from unless he had started absorbing moisture from the air?

The stream continued without pause and then began to slow. His sigh of relief echoed around the cold, tiled room. "ThankChristforthat."

If he was like this now, what would he be like when he was 70 and he had a less forgiving bladder? He would be awash with piss all the time. He looked down and his member had given up. (Story of his life.) There were drips but he wasn't going to be fooled. He waited. There was another slight burst of activity and then he decided he must be done. He had a little shake and then put his best friend away.

Washing his hands slowly he began to unwind a little. These days the stresses and strains of the day started and ended at his local bus stop. The moments of solitude he got during the day were like oases in a desert - few and far between.

Shaking his hands he reached for the paper towels. The recycling phenomenon was everywhere. Little did people know that recycling a paper cup was less expensive than washing-up an ordinary cup. If, your recycling facilities were in this country.

Being a government that wasn't prepared for anything and was more inclined to farm out any jobs they didn't like, they actually paid for most of their recycling to be done by other countries who had the facilities.

The cost of shipping, processing and getting raw materials back was astronomical. But they had to be seen to be doing it.

Other countries had invested in the proper machinery, employed people to run it. It had created jobs and less reliance on new materials but once again England wasn't prepared to pay for the initial costs of building such plants.

There was also the problem of where to put it. The NIMBYs were a powerful voice and could stop an anthill being built when the notion took them. Ask them to have a rubbish recycling plant near their homes and they would be up in arms. They would argue that it would bring property prices down.

Yes, in principle they wholeheartedly pursued the notion of recycling and saving the planet but 'Not In My Back Yard'.

He went back to his desk. Another day, another $1.42 dollars - or whatever the exchange rate was today.

8

Back at the desk, Jack began his morning. He put on his 'special glasses' the ones with the anti-glare, Ultraviolet and Infrared coatings and began his day-long stare at the screen.

He adjusted his seat. After years of working on computers he had seen colleagues succumb to something he called 'writer's back'. They hunched over their screens all day. With every passing hour they hunched ever downward and by knocking-off time they were bent double, their noses tickling their screens.

He had also called it 'the beast with no back' for two reasons; these poor malformed creatures were bent in half and more importantly when the account handlers came upstairs to the department with changes to copy, most would disagree for a while but inevitably they would acquiesce just to get the nagging, persistent person away from the desk.

'The beast with one back' was also his favourite term for masturbation. If Shakespeare can use 'the beast with two backs' as a euphemism for sex between two people, then he could have his own little private joke.

The email sluggishly opened its eyes and revealed the emails that had been sent on Friday night and the weekend. It didn't matter that it was the weekend. If someone could get a thought off their mind onto someone else, they would do it. There were quite a few of this type. He immediately weeded out the ones that were obviously no help to him.

"Has anyone got…?" "Can anyone…?" "I've lost my…" The subjects themselves merited no more attention. No, he hadn't got an adaptor for an *iPhone 6s*, No, he couldn't spare some time on Monday afternoon to take part in a video. And the person who had lost her earrings should ask reception if anyone had turned them in. If not, they had gone walkabout forever.

The email had become the corkboard for every company. Flats to let. My niece is looking for work experience. Would anyone be looking for a punch in the face? All offers considered.

As far as Jack was concerned, emails were for work and if someone put something vacuous up, then it was up for ridicule. Only a stupid or facetious reply would fit the bill. At which he was adept.

There were a few serious emails requesting his presence at meetings. He accepted two: one to discuss strategy, the other for copy comments on a piece of work. The rest were meetings to discuss upcoming meetings. There was also a post-post-post production meeting with the client on a photographic shoot. As far as he was concerned they'd already discussed what he and his art director had wanted and what could be achieved in the time. There was no need for another meeting.

He ran his hands over his smooth head. 'Meetings'. You'd think the company was selling meetings rather than advertising. Somehow he was supposed to attend all these meetings and do the work. At the same time.

The people who ran the company or its finances didn't quite understand creatives. What creatives did was something that was unquantifiable. They noticed that creative work appeared but had no idea how to do it themselves - or even how ideas came about. They knew about timesheets, meetings and how much money they were making, but plucking ideas out of the air and making them into something that was saleable was a skill they didn't possess.

One of the emails was asking how much time would he need to write a suite of 6 emails? It said 'ballpark it'. The question was ludicrous, as they all were when it came to time estimates. How long is a piece of string? You may as well say '12 inches' because when it came down to it they could only afford '6 inches' so his recommendation was pointless. Jack wrote '2 days writing' knowing they'd reply by saying they wanted to see something 'close of business'. It didn't matter. He could do it, but it would be a push especially since he was busy on other jobs.

But that was the nature of the business these days. They'd rush a job through because the client was expecting to see something at a time and date that no one had agreed upon. They'd show some initial thoughts and ideas only to be told it 'wasn't right' and the work would have to be scheduled again. 'There never was enough time to do the work but there was always enough time to do it again.' How many times had he said that?

Another email contained client comments on a piece of copy he had completed on Thursday night. Another rush job he'd done at home and emailed in Friday morning at 1am. The comments had come back in Friday night and they wanted them this morning, first thing. He checked it through. Changed a few words. Read it through, changed a few more. Read it through again, unchanged some words and then changed some others. He reattached the document to an email and sent it back. First thing. Done.

Jack made a point of turning everything off on Friday night. Phones. Computers. Tablets. His weekends belonged to him these days. There were occasions where he'd been asked to work the weekend and that was fine. But a call on Saturday morning to come in to the office would not be tolerated. They charged the client for weekend work but the workers never saw it in their pay packets.

There was more to do, but now he needed a cup of coffee. The urgent had been done. The necessary would be done next. The jobs that could wait were in a holding pattern waiting to land on his desk. He could relax for a few seconds.

Someone walked past the desks. He knew their face but not their name. It didn't matter, they never said 'morning' anyway. In a company this size you couldn't know anyone. In a company this size, pleasantries often went out the window. If there were any pleasantries to begin with. No matter, eventually that person would want him to do something and would be all smiles, pretending to be his best mate. Then after the job was done they'd go back to ignoring him as they passed one another in the corridors. It was the way it worked. Fake smiles and false interest. Welcome to advertising.

The coffee machine was an automated piece of crap that dispensed vile cups of chemical tasting filth. But it was free so he took the rough with the smooth. He probably wouldn't have noticed if it wasn't for all these beautifully smelling and personally crafted coffees you could buy from all the boutique shops springing up everywhere.

It seemed that whenever any shop failed, a coffee shop would somehow spring into being in its place. Where were they all coming from? There were now more coffee shops than any other shop. Jack put it down to the internet. You could buy anything you wanted online now but you'd have to find a place to go and sit and order your goods.

These shops came with their free wi-fi so you could sit and sip and click to your heart's content. The coffee was good, but Jack always thought £3 was a bit much for hot water strained through ground beans with hot foamy milk poured on it.

It wasn't the price that bothered him, it was the price related to what you got. He could say the same about beer. He loved a pint of Guinness. He adored 6 pints even more but £4 for a pint seemed more justifiable than £3 for a small cup of beans and milk.

Of course, early in his career, Monday morning breakfast was free. He'd come into work avail himself of croissants and coffee with jams and honey for everyone. Like everything, costs were cut, first the pastries went, then the croissants, then the good coffee. He never touched the croissants or pastries that arrived but the coffee was always welcome to oil the cogs and get his brain ticking.

Jack pushed 'latte' on the machine and stood back as the most unpleasant groaning sound came from the machine. Then it spat out a plastic cup and followed by a most unappetising sludge that reminded him of diarrhoea. The machine then spewed it full of some hot liquid that resembled coffee, smelt a bit like coffee and tasted like someone had declared chemical warfare in the cup.

"Needs sugar," he said, looking down at the concoction. He stirred in a sweetener from a little handy packet and then stirred it with a little plastic sliver of a thing that was a spoon 'substitute'. He put the lava like liquid to his lips and sipped.

"Ah. Absolutely shit."

He walked to the water cooler next and took another little plastic cup and filled it. At least this wouldn't have any harsh chemicals in it - he hoped. He walked back to the open plan area where his desk was and placed the two little cups down next to the *MacBook* which had already gone to sleep on him.

He bashed the keys. "Wake up, you bastard. Stuff to do." The computer winked back into existence. It looked far too sprightly for Jack's liking. It looked mischievous. It looked as if at some point during the day it would crash and wipe a whole document away. When asked to retrieve it, the computer would simply look at him innocently and say 'What document? There was no document here. Look, if there was a document I would show it to you, but there isn't, so start again.'

People were drifting in now. It must be getting close to 9 o'clock. You were supposed to be at your desk and working by 9:30am, but people wanted half an hour to settle into their working day. They didn't want to start immediately that would be madness. Gently does it, especially on a Monday. You didn't want to frighten your brain right from the start or the poor thing would go into hiding and you would have to coax it out with a biscuit. But since, there was no free food anymore you'd have to go out and buy your own biscuits.

Jack bashed through the remaining emails on his desktop, one by one. Giving his opinion, changing things, declining meetings and accepting briefings. When he was done he sat back and looked at the layout pad on his desk.

"Back to the real work," he said and picked up the *Pentel N50*. Opening the pad, he saw all the scribbles he'd done on Friday. They were trying to come up with a new campaign for a telecoms company and he'd been writing a few thoughts down. It was a telecoms operator that didn't sell you stuff piecemeal, it sold the whole package. Mobile, tablet, laptop and

TV - all linked with a fibre broadband for £25 a month. No connection charges, free installation. Minimum contract 2 years.

You choose the kit you wanted, anything from *Apple* to *Samsung* to *IBM* and *Sky TV* and this company would supply you, set you up and then leave you alone to enjoy it.

All the major suppliers had jumped on board and were willing to let these guys deal with the customers while they sat back and watched the cash roll in.

You could specify any piece of kit anywhere and it would be yours. It was everything. The full monty. The whole enchilada.

He'd written the line, *'Now you're talking. Texting. Surfing. And watching.'* The client wanted the *'one-stop shop for telecoms'.*

Everyone had agreed his line was better but the client was going to insist on the one-stop shop for telecoms. Even though one of their competitors had used it recently in a TV campaign.

Now they had to use the same idea and make it different enough so that the two companies wouldn't get mixed up in the customers' minds.

They hadn't got it yet. They were toying with the idea of pop-up shops that would only be around for a week in a town. There would be 4 different shop fronts but when you went inside you saw they were all connected.

It wasn't really a pop-up shop it was a 'pop-up street'. That's how he'd sold it in. Advertising would tell people where this pop-up street would be and they could sign up there and then. Or online. Whichever they preferred. But it was always best to get people talking to people. Especially older people, they weren't particularly happy about sending messages and visiting websites. They wanted to see how things worked in front of them.

The idea of bundling all these things together and setting them up was ideal for the people who weren't tech-savvy. It should have been done earlier but companies just wanted to sell the customer 'their' kit. They didn't see the benefit of selling some of their kit and some of another manufacturer's product.

What they didn't realise is that people bought that way anyway. Ah well.

Geoff, his art director, had sketched things out roughly. They had the bare bones of it all sorted. Emails, website, mini-mall visual on the website, they even had poster sites with the mini-mall where you just pointed your phone at the billboard and got all the information. It was all-singing and all-dancing. A complete campaign.

They'd even named the company Tottenham Court Road: the place in London where you could get great deals on electronic and telecommunication gear. Anyone who wanted anything could find it here.

For fashion go to Oxford Street, for music go to Denmark Street, for electronics, Tottenham Court Road. It made sense. Especially if you did a pop-up street. You could take Tottenham Court Road to any street in the UK. Or add it on to another.

The only gremlin in the works was the client. He was the one insisting on the one-stop shop and had gotten himself bogged down in the word 'shop'.

He didn't like the thought of showing so many shops in the visual when it's just the one-stop shop. They'd explained that it was just one shop called 'Tottenham Court Road' which is full of shops. The client was having none of it. He wanted the visual to be of just the one shop. They'd explained a pop-up shop had been done before so wasn't as intriguing as a pop-up street but he may as well have stuck his fingers in his ears and started saying 'La-la-la-la-la-la-not-listening.'

This was just one client however. There were layers of clients all stacked on top of one another. To get to the big decision-maker you had to go through all the little decision-makers. And their decision-making skills were based on what they thought the next decision-maker up the ladder would say.

The idea would die a death. The client's creative licence had expired, if in fact he ever held one. They had today to try and come up with something else or the 'one shop' would go ahead. With their workload they knew they had to let go of their baby and let it wander into the client's clutches.

Then, as if by magic, Geoff appeared in the distance. He looked calm but Geoff always appeared calm. Even when he was arguing he looked calm. He could be arguing about politics or religion, not that he would, but he looked calm. His words would betray how angry he was, but even in full rant his face never broke.

"Wotcha," he said with a brief wave of the hand and went to his locker. Then he stopped. "Have you done anything to my locker?"

"No, of course not," Jack replied.

"Because if you have, there'll be hell to pay."

"Haven't touched it."

Geoff turned back to the locker and punched in his code. He opened the door slightly, then stood back and threw it open and jumped for cover. When nothing happened, he put his bag inside and took out his *MacBook*.

"Can't be too careful," he said when he got to the long table and set up his computer.

Most teams sat side by side on the long tables. They faced other teams across from them and it was fine, but Jack and Geoff were old school. They preferred to sit facing one another. Just like in the days when there were offices for creative teams. You could face your computer and face the person with whom you were working.

"Good weekend?" Jack asked as Geoff was setting up.

Geoff blew out his cheeks and put his hands on his hips. He looked into the distance as if the weekend was some dim and distant memory. One of his hands came up to his face as if he was trying to wipe away the cloud that was covering his memory.

"Yes, I suppose so. Didn't really get a chance to relax, really. But, yes, it was all right. How about you?"

"The same," Jack replied.

"Same as me, or the same as usual?" Geoff asked.

"Same as usual."

"I'm really sorry," Geoff laughed.

"Hey, I'm fine," Jack replied defensively.

"You need the love of a good woman," Geoff chuckled.

"Why do you hate me? You know that every time I get set-up with a woman or I meet someone they all turn out to be complete nutters."

"So, how is Marianna?"

"Below the belt, bro," Jack replied. 'But the truth hurts. She is insane. We were supposed to go out on a date on Saturday. We were supposed to meet at the restaurant so I get there, sit at the bar waiting for her and on the stroke of seven she sends me a text saying that she doesn't fancy it. So, I had a few beers on my own and went home."

"I did say the love of a *good* woman."

"What did you get up to?" Jack asked, changing the subject.

"I linked all my speakers up so that I could play music through the whole house. It's great. It took a while but now I'm quadrophonic in every room."

"You're lucky your wife and kids have the same taste in music or that could end in tears."

"No, they get their choices as well, it's a diplomatic household."

"Justin Bieber?"

"Language! 10p in the swear box," Geoff said as he put the polyboard and duct tape constructed box onto the table.

Jack reached into his pocket and extracted a shiny 10p. Plopping it into the makeshift swear box he sat back. "How much we got?"

"Enough for a family vacation in Monaco by the feel of it. Anyway what's happening? I somehow get the feeling we may be stuck with a one-shop pop-up from the emails I read over the weekend?"

"Yes, fraid so," Jack said. "Let me fill you in."

"Oh good," Geoff replied and put his head in his hands ready for the latest bad news.

9

The 10 o'clock meeting was everything he dreaded. Long conversations which, if thought about properly, could be whittled down into one sentence, with two instructions neatly and eloquently put.

'One pop-up shop in 5 cities, just fucking do it.'

The JFDI or Just Fucking Do It, was becoming more commonplace these days. The clients believed they knew best. So as soon as someone came up with an argument which was contrary to theirs they became flustered, mouthed the words, 'I don't care,' followed by 'just fucking do it.'

There were even clients now who didn't want to talk to creatives because they used a despicable means to change their minds - words and reasoning.

There was a time when people listened to what creative teams had to say. The account teams and clients loved seeing work and we're always happy to follow their recommendations. Now they didn't see ideas, all they were bothered about was how much it was going to cost. Of course, if they blew the marketing budget in one fell swoop there would trouble, but the clients were the ones pushing the agency to do something new and different. Unfortunately, new and different, meant different processes which cost more money than usual. The problem was the clients just weren't willing to pay for 'new and different'. They wanted 'new and different' at a price that was 'smaller and more appealing'.

'I want something that's going to put us on the map; something that's going to make us stand out from our competitors, but I'm only willing to pay £1,000 and the loose change from my pocket - but not all of it because I want a Mars bar from the vending machine, later.'

This was now the hardest part of the job for the Jack and Geoff. Yes, the client had bought an idea. Yes, the client was happy, but it could be so much better. The Creative Director had caved and said it was still a good idea and they shouldn't be disheartened, but it wasn't quite the idea it could be.

Now they had the task of making the idea happen, one which they weren't totally happy with. It would have been interesting to do a pop-up street. It was different. It could have been eye-catching. Now they had another run-of-the-mill pop-up shop which was just like every other pop-up shop that had ever been done.

Half-heartedly Jack and Geoff sat listening to all the reasons why it was better to do this than go to all the trouble of creating their original idea. It was like listening to all the reason why you should behead a baby because as soon as it started to grow it would cost a lot of money to clothe and feed it.

The meeting went on for the best part of an hour. Geoff brought up the subject of using a professional model-maker to create the front of the shop.

"I think we've found a better way to do it," the account man said. "We'll just get some shop fitters to dress it as they would a normal shop."

"Is that better, or is it cheaper? If they make a pig's ear of it, we'll be left with something that looks rubbish," Geoff replied matter of factly.

"They'll be under your guidance; you tell them what to do and they'll work to your 'vision'," the account man said.

"Geoff's 'vision' as you call it, is to get a modelmaker to do the job, properly," Jack piped up.

The account man, never to be ruffled or deviated from his obviously pre-prepared script continued "Ok team, let's progress. The client is very excited about this, so let's make it happen."

As soon as he had finished the room of people started to mumble and grumble as they pushed back their chairs. The account man smiled as he left the room and Jack and Geoff just sat there.

"I suppose, when you get fucked in the arse you shouldn't sit down," Jack moaned as he pulled himself to his feet.

"You can tell why you're the writer, you paint such vivid pictures with your words," Geoff replied.

Like dead men walking they ambled back to their desks, the full horror of what they were about to face etched on their faces. They sat down at the desk in what was now a noisy room. There weren't any loud voices, there was just a constant murmuring that permeated the whole room. The carpet caught some of the sound but the concrete walls and large glass windows just bounced the sound right back.

The TV on the back wall was showing some military action somewhere in the world again, but the sound remained firmly 'off'. It was a strange thing to do because as anyone knows, turn on a television, even without sound, and your eyes are drawn to it. You could be talking to the most beautiful woman in the world, but as soon as a television is turned on behind her, your eyes will inevitably be drawn towards it.

Jack was sitting opposite so the competition for his attention was a hands down victory for the television. He was trying to read the news feed below but couldn't quite make it out. His glasses were for close-up work. Looking in the distance was another country as far as he was concerned. Even at this distance however he could make out a picture of some troops, a tank, some more armoured vehicles, an explosion outside some city and then the newsreader in the street with people running past him.

It was all very interesting until Geoff waved his hand in front of Jack's face.

"Hello, are you in?"

"Yes," Jack replied snapping back to the reality of the room and not the news. "What's up?"

"We need to write a full brief for what we need. Everything the shop should look like. Be made of. What the interior looks like...You know the drill."

"They want an idiot list you mean? Even after you drew it all up so they could see what it looks like?"

"Yes, but now they want it in words."

"I've got some words for them," Jack grumbled.

Geoff picked up the swear box ready to hear what Jack had to say on the subject. His expectant smile radiated from his face as he shook the coins within it.

"Fiddlesticks," Jack said po-faced, looked back at his computer screen and began to open a new file on his *MacBook*.

Geoff laughed and put the swear box down. Even Jack knew it wouldn't be long before he slipped up and there would be the fresh jingle of change in the bottom of the box.

An hour later Jack was still tapping away on the *MacBook* when Geoff jiggled his hand in front of his face again. It either meant he wanted a pint or he was going out to get a coffee. Either way Jack was ready for a caffeine pick-me-up and was in dire need of something that was drinkable. A good coffee would hit the spot, not that industrial solvent from the machine.

"Yes, that would be great," Jack said and reached into his pocket. He gave Geoff £3 in pound coins. It was £2.95. Once again, a huge amount of money for hot water percolated through ground beans but he thought *'what the hell?'*

"I expect to see some change," Jack called.

As Geoff turned and walked away he gave Jack the finger over his shoulder.

"No, not one, I want five pence change."

With the break in his concentration he was immediately drawn to the television again. The news was still on. Normally at this time of day they'd changed it to something else. That Jeremy Kyle fellow or those women on a panel all talking about men and things.

He'd never got that *'Loose Women'*. He knew he wasn't supposed to, but even on the occasion where he had drifted onto it by accident, he was lost by some of the comments. It was a tamer version of a night out with a bunch of girls. On TV they really couldn't let loose, so it was a PG version of a conversation with a bunch of drunk girls. God help the rest of the world if someone gave them a drink. 'Loose Women after dark' could be a thoroughly frightening experience for everyone. Especially if the prosecco came out.

Why wasn't that or some other daytime rubbish boring the creative department? He still couldn't make out the screen properly or the ticker below but now the Prime Minister was being interviewed and the President of the United States. Then there was Putin at a council meeting or something, then Kim Jong Un smiling and waving as troops marched past. He'd got his toy soldiers out and he was going to play with them.

After a few minutes Geoff plonked a large latte in front of Jack complete with sweetener, a stick to stir and 5p change.

"Enjoy," he said as he went back to his side of the desk. Another team had plonked themselves down next to Geoff and had decided to move his stuff. Geoff looked at the pens and ruler that had been shifted and instantly moved them back to their original position. It earned a glare from the writer who was about to say something. Geoff just stared at him and gave him one of the falsest smiles he was capable of.

"Cheers, mate. Any idea what's happening there?" Jack asked pointing to the screen and sipping through the white plastic top of his cup. The coffee was good. Real coffee. None of that machine 'muck'.

"Near as I can make out, Korea and Russia are at it again. Some sort of border dispute. Some tanks crossed the border 'by mistake' and everyone's getting hot under the collar again. They even launched some fighter planes too. Doesn't look good."

"Great, another war. Why are the PM and the President renewing their love affair?"

"They've got troops in the area, they're talking about sending them in to 'calm hostilities', though how you calm a situation down with 2,000 troops armed to the teeth with the latest hardware is beyond me."

"No, it really doesn't look good," Jack mused as he turned back to his computer screen. He'd lost his thread of reasoning now and would have to read through what he'd written to get his mind back on track. It wasn't too difficult, it was just annoying. He began bashing away at the keys again and vanished back into his own little world of words.

Geoff meanwhile was searching for reference for the shop. It had to look like Tottenham Court Road shop without actually being a Tottenham Court Road shop. Everyone was ready to sue if something looked like something else so he had to make sure 'it was in the *style* of Tottenham Court Road'. A representation, not an exact copy.

Another half-hour passed before either one raised their heads. The bad thing about open plan was you could hear everything.

One particular thing about working in creative departments Jack and Geoff had both learned was that creatives were noisy animals.

In the old days, someone would be letting off fireworks down the corridor, someone may be chasing an account handler because he hadn't sold an advertising campaign to the client. At least once a week someone burst into tears because the creative team were 'beastly' to them.

The good thing about Jack and Geoff was that they could switch off their hearing at will. There could be someone performing an erotic dance to the tune of the stripper and neither one would bat an eye. They didn't need earphones. The job needed doing, so get on with it.

It was some time before Jack realised that there was something happening. There seemed to be a shift in the mood of the department. Something menacing and electric was in the air. Jack spotted it first out of the top of his glasses. A group of people had gathered round the big screen at the opposite side of the department and the sound had been turned up to normal levels. It was odd. He could understand if it was football. The rest of the creative department seemed to have some unhealthy obsession about who was losing at football when in Jack's humble opinion the only people who weren't losing were the footballers earning millions of pounds every year for kicking a ball.

Intrigued Jack saw more military vehicles travelling across the screen. Which wasn't unusual. The reactions of the little crowd were. There were hands over mouths and a few gasps of disbelief. Little rounds of muttering erupted from the little group every few minutes, so Jack guessed it must be serious.

He tried to attract Geoff's attention but his head was down behind his computer. He couldn't be roused by conventional methods now. He was lost in work.

There was only one thing to do Jack threw his pen in the general direction of Geoff's head and it bounced off his shoulder onto the desk in front of him.

"Oi, Geoff, look," Jack said pointing to the far side of the department.

Geoff picked the pen up and threw it back at Jack. It bounced off the back of his *MacBook* and dropped to the floor which immediately ate it and swallowed it from sight, never to be seen again. Calmly, Geoff turned around to see the spectacle and stood up.

"That's very odd," Geoff agreed. "Best see what's going on."

They both slowly walked to the back of the crowd and joined them to see what the kerfuffle was. This was probably the first time the creative department had taken out their earbuds. They stood together and in silence. Even John, who liked the sound of his own voice, was speechless at the front of the crowd his hand over his mouth and desperately rubbing the side of his nose as he always did when he was stressed.

The BBC reporter on the ground in Korea looked to be in a state of panic. He was almost shouting at the camera and seemed to be engulfed in a dust storm that flashed from time to time as small explosions burnt through the gloom. But that was nothing, BBC reporters always seemed to carry around their own dust storm with a complement of scared people running to and fro in the background. It was almost like their calling card.

His voice however said it, "was a minor skirmish that has now escalated into full conflict. The warnings from both sides were clear. Unless there was a retreat by the Russian forces, North Korea would use force to remove them. This did not happen so Northern forces engaged in an attempt to push the Russian forces back across the border. The Russians still believed they were on their own soil when the bullets started to fly, so they returned fire..."

"Fuck," Jack said. Then Geoff put the swearbox under his nose.

"Thought you might," Geoff said as he shook it.

It was a tremendous testament to his art direction skills that the box held together despite the weight of the coins inside.

Jack grudgingly put another 10p in the box and returned his gaze to the television screen.

"Never quite seen it like this before," Geoff said out loud.

"That's not the half of it," Kes said from somewhere near his right ear. "The President of the USA is demanding an immediate ceasefire or he's going to send in the troops himself."

"And the PM's saying pretty much the same thing, even though Russia is saying they'll attack them if they put their oar in," Matt said from somewhere near the front of the little crowd.

Jack turned back to his desk. It was a war half a world away, it was either going to blow over or carry on. Wasn't there always some sort of conflict over there any way? It made no odds to the situation here. They would have their little battles then there'd be a stalemate and then everything would go back to restrained animosity. Meanwhile he had to get this treatment finished. He wanted Geoff to have a good read through before he sent it upstairs. He wanted to make sure their arses were covered.

He didn't know why he was doing this particular job. If they had got a modelmaker in to do the job, they would be the ones doing all the donkey work and Jack and Geoff could move onto other jobs.

It seemed like every day they were doing more of other people's jobs for them. It started with timesheets. Went on to expenses, then typing, and then dealing with clients directly. Soon they would be budgeting jobs and running financial reports. They weren't far off that now considering they had to write wash-up reports on jobs that had gone 'tits-up'.

There had been a big problem a couple of years ago. A lot of time was going down on their timesheets for a particular job. Jack had written an entire 20 page document of the timeline of the job explaining what had happened and why. No opinions or 'the client is a twat' comments. It was just pure fact. He'd linked it to printouts of timesheets and his diary of meetings. The client was refusing to pay for all the time used but when his lawyers had read Jack's report they ordered him to pay up.

This wasn't what the management wanted to keep the client happy, of course. They wanted the client to pay half of what was expected and then they would make overtures to keep the client, even though he was a drain on everyone's time.

He paid up and fucked off. The last anyone had heard he was pulling the same stunt with another agency up the road. Lots of work, lots of hours wasted, nothing going to print and no pay either. They were well rid of this man but the powers that be blamed him for losing a client when all he had done was point out that the Emperor had no clothes and was wasting their time and money designing a whole wardrobe to match its colour scheme.

It seemed like whatever happened it was the creative department's fault. Seeing as how the creative department was involved in every job it was easy to pass the blame to them. Even when the creatives warned the account teams that certain situations were bound to arise, the account team carried on and then complained that the creatives had fucked up.

Jack was sitting back down writing again making sure that everything he wrote had 'anti-fuck-up' built into every stage. You couldn't second-guess everything but over the years he had learned he could prepare everyone for almost anything. He'd worked closely with a lot of great production men and women and they knew all the pitfalls of every job. They knew what to expect. So, he'd always picked their brains. He'd always listened whenever they had that 'funny look' on their faces as well. Their intuition coupled with his gut sense meant they could head a lot of problems off at the pass.

Today, he had warning bells going off everywhere in his head - it was like Westminster Abbey up there during a royal wedding. He knew Geoff could keep control of almost anything and everything. The one wild card was the client. He was what Jack called 'a cushion' - he had the impression of the last person who sat on him. And in his company that was a lot of people.

Like every job that had 'Danger' flashing in his mind, he'd already started his 'Wash-up Diary' which had dates and times and comments from everyone written in it. He hoped he wouldn't be writing another report on a job gone wrong, but you never could tell these days.

"Jack, quick, check out the news," Geoff said as he came back to his side of the table and started to pack his gear away. The crowd had dispersed at the big screen except for a few people and all the people around him were frantically packing their stuff away.

Confused, he clicked over to the BBC News website which he had bookmarked many years ago. The ticker was too slow and the news reporter was apoplectic now and wasn't really making much sense anymore.

"What the f...?" He couldn't finish his sentence. The top headline of the day was across the World page. It was even across the UK page. In fact, some variation of it was across every header. He almost expected some variant across the sports pages but they were still carrying some Manchester United story.

"War declared." Read the headlines. Updated 5 minutes ago.

The article explained that diplomatic relations had finally broken down. Russia and North Korea had begun hostilities at the border. The USA had thrown its hat in the ring with North Korea and dragged the UK along in its slipstream. The UK's 'special' relationship once again proving useful to the Americans despite all their 'back of the queue' talk during the Brexit campaign.

China and Japan had sided with Russia. India was sitting back at the moment but was expected to side with Russia.

For Jack it was 9/11 over again. When the first plane hit the towers he'd been transfixed. The full enormity couldn't quite reach his brain. He had just sat there and waited. And then the second plane hit. That was the moment he felt his depression begin. The horror of it all. The hope he had for a peaceful world. Gone. Before that moment he had been optimistic.

Something similar had happened during the Brexit Referendum. He'd hoped that unity would survive. That the United Kingdom would vote for a future where humanity banded together and fought the real enemies. Poverty. Disease. Famine.

Instead they had chosen to leave and the world seemed to slip back in time. Union flags seemed to be flying from every car and house window. There was talk of a British Empire again. Jack had watched as racist attacks increased.

Now something even more frightening was reuniting countries. Nations were picking their sides and gathering together. Standing shoulder to shoulder. The rhetoric of war. Diplomacy had finally failed and countries were girding their loins for what could only be a major conflict.

Jack closed his computer just as the announcement came over the Public Address system.

"In the event of the current crisis, we would ask you to vacate the building slowly and return to your homes. We repeat, in the event of the current crisis, we would ask you to vacate the building slowly and return to your homes."

By the time the second announcement had finished Jack had stowed his gear in his locker and his jacket was on. Last time there was an announcement like that was when the planes hit the Twin Towers and the warnings were all over London as they expected the same here.

He was going to leave his bag in the bottom of the locker but stopped. He thought for a second. A huge feeling of deja vu hit him. He'd been through this in his head many years ago. Reaching down he picked up the bag with a grunt. He would probably need what was inside. You never knew. There had been many a bomb scare in his time in London, but never a nuclear bomb scare. This was a first for him. The bag was heavy, it was really heavy. Then he started to move towards the stairs with slow purpose.

Some people were standing at the lift waiting patiently but as soon as the doors opened you could see it was already full to the brim with frightened people who were a little upset to see that they were at the creative floor and not on the ground. The doors slid shut and the people continued to wait at the lift doors.

Looking back over his shoulder he could see other people milling around asking stupid questions. Looking at their computer screens. Watching the big screen in the department. Geoff had packed his gear away in record time and had vanished. The door to the fire exit was still ajar. Which meant he had seen what was happening and taken the quickest way out. It may say 'Fire Exit' but it also said 'Only to be used in an Emergency'. Jack thought this qualified and followed the invisible trail of his partner.

He was no coward but he wasn't stupid either. When the going got tough, he was all for scarpering. Forget heroics and waiting to see if it would all blow over in the next few hours, he was leaving London. This was one of the places in the world which had one of the biggest bullseyes drawn on it and he wasn't waiting around for the arrow to hit.

He jumped down the stairs taking one flight in two dangerous bounds. The same with the next. His momentum was such that he had to stop himself from head butting the wall at each level with his hands. The weight of the bag was pushing him faster than he was used to.

He pushed the door exit button at the bottom of the stairs and emerged into reception as if he had quite literally fallen from the creative floor. Even that had been too slow; there was already a crowd of people crammed against the front door of reception, all trying and failing to get out of the building at the same time.

Panic. In their fear, they had pinned the doors closed. A whole mass of people now stood between him and his exit.

10

The narrowness of the door meant the people could only get out one by one. Which was made more difficult by the press of the crowd. They dribbled into the streets while the rest pushed and shouted behind them. The receptionist was battling to open the other doors but they were firmly bolted to the floor and no matter how she tried, she could not reach down to pull the bolts free without someone pushing her face into the door.

Jack waited for a second. Will they actually realise by pushing that they were effectively blocking the person who could let them all go free? No, they didn't. They weren't thinking at all. 'Mindless mob' was the phrase that sprang to mind. And these were some of the people he considered to be intelligent.

Jack sighed and climbed onto the reception desk. He walked its length to the front of the crowd and pushed the panicking people back with his feet so he could ease down at the front of the doors. They weren't happy with this turn of events but Jack's cold stare made them keep their distance. He had the look that could sometimes curdle milk. Either that or he wasn't paying attention to sell-by dates.

He stood next to the receptionist, who looked battered and bruised already. The people ignored her and pushed her back and forth as she fought to open the door.

"GET BACK!" Jack shouted at the top of his lungs and pushed the front of the crowd. The mob looked at him shocked. He stared at them one by one, and one by one his eyes pushed them back a few more steps.

Just for a few seconds the people were stunned into inactivity and stopped their wailings. They looked at him with frightened expressions and hang dog looks that showed their submission.

"Let us open the doors properly and we can all get out," Jack said matter of factly.

When the crowd had stopped moving completely, he bent down next to the poor receptionist and calmly pulled the bolt from the floor. The doors opened and Jack moved the receptionist aside. Like a swarm of locusts, the people ran out onto the streets careful not to get in Jack's or the receptionists way again.

"Thank you," she muttered breathlessly. "I thought I was going to be crushed to death."

"Judging by the ways things are going, that's exactly what's going to happen to a lot of people out there today. Why aren't you following them?"

"I'll be fired, if I leave the desk," she replied glumly.

"There may not be a desk in an hour or so. Go on, get the fuck home."

"But…"

"No buts, go. I have a bad feeling that the day's going to get a lot worse and you staying at your desk won't make a blind bit of difference."

The receptionist looked at him thoughtfully then picked up her coat and handbag from behind the desk.

"Thank you," she said sincerely then vanished out of the door and into the passing crowd.

People were still streaming down the stairs and out of the lifts. Outside they split into two groups; one headed north and the other south. He thought it through. *'If it was war and there were bombs on their way. What should he do? There were no bomb shelters here. Well, not for ordinary people. He had to get home. Which meant he had to go out into that insanity.'* When they were calm or comatose, Londoners were a danger to life and limb. Now that they were emotional and scared, anything could happen.

Jack stood for a moment and considered his plan of attack, or plan of retreat if he was to be honest with himself. He watched as the crowds slammed into one another and people pinballed from one person to the next.

Everyone was panicking. Everyone. If he could keep a cool head and think this through, he would be all right. He made a decision. Time to get moving. See how bad things were before he really decided what to do.

For some reason a quote from Abraham Lincoln sprang to his mind:

'If I was given seven days to cut down a tree I would spend the first six days sharpening the axe.'

Then he started walking South. He wasn't going to get caught up in the hysteria of the situation. He wasn't going to give in to panic. If he was going to die today, he wasn't going to die terrified, he was going to die undertaking the best course of action given the situation. After all, this was just another problem to solve. He had to solve it piece by piece. Slowly but surely. That's what he did.

It was easier said than done. Jack wanted to walk down the street but the people behind him wanted to run down the street. They were pushing at him from every side but he would not deviate his direction. Thankfully, the weight of his bag added to his own weight, helped anchor him to the pavement. If he was toppled however he would be done for. Trampled to death under a hundred feet in under a minute.

Running and large crowds were a mistake. People were falling all around him. Whether they had tripped on the edges of the pavements as they swarmed down the roads he didn't know, but the people immediately behind fell over them. Little cascades of human beings were happening everywhere. Some picked themselves up. Others remained on the floor where they tripped the people behind.

There were cars and buses on the street trying to travel North, people too. They collided with the

Southern travellers like two armies on a battlefield. Leaving casualties littered across the street.

This was impossible. There was no way he could travel straight home through all this. It may be time to take a different tack. In his opinion, he had assessed the situation and found it to be stupid. Jack slipped down a side road. Hopefully the human stampede would be less powerful in another direction and he could make better progress.

It was no use. They were everywhere. The panic had everyone running for their lives in every direction and despite shouts to 'remain calm' from what seemed to be from a Community Police Officer, no one was.

There was only one thing to do in this situation. He'd done it many times. Whenever there was a tube strike, the trick wasn't to get dragged into the melee, the trick was to either get right in front of it, or get left at the back of it.

Since there was no way to get in front of it - except if he had a train with a cow-pusher on the front. He had to wait for it to pass. That way he could progress in his own time and not be crushed by the mob.

It was probably not the most sensible idea; the missiles could already be on their way but, he decided, he would rather be destroyed in an instant by enemy fire than trampled to death by 'friendly feet'.

There on the corner, was his answer. He'd spent many an hour sat outside with his pad and pen watching the world go by, now he could watch it swarm by.

He walked calmly into the *Caffe Nero* and looked around. It was empty. No one had even seen fit to lock the doors. Like him they had downed tools and just left. The customers must have done the same because it was like the Marie Celeste. The power was on and even the tables still had a few half-full coffee cups on them and uneaten bits of cake and sandwiches.

For a moment he thought about drinking one of these, then thought better of it. *'What am I, some sort of savage?'* he chastised himself.

Instead he put his bag carefully on the tiled floor and sighed. It was always such a relief to put it down that he wondered if he should pick it up again, or at least empty the weights out.

'No,' he said to himself, take the weights out now and he'd probably go running down the road shouting 'the sky is falling'. Keep them in for now. It would slow him down. Step by step not gallop by gallop. Keep calm.

Heeding his own advice, he looked around again to make sure he was alone then walked behind the counter. He saw the 'thingummybob' and the 'whatchamacallit' and pumped some coffee grounds into the 'scoopy thing'. Tapped it down and attached it to the hot water. He put a cup underneath and pressed 'go'. Taking one of the milk jugs he started to steam some milk.

Slowly the milk began to build up nicely. He was hoping for a latte but the way he did things, it always ended up as being a cappuccino. He'd had his own machine at home once and had learned one thing; he wasn't all that good at making coffee. He frothed it gently every time, but he always overdid it. Rather than a smooth consistency of frothing milk he was left with a 'globby' mess.

He was lost in spoiling his coffee when a scream came from the street. He glanced through the window which was difficult because they were half opaque. From what he could see, an old woman was being knocked to the floor by one of those young man who appeared to be in possession of more beard than face.

"Oh no, you don't," Jack muttered to himself. He dropped the milk jug instantly and sprang into action. Forget all those thoughts about keeping calm. He wasn't about to let something like that happen. Without the bag slowing him down he moved like lightning. He almost flew across the cafe and out the door in a blur.

"GET OUT THE WAY YOU STUPID CUNT!" Beard-face yelled at the woman's back. He punched her but the blow glanced off her side. There was no direction to his attack, he was just flailing around in a frenzy. The man was lost. Fear and panic had him in their grip and he was completely out of control.

Jack aimed a side kick at the man's left knee. There was a scream of pain and the man crumpled instantly to the floor. His arms instead of flailing around now cradled his poor busted knee. But that wasn't the end. Jack leant over him. He grabbed his beard with his right hand and punched down with his clenched left fist. His strongest hand. He kept the punches short but powerful. Little thunderbolts that would disorient the man and would allow Jack to punctuate his words with blows.

"Where." Punch. "Are." Punch. "Your." Punch. "Manners." Punch. Jack stopped when he got no answer. The man fell back bloodied and unconscious. Jack released his beard so that his head made a nasty thud on the tarmac. He stared down at him for a few moments just in case the man decided to wake up and prove beyond doubt that he had no manners by attacking him from behind.

When the man didn't move, Jack stepped back. The adrenaline that had been coursing through his veins began to slow and his breathed relaxed.

He felt good.

The anxiety that had been building up through the morning was gone. It was true; stress was a condition brought on by resisting the urge to punch the living shit out of someone. Punching Beardface out of the conscious world had made him feel a damn sight better.

"Thank you," a small but surprisingly young voice said from the bundle of old clothes Beardface had been attacking.

Looking over to the old woman he realised he had been wrong. It wasn't an old lady at all, but a young one. She was one of those girls who favoured old hair styles and old- fashioned clothes. Looking at her now he guessed she couldn't have been more than 25.

"You're welcome," Jack said offering her his hand. "Are you alright?"

"Yes, I think so," she replied. "Just a bit shaken up."

"Sure you're not hurt?"

"I'm fine, I think."

Jack pulled her up by the hand and righted her on her feet. She was beautiful with white hair that had been coloured. She wore strong dark lipstick, dark eyeshadow all daubed on a white pancake make-up background. She looked more like a ghost than a human being. A beautiful ghost.

"Would you care for a coffee?" Jack asked as if they were observing social niceties at a social function.

"Pardon?" she asked a little dumbstruck

"A coffee?" Jack asked again. "I'm making one, and it looks like you could use something to calm you down."

"Er, sure," she replied, looking around at the people who were still running down the streets. "But shouldn't we…?"

"Run?" Jack finished her sentence. "Best not, you look a bit too shaken at the moment. Have a quick coffee and a sit down. Then consider a swift walk, when the crowds have cleared."

"Ok, sounds like a plan. What about him?"

"Let him get his own coffee," Jack smiled.

As Jack walked into the coffee shop again, the girl followed but not before kicking the unconscious man in the groin with her pointy shoe. *That was cold,'* Jack observed. Utterly called for, but cold nonetheless. He liked this girl.

11

She'd asked for a decaf, skimmed milk latte with a few sprinkles and Jack had apologetically supplied her with a cappuccino. With some sort of milk and some dry brown stuff on the top that could have been anything. But she took it gratefully and with a smile that made her dark lipstick race across her white face.

"How are you feeling?" Jack asked, sipping his equally bizarre drink.

"Much better, thanks," she replied as she examined her old ripped dress at the elbow. "Could have been worse. I'm Trudi, by the way," she said. "Trudi with an 'i' not a 'y'. Why? I don't know."

"Jack," he replied, offering his hand which took carefully so as not to exacerbate her injuries.

"So, Jack, why aren't you running for your life?" Trudi asked chirpily, considering the whole situation.

"I thought I'd try and wait until the initial panic died down a bit, then head off."

Trudi raised an eyebrow quizzically. "And what if they nuke us while we're having tea and cakes?"

"Then we die with some grace, not screaming in panic," Jack replied with smile.

"You are extremely weird," Trudi said clasping her coffee cup both hands and smiling at him.

"I have this saying which I use quite a lot, 'Men are from Mars, women are from Venus, I'm from Earth'," Jack said. "It's the rest of you who are strange."

"Well, I'm not from Venus, either. I'm an Earthling. But it looks like I'm going to be blown to high-heaven with the rest of the world today," Trudi reflected.

"Maybe not," Jack opined. "Get far enough from the centre of London, Parliament, Power plants, military bases and there's a good chance you'll survive."

"They'll be sending nukes not fireworks."

"Nukes have a blast radius, get far enough away from the epicentre. And underground, and you'll probably survive."

"Probably? What about radiation?"

"Stay underground for as long as you can. Most of the radiation is from the initial blast. Most of it will have dissipated. Today's bombs are more devastating than dirty. You still have to watch out for radiation but after a couple of weeks most of it will have gone."

"You're kidding me."

"Nope, you'll get a huge burst of radiation at first, then over the space of a few weeks, normal levels."

"That's absurd."

"Not really, if the earth is left completely uninhabitable. Who wins?"

"No one, but that's the deterrent isn't it? Mutually assured destruction and all that."

"And what would they do with a completely irradiated Earth? The leaders who ordered the strikes would be stuck in their bunkers forever. No, they want to come out and invade the countries they have bombed to shit. So, all the bombs are cleaner, very destructive but they're not going to ruin the planet so they have to spend umpteen years in the bowels of the earth."

"All sounds a bit iffy to me."

"Trust me on this. Get as far away from London as possible and get yourself underground if you can with a few supplies. Get in a cellar if you can. Come out 14 days after the blast, and avoid the rain, it will most likely be acidic for a while."

"How far do I have to go? I mean I have family in South Kensington, will that be enough? I've tried to call them but the whole phone network must be clogged up."

"Everything's clogged by now. Start walking, walk as far as you can get until you hear the 4-minute warning, then get underground."

Standing up Trudi slung her bag over her shoulder. "Well, I'd best start out if that's the best advice I'll get today. What about you? Have you got somewhere to go, family to hole up with?"

"Not anymore," Jack said sadly. "Good luck."

"You too," Trudi smiled. 'Have a nice apocalypse."

She turned and opened the door and then she was gone. The door took its time to close properly and he could hear the distant sound of running feet and shouts of anger. The worst of the mob had passed now. Like a rainstorm that had moved on, its wake was evident by what it left on the pavements.

Jack collected the cups on the table and took them to the back of the shop where the dishwasher was situated. He closed the door and pressed 'wash'. Never let it be said that he left a dirty cup.

Walking back into the main shop he picked up his bag with a grunt and left. It had been a long time since he'd had coffee with a young lady and he quite liked it. Of course she was too young for him. And too pretty. And they probably didn't have much in common. She was better off with someone else. If she made it.

He hoped she would make it. Hoped she would find her family. Hoped that she was safe when the bombs started falling. He'd read all that gumph about the bombs and blast radiuses and fallout rates. For once he hoped what he read was true, else they were all in for a very unpleasant death.

All? No, the privileged few would now be heading to their bunkers. The war wouldn't start without giving them time to reach safety. Get to their seats. Order their popcorn, and put on their 3D glasses.

He may have a few hours if he was lucky. Time to reach home maybe. He hoped so. He didn't want to be vaporised today. Or any other for that matter. But today in particular when the likelihood was high, he'd much rather be hiding in a dark cellar. His dark cellar preferably. If he was going to die, he wanted to die at home.

Jack wondered if it would hurt. The only answer that came to his mind was, *'probably'*. Although they said that your nerve endings would be fried so quickly, your brain wouldn't have time to register any pain.

There was more to his little nuclear survival lesson but he didn't want her to give up hope. He didn't want anyone to give up hope. If the bomb and the fallout didn't get you, the acid rain and the nuclear winter would. Then, if you survived all that, there was the scavenging mutants. He wasn't sure if there would be scavenging mutants, but it was always best to be prepared for such things.

There wasn't much you could do to survive, really. Unless she had built herself a nuclear bunker in her spare time out of old clothes and sticky back plastic, Trudi with the cute little 'i' at the end of her name would probably be dead soon.

Jack pulled out his mobile phone and checked the screen. It was a *Windows* phone so all the squares on the front told him all he needed to know. No calls. No texts. There was an email however. *Holland &* *Barratt's* 'Buy One get one half price' offer was ending on Thursday. Everything must go. *'You're not kidding,'* he thought to himself.

He tried to call Geoff, to see if he was out of the city, or had got anywhere yet. But the phone didn't even ring. Everything was dead.

Chuckling to himself at the irony of the situation, Jack put the phone back in his pocket. After years of texts, emails, missed calls and messenger texts, the first time he really wanted to use his phone and the damn thing wasn't working.

"Figures," he said to himself and began his journey.

12

By the time Jack left the cafe, the crowd had thinned out completely. Even the bearded man who had attacked Trudi had slunk off somewhere leaving a few drops of blood and what looked like a patch of urine on the pavement.

That was good. He didn't want to beat some more sense into him. It would be a little too tiring on the arm. He had better things to do with his strength right now than re-educate 'Beardface' on how to treat people.

He could see the back of the crowd shuffling off in the distance and a few stragglers were walking down Charlotte Street heading in a northerly direction. Other than that the place was quickly becoming deserted. *'New Year's Day,'* he thought to himself. *'It was New Year's Day.'*

The crowd in the distance sounded like a beehive buzzing angrily. While car horns cut through the air with their endless 'parping', little good it was going to do them. The whole of London had decided to leave at the same time and the roads weren't made for it. Even rush hour took 3 hours these days.

Alone in the street all he could hear now was the clinking of the weights in his bag. He had about 7 miles to get home and about 2 million people in between him and his destination - all of them terrified. He would have to lose the weights soon. Stash them somewhere. Even get rid of the bag but not before he removed his little helpers. First he had to get out of the view of the general populace and the CCTV cameras - he didn't trust them. It wasn't 1984 but it was damn close. Any infringement and he would have the police waiting on his doorstep when he got home ready for him to slip into a nice pair of warm handcuffs.

The other plan that was running through his mind was the scenario where he didn't make it home. If the worst came to the worst he may have to find shelter somewhere else and the rest of London wasn't particularly welcoming visitors, right now. They were locking their doors and hopefully heading down into cellars.

As he trundled his weights down the road he noticed that the few people who had no interest in finding safety were more interested in finding liquor. The few left on the streets had already turned feral. Most were breaking windows while sipping from bottles of whiskey. One was supping from a bottle of Champagne. Jack had no idea of these things but if one was going to drink to the end of the world, one would do it with one of the most expensive drinks you could loot from the nearest Oddbins.

"It's the end of the world as we know it," one sang, badly. "And I feel fiiiii-nnnneee."

REM's song seemed appropriate for today, if only the gentleman singing it could hold a tune then he would have been mildly amused. Singing out of tune wasn't funny in his mind. If you can't sing, don't. It should be a rule enforced by very large policemen with big truncheons. Or maybe large vicious-looking tuning forks.

Come to think of it, where were the police? This was a catastrophe. They should be lining the streets, protecting property. Or beating the crap out of anyone who stepped out of line, if you prefer. This was the ideal opportunity for a bit of police violence. Or had they learned their lessons over the years? They'd been caught so many times on camera now they could have a whole TV series just called 'Police Brutality'. That's if the footage didn't go missing. CCTV could mysteriously vanish or a technical glitch could turn the cameras off. But there were now thousands of cameras. Everyone carried their own video camera. It was right there on their own personal phones. One step out of line and the police were on candid camera for all to see. And it would be admissible in court.

Another window smashed down the way and someone was helping themselves to an electric guitar. Much as Jack liked guitars he could think of more practical things to steal at this time. Food would be one. Water purifiers would be another.

Atomic bomb proof umbrellas would be ideal.

Having said that, hadn't he helped himself to a couple of cappuccinos/lattes not so long ago? You could hardly call that practical.

Maybe in the thief's mind he was going to compose a song to mark the occasion? Maybe a little Apocalypso music?

Jack smiled to himself. That was dreadful. Truly dreadful. If anyone saw him now they would have thought him insane. He was walking down the middle of Rathbone Place towards Soho with a bag of weights on his back, smiling, in the middle of what could be the end of the world. The only thing missing from this scenario was him whistling a merry tune.

'Oh fuck it,' he thought to himself and fished his earphones out of his pocket. If he was going to be melted in the path of a nuclear firestorm he may as well go out listening to some music. But what would be appropriate?

Jack put on his earphones and immediately felt better; disconnected from the madness that surrounded him. He put away his CD player and fished out the Kindle with its list of downloads. There was no way he could connect to the Cloud and download anymore tunes so he would have to make do with the ones stored on his device.

Fortunately, one of his recent downloads was the 'Slash' album and Jack remembered there was a song with Iggy Pop called *'We're All Gonna Die'.*

Jack pressed the 'shuffle' icon on the album and the song *'Ghost'* featuring Ian Astbury banged through his head.

"Cool," he muttered to himself as he picked up the pace to the beat.

Then he started whistling.

13

That's when people started to look at him as he passed. They may be intent on looting or performing some other criminal activity, but here was something far stranger. A man walking down the middle of the street, smiling to himself and whistling.

For some reason it just didn't compute. It was like whistling nonchalantly as you walked through customs. It was just asking for trouble.

Then they looked closer. At first glance he just looked like a typical middle-aged man, but he was tall, broad shouldered. Not an inch of fat on him. Someone who looked like he used the gym and not just to sit in the juice bar reading a book.

"Problem?" Jack asked the man pulling the *Fender Telecaster* out of the guitar shop window.

"No," the man replied. "Have a good day."

"You too," Jack replied. "Better put on some sun factor 10 million, looks like it could be a hot one."

"Yeah," the man agreed then began to run in the opposite direction, leaving his booty behind.

Jack carried on walking. Now that the people were mostly out of his way he started to enjoy the day. It was quite beautiful. If it wasn't for the mayhem, he would have probably enjoyed it a lot more. But he reasoned that you can't have everything.

He reached Oxford Street and stared up and down what was one of the busiest streets in London. The traffic was at a standstill. Every car was parked in the middle of the road higgledy-piggeldy and empty, or so he assumed. The people had abandoned their cars, buses and taxis. The road was completely gridlocked. Except for motorbikes and scooters which could dart in and out of the carnage. He could see a few in the distance crossing the road jam from other side streets.

That's what he needed; a bike or a cycle. He could walk home but it would take time. He watched as these lucky bastards zoomed in and out of the traffic and headed off to safety. Now where could he get a bike? His brain computed for a while. What had he been thinking in all his previous mental simulations?

In the distance, one biker rode too close to a gang of people and was pulled to the ground. There was a mad scramble as they all tried to get on it and Jack turned away unable to watch these people desperately club one another to death.

There was nothing he could do about it he reasoned. Even if he could he was too far away to wade in and ...Do what exactly? Beat the biker to death? Beat the crowd of people to death? What should he do? Somebody should be doing something.

The truth was, everybody was doing something. They were trying to save their own lives and selfish as that may sound, it was the right thing to do. He should be doing the same.

Soho Square was just ahead so he left the worries of Oxford Street alone. He'd had many an impromptu picnic here in his time. Now, there was just litter. He never did quite get to grips with this sudden desire to go roll around on the grass outside when sunshine hit the city. Although he'd followed and tried to understand. People would descend on patches of green, loll about in the sunshine for an hour then go back to their fluorescent offices feeling as though they had communed with nature. *'No, you sat on some grass in the middle of a city full of brick and concrete, that's all.'*

There were precious few of these green patches dotted around now. The expanding city had eaten them up and spat out huge curtain walled buildings where you could see people unhappily incarcerated from 9 until 5.

Rather than walk around, Jack thought it would be nice to walk through the centre, maybe even pick up a few lost memories on the way. Even now the pull of 'green' was too much for him. Maybe he wasn't all that different from other people, after all.

Again he noticed that although it was a fairly sunny afternoon and there was enough discarded food on the pavements, there were no birds pecking at the paving slabs. Surely, there should be some. Had they all flown away knowing what was to come? It wasn't as if birds had their own built-in nuclear warning system. Did they?

Could they have sensed something all along? This morning when the birds were conspicuously absent, had they known back then that the world was going to turn into a fireball and had gotten the fuck out before they got their feathers burnt? He knew they had their 'instincts' and some had their connection with the magnetic fields of the earth but had they also some sixth sense that could help them get the hell away from trouble spots?

If he had the same' danger sense' he would have phoned in sick and wouldn't be here, now. He'd be miles away with his fingers in his ears and his eyes tight shut waiting for 'the big one'.

Wrapped up in his thoughts he saw the figure step out from behind the little building in Soho Square's very centre. What was it? A hut? A pagoda? Some other description? He'd never asked and so he'd never found out. If he had an internet connection maybe he could do a search. Later maybe, for now his focus was on the hooded figure pointing a knife at him.

"Put the bag down and step back." The figure motioned with his knife to where the ground was - as if he had somehow forgotten where 'down' was.

Jack did as he was told. Holding the bag firmly, he slipped the straps off his shoulders. He achieved it in a fluid easy motion without giving away how much of a weight it was. He was used to its weight. So he carried it as if it was normal. Nothing strange here, honest.

"Go on, step back." The hood again motioned with his knife so he knew where 'back' was.

Jack took one step back without breaking his gaze from the mugger. He raised his hands to signify his surrender. His eyes however burned pure hatred into the mugger's face. *Just break eye contact fucker and we'll see what we will see,'* Jack thought

"That's it, Grandad. Keep them hands up."

Grandad! Grand-fucking-dad! Who does this little cunt think he's dealing with? A pensioner on a zimmer frame? Just look away for one second you little cunt I'll rip that little shit-eating grin off your fucking face.

The youth moved closer, bending down to reach for the bag, but not daring to move his eyes away from the man in front of him.

Jack stared and then smiled slightly. He knew what was coming and he wasn't about to let his chance slip through his fingers.

Just as the youth's hand grasped the straps of the bag he started to move away. Unfortunately for him, he didn't move far enough and fast enough. He'd assumed that the bag was an ordinary weight. Something you could pick up and run with. Big mistake. There was at least 45 kg in there and he wasn't ready for it. Especially with his arm at full stretch. He jerked backwards as the weights anchored his arm to the ground and his legs gave way. The last thing he thought was, *What the fuck has he got in here?'*

The second the youth looked down and went off balance, Jack gave him a short sharp punch in the face to disorient him. With his attacker more off-balance Jack clenched his hands together and brought them down with all his strength on the back of the youth's head.

There followed a sickening crack as the front of his skull hit the unyielding pavement. Then he lay still. His knife skittered across the paving slabs as Jack lifted the youth's head and smacked it face first into the ground once, twice three times. Just to make sure.

Jack stood up and watched the blood start to spread from underneath the young man's head. The eye he could see on the one side of his head stared forward. He was like a fish on a slab.

He'd killed him. Not murdered. He'd killed him. There was a difference. This human had tried to rob him, would probably have killed him given half the chance. Somehow the rules of society had changed the moment the alert had been given. This was the start of something different, something more barbaric and uncivilised than all the rush hours or tube strikes he had endured in his life.

"I'm very sorry," Jack exclaimed, as if that would make everything better. "But you started it."

Looking around he saw people in the distance. A CCTV camera on the corner of a Greek Street building was busy monitoring empty space. It was pointed in the complete opposite direction. He picked up the bag and walked slowly away from the body. If he ran it would surely draw attention. So, he walked. His weights providing a comforting pressure on his gait.

Besides who would be manning the cameras at the moment? And if they were what could anyone do about it? There were probably 10 crimes being committed every second right now. Martial law might even be in place but it just might be looking at another place.

Even then there was probably a camera that he hadn't seen. One that had recorded everything that he'd just done and had sent a SWAT team his way with guns and vests and big knives to slit his entrails from his body.

No, that was ridiculous. No one would be watching him. He didn't know why he was panicking. He was fine. Nothing like that would happen. It was a good job he'd taken his anti-depressants this morning or he would be all over the place.

Then he stopped. Did he take his pills this morning? Surely he did. He almost did it automatically these days. He remembered seeing his 'Post-it' that said 'Don't worry it's just the drugs'. But did he take his pills? He remembered the cup of sweet red tea but his pills? Not really.

Like a man who had left the stove on, he walked and then stopped. Walked a bit more, then stopped again. It would be some time before he could walk properly again. His brain was in need of the blood from the rest of his body. It needed to stimulate his memory centres and pluck out an answer.

The problem was, the pills he took sometimes made him forgetful. So even if he had taken them and forgotten, his brain couldn't go back and remember he'd taken them. 'Aaaaaaaaarrrrrgggggghhhhhh!'

It was infuriating. He should get home as fast as possible and check the box of pills with the days printed on them. It was the only way to know for sure.

14

What was wrong with him? He'd killed someone and he was walking down the street as if he was going shopping. He was more worried about the fact that he hadn't taken his pills than the fact that he had just pulverised someone's skull with a pavement.

Thinking about it, he actually felt a lot better about things. The anger he had released when he pounded to the young man's skull was exhilarating.

After years of stress and strain, turning someone's skull into porridge made him feel fantastic. The same with punching 'Beardface'. It was like all his angst had been released with every violent act.

Who knew? All those years of psychoanalysis and the answer was staring him in the face. Forget the pills and potions. Forget the nights self-medicating with alcohol, go outside and kill someone and watch the stress and strains of everyday life just wash away with their blood.

In another life he had followed martial arts for a while. He'd followed the theory but was never much good at the practice. He'd tried to control his seething mind, his body, his breathing, his thoughts even. Slowly but surely he had left some of that anger behind. Some of it had helped but there was still something dreadful lurking behind his eyes. Coiled around his brain.

He'd spent decades trying to fit into society or at the very least try to understand it but somewhere along the line he had realised there was something different about him. Especially his tolerance for the mundane and the stupidity of other people.

This now, was an elation. The world was going to end. The rule book was going to be burnt in a nuclear fire. Maybe a better world would rise from the ashes and he wouldn't feel so isolated from it. *'New world. New rules.'*

So what if he killed someone? It was the right thing to do. The man may have killed him and no one else would have given a fuck. It's now a dog eat dog world.

Jack stopped again. Would anyone give a fuck? Really? If he had been killed back there, would there be scores of mourners wandering around weeping and wailing and throwing themselves onto his grave? No, there wouldn't.

He started walking again. Damn it, he'd done the right thing. So, why did he feel so terrible? His conscience was playing with him. Trying to drive him back to face his failings. No, that wasn't going to happen. Look at the innocent people lying by the roadside. Dead, killed in the crush of 'humanity' that was only thinking of itself. It was one of the basest instincts. You had to survive. You had to keep going. You had to pass on your genetic code. Make sure you lived on in your children. Fulfilled your biological imperative. If anyone got in the way of that you pushed them aside. If they wouldn't be pushed away, you had to make sure they couldn't stop you.

As his anger rose and fell with his logical mind trying to reason with his conscience, he wondered if it was too late to have children? In the midst of the end of the world could he be an Adam and find an Eve to begin anew? Then another horror hit him; if Marianne was his Eve he may have to do the decent thing and kill himself. He couldn't bear the idea of spending the rest of his life listening to her moan every time she had a child.

"But look what it's doing to my figure."

"We're trying to repopulate the earth, dear." he would argue.

"Not this girl. I've got my looks to think about."

Then he would either kill himself or kill her. The lack of mirrors and hair and nail salons would drive her to suicide anyway.

These were all useless thoughts at the moment. The more he walked, the more his mind wandered off the beaten path. He was trying to forget the horror of the murder. It was as if it was a story. Something that had happened to someone else in a book or a film.

That was it, he'd read about it somewhere. It wasn't real. It was a dream maybe. Or a story told in his childhood to frighten someone. Then he felt the heavy weights in his bag again and realised it was all true.

The weights were keeping him grounded.

Why couldn't he be one of those people who could let things go without going back to them. Of course this wasn't a faux pas that you could just apologise for but he could at least concentrate on the matter in hand. He was walking for his life now and all that other stuff could just take a backseat. A silent backseat passenger that wasn't forever asking, 'Are we there yet?'

If only he could forget it, rationalise it, or better still, believe a lie he had made up.

He'd actually seen people rewrite history in their heads. They denied something had happened. Told a lie and then continued to repeat that lie until they themselves believed it. The 'It wasn't me' syndrome.

His father had done it. He'd caught his father in an affair. He hadn't caught him having sex but he'd seen all the clues. His father was behaving strangely. Secretively. There was something a bit 'off' about him and a young Jack couldn't quite put his finger on what was wrong.

He'd followed his father when his mother wasn't around. Seen him go up the road. Seen him knock on a door. Saw the woman open it and kiss him. Then invite him in. His father had looked round but not seen him crouched down in the alleyway. He watched and waited. As his father went into the house. A couple of hours passed and his father re-emerged. His father was dressed but the woman was in a dressing gown. They hadn't been having tea and cakes in there.

Years later after his mother had died, Jack's father had told everyone that he'd never even looked at another woman during his marriage. He had always been faithful and now she was gone. The thought of looking at another woman had made him feel unfaithful. Never even thought about it because he had loved Jack's mother so much. The women all around at the time had sympathised with him. Told him it would be all right. If he needed someone to talk to they would be there for him. He was lining up his next conquests on the sympathies of his wife's death.

Jack had wanted to scream at him. *'Liar.'* Jack had wanted to pound his filthy lies out of his mouth. Make him admit he was a foul human being for cheating on his mother. But reason returned to him and he let his father tell his lies.

What use was there in telling the truth or beating his father within an inch of his life? Mum was dead. Exposing the lie wouldn't bring her back. He'd always looked up to his father. He was a hero. Larger than life. After Jack found out about the affair he just became another man. Flawed. Lacking integrity. A breaker of vows. A weak man who couldn't keep a marriage vow to his wife.

Had she known how her husband had cheated on her? Had she put up with it because she didn't want to face the truth? Had she tolerated his womanising because she was getting older and maybe wouldn't find someone else?

When she was dying did she regret her life? Could she have had a better life with someone else? Someone who wouldn't cheat on her?

There were tears in his eyes now. Angry tears. His anger was back. His emotions were becoming his fuel and he was going to use them to get home. And if he has to kill someone who gets in his way again. He would. It was their fault for getting in his way.

15

He walked. That's what he did. When things got too much for his brain. When he was stressed, tired, angry or losing his mind, the first thing he did was put on his shoes and walk. Sometimes he would carry the bag of weights when he went out for a stroll. Something to fight against. Something to hold him back.

He'd read somewhere that walking was the best thing for depression too. It worked for him. There was something soothing to his mind and body about the motion.

The day his mother had finally died of cancer he'd walked. He remembered talking to a MacMillan nurse and then he'd excused himself and just started walking.

He'd arrived at his hotel the next morning at 2 o'clock. He'd no idea how he had got there. His mother had died at 4 o'clock the previous morning.

22 hours had gone by and he didn't know what had happened.

The hospital was 12 miles away. Even if he'd walked at one mile per hour it would only have taken him 12 hours, so where had he been?

Maybe he had stopped for a sleep, but where?

His brain wasn't working very well then. Since he'd started taking the pills his day to day thoughts were a lot clearer. And because they were a lot less 'fuddled' he tended to remember more things. There was a gap, however. The years his brain had run riot at every little thought. Those years were a mixed mess of strange thoughts and disjointed memories.

The booze hadn't helped, of course. Years of drinking and trying to pour oil on the turbulent waters of his thoughts had also taken their toll. If his troubled mind hadn't taken his senses, the booze had. There were big gaps. Sometimes they would reappear to him as deja vu or as little snippets of memories when he had a drink, but they were few and fleeting, so he disregarded them. The only thing he retained from those days was information.

On the whole, today he was in better mental health than he'd ever been. Which didn't say a lot for his mental health before.

'If you can't remember your childhood it was a happy one.' That's what they said. But what if you had suppressed the memories because they were too hard to bear? Well, he remembered his. He remembered too many. Too many times being terrified. Too many times sitting in his bedroom. Hoping he would be left alone.

After his father's affair he became a bitter man. He drank and would come home full of beer and resentment to his family and especially his little boy.

It was probably why he wasn't scared of anything anymore. He had gone through so much fear as a young man that he must have exhausted his allotted supply.

Today, he'd faced claustrophobia, deadline panic, fear of a stupid client and fear of a desensitized human race of robots. Nuclear Armageddon was somewhere in there but he was dealing with that that now. This was no time for fear. And to be honest, it wasn't all that bad. All things considered.

16

Jack decided to cut down Compton Street - right into the heart of gay Soho. He hadn't been down this road in years and the little boutique shops and Old Compton's itself were deserted.

An *Ann Summers* shop stood unmolested. Even the looters weren't in the mood for some frilly underwear or chocolate body paint at this point of the apocalypse. But down one of the little alleyways at the side there was movement. It caught his eye because it was the only movement there was. It wasn't hurried. It had the appearance of someone calmly smoking a cigarette. Then a plume of smoke filled the air and caught the light as it puthered from the shadows.

A young lady stood in a doorway watching him. A young lady with a look of disinterest. She didn't care what was happening around her. From her appearance she looked to be 'looking for business'. But that would be completely unheard of. Was she offering 'a bang before the big one' discount?

Jack stopped himself. *Some people were stealing Fender Telecasters, some were drinking themselves stupid, others might just prefer to go out with a bang,'* so to speak. But he couldn't quite figure out what was in it for her. She might get a £100 but what would she do with it? It was just another thing that didn't sit right in the logical part of his mind.

"Looking for a good time before the end of the world?" she shouted, stubbing out the cigarette under her too-high heels.

"No, thanks," Jack replied. "Getting out of here before…"

"Yeah, I know," she interrupted. She looked to the other end of the alleyway visibly turning her attention away from Jack. It was as if she had lost complete interest in him and was looking for her next 'mark' or 'john'.

Jack watched her body language for a second then walked forward. There was something wrong. There was also a strange feeling about her voice. Something fearful. The place itself felt 'wrong'. Why wasn't she running like everyone else? If it was the shoes he definitely understood. She could barely stand in them let alone put one foot in front of the other. But with her job he imagined she wasn't required to be on her feet all day.

"Are you going to stay here?" Jack asked as politely as possible.

"Nowhere else to go," she replied lighting up another cigarette a little too nervously.

"Surely, there's somewhere…"

"No, now if you don't want a fuck, get the fuck out of here."

Jack saw the shadows move slightly. It could have been a trick of the light but he wasn't sure. "Hey, ok, I'm going. No need to be like that."

"Well, do one, Mr Good Samaritan."

Jack turned to the left and started slowly down the road. Walking normally as if he was just 'passing through'. If anyone was watching him from the alley they would have thought he suspected nothing.

As soon as he was out of eyesight, he placed his bag in a doorway and jumped around a corner. He could pick up the bag later. He needed to move fast again. He just wanted to see what was going on. He wouldn't need the bag. Or so he thought.

One of the good things about Soho was that there are lots of little rat-runs. Alleyways where you could walk in circles. It probably made it good for picking up the punters but it also made it easier to double back easier and see what was going on from a different angle.

A couple of quick right turns and he approached the alleyway from the other side. He peeked his head carefully around the girl's little stretch of alley, he saw he was right to have his suspicions. Two men had emerged from the shadows and were talking to the young girl.

"What you send him off for? He could have had some money?" the first man said.

"He wasn't interested," she stated. "I thought you just wanted to stick some pervs?"

"We'll stick anyone who's got cash to spare," the second thug muttered.

"Why? she pleaded. "We're all going to die. Please, let me go."

The men laughed. The rules had gone. You could do anything you wanted to now. Some people just wanted to kill. And these two were going to do just that.

As they carried on talking, Jack saw the gun in the first man's hand and the knife in the other man's. They meant business and if the girl hadn't shooed him away he might be on the other end of that business. Now she was in trouble for saving him.

It felt odd. He'd never been saved before. Or at least he couldn't remember anyone standing up for him. He'd just done it himself. It was kind of touching that this whore with a heart had defended him from these two monstrosities of human beings.

It would only be gentlemanly to repay the favour. Jack paced the steps out in his head. Watched them as they all turned their backs to him. They weren't expecting anything. He realised he better do something soon.

"Well, if he wants to pass up a fuck, I think I'll take a little for myself seeing as how business is slow today," the man with the gun said.

The girl just shut her mouth and waited. The man was undoing his jeans while the other man watched on. The look the man gave just showed that he was used to this kind of thing.

Jack walked slowly up behind the two men. He wasn't trying to be quiet, he just was. He was seeing red now. Acting on instinct again. When he saw Trudi take a hit earlier on he couldn't control himself, and now was no different.

He walked up behind the second man and simply took the knife from his relaxed hand. He wasn't expecting it so it was easy. Jack then took firm hold of it and thrust it where he thought the man's anus was. Then he just pulled it out quickly. It cleaved through material and flesh like it was nothing. A good knife kept sharp. He obviously loved working with it so had kept it in good condition. What he never prepared for was the knife which he loved to be used on him in so lethal and intimate a way.

The resulting shriek was enough to raise the dead, and the man fell clutching at his backside in agony. His eyes were staring and his body twisting in pain. Shock would take him quickly. Blood loss would do the rest.

His accomplice only had a few seconds to realise what was happening but instead of levelling the gun at Jack, he decided it was better to pull up his trousers.

Jack had read somewhere before that faced with a decision to fight naked or fight fully-clothed, men would always favour the latter. Being such strange beasts, men didn't really want people looking at their todgers. Not even in the midst of battle.

It was the wrong decision of course, while the man was making sure he was appropriately dressed for a fight to the death, Jack plunged the knife into the man's exposed navel and pulled upwards. The man's abdomen opened like a red flower and began to belch its contents onto the pavement. The man shrank to his knees desperately trying to hold his body together. The look of horror on his face seemed quite comical. Until he collapsed on to the pavement, a pool of crimson surrounding his body.

The girl saw everything but only had time to step back to avoid the ever widening lake of blood that was seeping from both men.

She stared down at the men and then glanced into Jack's face.

"Now, let me ask that question again. Have you got somewhere to go?"

"Yes," she replied without a single stammer or look of fear.

"Then go," Jack answered. "Don't wait around here for any more shit to catch up with you."

The girl reached into her doorway and pulled out a coat that hid her strange apparel. Then she kicked off the too-high heels and carefully strapped on some flatter, more sensible, trainers.

"I don't know who the fuck you are, but thank you," she said as she began walking away.

"You forgot something," Jack called. He bent down to the red body of the first man. In his panic to do up his flies he'd completely forgotten about the gun and had dropped it as the knife cleaved his abdomen into pieces. Jack picked it up. He slid the safety off and handed it to her. "Point and shoot, don't let anybody else stop you."

She looked down at the gun and with a smile put it in her pocket. "What if I wanted to shoot you? After all, you are a very dangerous man."

Jack smiled and started to walk back towards where he'd dropped his bag. "I wouldn't recommend it," he said waving the knife. "You saw what happened to them."

When he turned back around she had gone. Wise girl. The men on the floor were dead or dying, he didn't care. All that mattered was that he got a move on. There had been too many distractions to his journey already and he had barely made any headway.

'Well, what were you supposed to do? Ignore them?' The voice came from nowhere it seemed. But he had to agree with it.

As he passed a doorway he mailed the knife through the door. It was sticky and covered in evidence but if it wasn't in plain sight no one could pick it up and use it against him. He wiped his hands on his jeans and made his way back to the doorway he had stopped at earlier.

The bag was where he left it. He picked it up with a grunt, a muffled 'fucking weights' and then started walking again. He hit Shaftesbury Avenue and turned right. Jack had considered heading towards Waterloo Bridge but for some reason he believed 'traffic' would be bad there. It was a very popular bridge. If he was to guess most people heading south would pick that as first choice. Better to head for Westminster Bridge. Much as he loved Waterloo Bridge, by his reasoning most of the people would have been evacuated from

Westminster before the warnings. Which meant clearer roads. He hoped.

Besides, he had to say goodbye to Piccadilly Circus. It was one of the first places he visited when he came to London. He'd also spent a lot of time at Tower Records before everything went online. Inexplicably he felt drawn towards that part of town. He had to see it one last time. He couldn't imagine there would be much left after a nuclear blast.

Piccadilly Circus wasn't how he remembered it. All the usual landmarks were there but without the crowds milling around and walking to and fro the place just seemed alien. He couldn't believe the difference. Yes, it was choked with traffic, but there was barely a human being there. There were a few picking their way through the abandoned cars but not the mass of heaving flesh he was used to. What worried him the most were the bodies.

They were piled around the entrances to the tube station. The gates were locked and the bodies were smashed against the metal railings. They had tried to catch the tube. What were they thinking? As if the tube drivers and staff were going to stay at their posts while the city was bombed to fuck. No, they were on their way as well. Every single employee was on their way home and weren't going to stick around for some besuited individual who thought it only proper they should stay at their post while megatons of explosive nuclear power turned them to dust.

You could argue that they would be safe underground but an explosion of atomic force wasn't going to shatter a few windows, it was going to rip up the floor of the world and send it into orbit. It didn't matter how deep the tunnels went, as soon as a bomb ripped the top off London, heat and radiation could get down there. Plus, he imagined that most of the tunnels here would collapse from the force of the explosion or explosions. There may be more than one bomb. The 'enemy' would want to make sure they were doing the job properly.

Jack decided to walk in between the cars on the road. The pavement was too close to the edge for his liking. Anything could jump from a side street or alley and attack him.

He stopped and gave a long look around. No police, no army, no 'peace-keeping' forces. There were a few dazed people running in strange directions but no one you could call 'authority'. He was probably safe enough, here. He may have been safe enough before but somehow he didn't feel right arming himself so close to Oxford Street. That's where the normal people lived. Here was just a bit more lawless. This is where male and female prostitutes hang out. This is where the pickpocket signs were. This seemed to be the place where you should 'tool-up'.

Putting down the bag of weights he opened it up and split the false seam he had sewn in many years ago. It took a fair amount of effort. When he had sewn it in, he'd made sure that this false seam wouldn't unravel as he was carrying his bag around. A hard task because the damn thing wasn't light.

Inside was a kukri, a bent bladed machete-like knife issued to the gurkhas, in a leather sheath. He placed that on his left hip and fastened it to his belt.

So he could draw it across his body with his right hand.

Also, hidden in the bag were a pair of thick weight lifting leather gloves with knuckleduster blades.

He pulled them on and then fastened the Velcro straps around his wrists. No one was going to get these suckers off him. To be fair no one was going to get in arm's reach of them. They had been normal knuckle dusters until he'd filed the knuckle part of the metal to a ragged and deadly point.

You wouldn't just be hit by metal, the jagged part would take away the top part of a throat or a face with little effort. Maximum damage for minimum effort. It was good to see his old friends again.

He'd hidden them years ago. It was his apocalypse pack and it had started out as a half-thought through idea; one of those 'nerd' things they always talked about.

'What would you put in your zombie apocalypse pack?' his friends had asked.

'Good knives,' he replied. 'Ones that could do the most amount of damage with one swing.'

They laughed. 'Just remember, this is England with knife and gun laws. How would you get them through any metal detectors?' they mocked.

Jack thought for a moment. 'Metal detectors found metal, so why not give them some metal to detect? A whole lot of metal.'

"I'd carry metal weights in the bag, so no machine could find them. Maybe sew them into the lining so if anyone did get curious about searching it, they'd just see a bag with weights in it. They would be looking for something that set the detectors off. When they found their answer they'd move on."

"Why carry metal weights around?" Mike had asked.

"Because, I'm in training and carrying weights around is what people do, for exercise," Jack had replied.

He'd been joking of course. His friends had nodded their drunken agreement and changed topic. But Jack being Jack, he'd mulled the idea over in his head and then wanted to see if it could work.

He'd found all the knives at an army surplus depot. He'd sharpened the knuckledusters at an old garden centre in Mitcham that had a grindstone for sharpening garden shears. The owner had asked what he wanted to do 'a damn silly thing like that for?'. He'd explained he was testing out a theory and the man had simply shrugged his shoulders and left the lunatic to his strange work.

When he had finished his preparations he had sewn the 'knives' inside. Not before making sure the knuckle duster's new 'blades' were wrapped in metal. It would be bloody stupid trick to lacerate his back every time he put on his bag.

Then he'd placed the weights inside. You couldn't tell there was a secret compartment. It looked like a bag with weights inside. That was strange enough. He couldn't imagine anyone looking for anything stranger.

Then he'd taken the bag out for a few practice 'walks'. The stitching had come undone a couple of times because of the stresses and strains of the weights. That was, until he swapped out the nylon thread he was using for fishing line. It held. He carried the weights around in the bag. The stitching held again. Zombie apocalypse pack was ready. All he needed were the zombies now. But looking around at people staring blank-eyed into their devices he realised he'd been surrounded by them all along.

He hadn't had a chance to try it on a metal detector but a bouncer at a pub once stopped him and asked what was in the bag.

When he replied 'weights' the bouncer looked inside and saw there were indeed weights in there.

"Why do you carry weights around?"

"Broke my hip in a car accident a few years back. Been through years of therapy, carrying extra weights helps the bone mass regenerate."

It was sort of true. Another little known fact that weight and exercise do this. He had broken his hip years ago when a car had hit him. He was better now but there was a truth in it. Putting these two truths together made a lie that was completely true. Two positives made a negative. Well, sort of.

The bouncer made sure he left the bag at the door but didn't search it any further. He just thought Jack was a little crazy and left it at that. He'd dealt with crazier.

Now that he had his knives out of the bag, he didn't need it anymore. It was a shame. Him and his bag had walked many a mile together. Now he had to discard it. With an uncomfortable grunt he swung the weight of it under a car and let go of the handles. He listened as the weights 'clunked' somewhere out of sight. He was sad but relieved; the weights were killing him. Carrying the weights short distances was fine. But carry any weight too long and you'd be exhausted.

He'd read a story about a lecturer at a college. He walked in one day carrying a glass of water. He said that this glass of water represented all his worries. Carry it around for a short time and everything was ok. But the longer you carried those worries around with you the heavier they would seem. Nice story. He must have read it about 10 times on people's feeds. It had been shared in circles for the best part of two years.

Jack relished the loss of the weight. Even though he changed shoulders frequently he did worry that it was throwing his back out. Without the bag he would be racing around trying to get everywhere at breakneck speed. That was the thing that was killing him most about London. Rather than set his own walking pace he found himself following everyone else's. The weights slowed him down enough to take a walk, not a frantic run around the city every day.

The one thing he'd miss was his Kindle and his headphones. He'd stowed them in his bag by force of habit. But that was a good thing. He had his back-up at home. This wasn't the kind of day where you could cut yourself off from what was happening around you. Any little sound could warn him of another attacker. He had to be alert. He had to walk until he found what he was looking for next.

Today wasn't a 'saunter kind of day' though, so he picked up the pace a little and began whistling again.

He felt safer than he had before and believed he was ready for anything.

He waved goodbye to the statue 'Anteros' and headed down Regent Street. How many times had he wandered through here and never even looked up at his little buddy? Tourist and Londoner alike had thought the statue was Eros but that was another fact that he liked to disprove. He'd won many a bet, when someone had said they'd been to Piccadilly Circus and taken a photograph of Eros.

"Really?" Jack had asked. "I think you'll find there isn't a statue of Eros in Piccadilly Circus."

"Bet you there is," they'd say all puffed up and ready for an argument.

"How much?" Jack would ask.

"Ten quid," they'd say and they would shake on it. A little phone research later and they found the statue was Anteros, Eros's brother. He would take their money with a smile and then buy a drink for the both of them with his winnings.

To be honest, someone had pulled the same trick on him and suddenly realised that what he thought he knew and the actual facts were two different things.

Now Jack was used to the idea that everything he knew was probably wrong. He'd started watching QI on Friday nights and every question was an eye-opener. How many moons does the Earth have? Custard explodes. The female owl says to-whit, the male owl says to-whoo. These days he was a mine of useless information that could prove useful at some point.

He also remembered some story that Piccadilly Circus was named after a tailor who sold 'Piccadills', a sort of collar. He didn't know all the facts but his memory was powerful enough to pull out the relevant bits when he needed them.

Smiling to himself he walked past Jermyn Street. He remembered there was a perfumiers down that way called 'Trumpers'. It always made him smile. Of course now wasn't the time to get lost in his thoughts, he had to concentrate. He had to get to the safety of home. It was time to pick up the pace and stretch his legs out.

Years of carrying the weights in his apocalypse pack had strengthened his legs and his core. He didn't want to run or jog. That was too tiring. Walking was good enough. He could be home in an hour or so if he kept a good pace. Decades of tube strikes, bomb warnings and defective trains had given him many opportunities to walk home. He'd been stranded in many different parts of town and rather than wait for another train or try and get on an overcrowded bus, he'd walked. Some days it was a relief to get off a stuffy train and wander back home under his own steam.

Down one of the side-streets, a police car caught his eye. That too had been abandoned and there was no sign of the officers who had been in it. The car was at an angle to the pavements with both doors left open. It looked like it had come to a halt and both police officers had left in a hurry. Some emergency perhaps but the roads at either end of the side-road were jammed with cars; there was nowhere to go.

Maybe they had decided to escape on foot when they had been boxed-in?

Even on Regent Street, one of the wider roads in Central London, the cars had somehow bottlenecked and crunched together. Cars were on the pavements, in the central reservation, everywhere. There were even a few bodies in the road. There had been road rage, pavement rage and in one case on the bonnet rage. One man lay with blood congealing on a head wound that left you in no doubt that he wouldn't be getting up anytime soon.

17

He'd been right to sit down and have a coffee earlier on. He'd managed to avoid most of the panic. It had been a warzone. The grim aftermath painted a violent picture of the frenzy before.

It wasn't just the dead bodies that worried Jack. It was the evidence of the savagery that these bodies wore. Their battle scars were horrific. Londoners weren't exactly known for their politeness but to turn into violent monsters just seemed too unreal.

He'd played this sort of scenario out in his head before, but seeing it for real was another matter. His imagination although dark and savage bore no resemblance to the evidence of real life, 'or real death', as his mind corrected.

Another body lay in front of him between two cars. It looked like the person had been crushed between them. There was blood on the tarmac and the white of bone could be seen sticking through the man's trousers. Almost like he'd been impaled on his own skeleton.

Approaching carefully, he looked down at the man. 35, good suit, tie missing, pale blue striped shirt, dripping with blood.

"Help me," the man suddenly croaked. "I can't move." He motioned with his eyes down his body. It wasn't just his legs that had been broken. It looked as if his hips and his rib cage had been pulverised too. He needed an ambulance and a hospital. But by the looks of things, he wasn't going to get what he needed.

Jack knelt beside the man. "Ok," he said. "Just a second." Jack braced himself and drew the kukri from its sheath out of the man's sight. He took a breath then slashed the knife deep across the man's throat in a single swipe of his hand. The little amount of blood that was left in his body gurgled out quickly and then the man's eyes went blank.

He wasn't going to leave the man to suffer. He also wasn't going to let him slow him down, either. This was the logical choice. Quick, and as painless as possible. He stood for a moment and watched to make sure the man was gone. Then started off again.

Returning to his journey Jack wondered how many more 'mercy killings' he would have to perform today? Would he have to do the same thing to himself? *'Let's wait and see, shall we? No point looking on the dark side, just yet.'*

The next question that started its long journey across his mind was, *'What had he become?'* He had just killed a man and felt no remorse. He'd killed the other guys too but they deserved it. This was an innocent man who needed his help. *'No,'* he replied to himself. *'That was a dead weight that would have got you and him killed. This way, it was just him.'*

'Best not to think about it,' he muttered inside his head. *'Keep walking'.*

"Hold it, right there," a voice commanded from over his left shoulder.

Jack sighed to himself and came to a dead-stop. He turned around slowly. There were the two missing police officers. The mystery was solved. They hadn't run off they were still here upholding he law. God only knows what they were doing here but now they were standing 10 feet away from him and a slight distance apart. How he hadn't seen or heard them approach was another mystery but not an immediate worry. One was pointing a taser at him. The other had his hand on a small pouch attached to his belt.

"We saw you murder that man," taser cop said.

"I put him out of his misery, there was nothing anybody could do for him," Jack replied.

"You're under arrest."

"No, I'm not."

"Oh yes you are."

"Don't be ridiculous," Jack said. "In case you hadn't noticed, there are far more worrying things heading this way and they're about to blow this place to Kingdom Come. Do you really want to play cop? Or would you rather be running for your life?"

"You are under arrest. Do not resist or we will have to use force."

He stared at them with his serious face. The one that said 'don't mess with me'. Sadly, no one took that face seriously. Most people thought his serious face was funny. But the policemen weren't laughing. They were sticking to their script and weren't going to change it.

Jack shook his head in disbelief. He gave them another look and then began to turn away to leave. Taser cop's finger started to tighten the moment he started to turn.

He knew he couldn't avoid a bullet, but this was a glorified dart gun with wires. A lot slower. A hell of a lot slower than a speeding bullet. Instead of turning, Jack twisted and stepped aside. The darts from the taser went sailing past his right arm.

The officers both looked at him dumbfounded as the darts jiggled on their wires on the floor behind him.

This time the other officer decided to take a shot. He pulled out his taser from the pouch he had at his waist and shot it at Jack. Jack simply stepped to the other side and watched as the darts went to his left.

"What now?" Jack asked.

Both officers dropped their tasers guns and pulled out their truncheons. Well, Jack thought they would be truncheons. Instead they were more like the night-sticks he'd seen on American cop shows.

"Oh great, even the police have turned American," Jack said. But to be fair when it came to close-up violence you couldn't beat a good old 'nightstick'.

It was then that they made another mistake. They moved towards him one at a time. Police training meant they should have taken him together and they should have stood apart. Provide two separate targets. But because he was standing between a line of crashed and crunched cars they had to wait in line to have a go at him.

The first officer swung his night-stick in a short arc, Jack caught his arm with one hand and open palmed his chin so it snapped his head back. He used enough force to knock the officer down but not out. He also knew he had on his knuckleduster blades. He didn't want to slash the constabulary to pieces. No matter how stupid he was being.

His partner came up behind and stumbled over the first officer. As he went down Jack gave him an encouraging push so he fell into the side of the car. There was a sickening crunch as flesh and bone slammed against metal and the second officer rolled awkwardly onto the struggling first officer in an almost homo-erotic way.

"Please, stay down," Jack said as both officers looked hate up at him. "The man was beyond help. Now get the fuck out of here before we're all fucked."

Jack turned his back to the officers and began to walk away. He hoped they would take the hint, lick their wounds and go away.

It wasn't going to happen. He heard the frantic scuffling of the men getting to their feet and then a few hurried steps in his direction. Jack turned back round just in time to deliver a knife hand to the second officer's solar plexus.

As he doubled up in pain, Jack performed a two-handed smash to the back of his head. He didn't fall to floor, he jumped, then lay still. Jack looked up and the other officer just stood watching from a distance.

"We'll remember your face," he mocked.

"Not much good it will do you," Jack turned and walked on.

He heard the squawk of a radio and the officer talking into it. *'You're kidding me?'* he thought to himself. The thin blue line was coming after him when there was all this chaos to contend with?

He almost stopped in his tracks to give himself a face palm but there were things to do. It added another complication to his escape plan but it wasn't something he hadn't thought of before.

Probably best to get off the main roads and stick to the shadows. The last place he wanted to be was in a prison when the bombs hit. He could bet that Her Majesty's Prisons weren't built to withstand a nuclear blast.

He turned left at the bottom of Regent Street. His plan was still to head across Westminster Bridge but he may have to find a longer route. Christ, he didn't need this. Why had he gotten involved again? He could have left the man to die without killing him. It wouldn't matter in the long run. The man was dead anyway, cutting his life shorter would make no odds.

Technically, yes, he had killed him, but what sort of life would he have left crumpled and broken in agony just waiting to die?

What would the policemen have done? Called for an ambulance? Would they have waited there and got crispy fried? Don't think so.

A little on the way down the road he saw what he was looking for. Or hoped he did. Another man was sprawled out on the road. Jack hurried over to the still body and checked his pulse. The body was warm but the man was dead. At least he wouldn't have to put this one out of his misery.

There was blood all over his head. It looked as if he had been bludgeoned with something. There was a little blood on his shirt but that was fine. It would all add to the effect he wanted to achieve.

He quickly removed his jacket and his Bring Me the Horizon t-shirt and threw them under a car. Removing the shirt from the dead weight of the man was not an easy task. But seeing as how he wasn't concerned about hurting the man he performed it with a roughness of a wrestler about to drop his opponent on his head - much to the delight of a blood-thirsty crowd.

Dropping the body and putting on the shirt he realised it was too tight on the shoulders and a little too loose in the waist. But as a disguise it would have to do.

At a glance and at a distance he didn't look like the same person who had slit the throat of a man on Regent Street. With the blood spatters on his shirt he looked more like he was a victim of a road crash. Or a trampled victim of the mob that had passed by earlier and was now stumbling his way home.

If they got close they would realise there wasn't a single drop of blood on Jack's face that would explain the bloody shirt. He took a palm full of blood from the body that hadn't congealed and smeared some round his neck and on his right cheek.

He didn't have a mirror to hand but hoped that it would be enough to hide his features, slightly. If it threw off any pursuers a little bit, then he would be happy.

Then he started off again. He was all too aware that his kukri now stuck out more than before but that couldn't be helped. The shirt was loose enough at the waist to hide most of it from the casual glance.

The knuckle dusters on his gloves were a different matter. They looked out of place. They attracted attention. Why would a man be wearing weight-lifting gloves? Unless he'd just come from the gym. But even then he'd take them off when he left, surely? If anyone looked at them with more than a passing interest, they would see the knuckledusters and their strange sharp appearance. They were cycling gloves. That's it! Cycling gloves with knuckledusters on them to ward off cars who got a bit too close.

It was a reason but not a very good one. It still screamed 'psycho' about him and that was one thing he wanted to avoid. He couldn't dwell on that at the moment, there was more to do.

As a final touch to his disguise he put some of the drying blood on his shaved head. With its stickiness it would make a great hair gel. If he could market the 'hold' of blood to hair stylists he could make a fortune.

Then he took the kukri and removed his pride and joy. The beard he had been cultivating was a giveaway. He held the beard firmly and then proceeded to slice his beautiful soup strainer and removed as much hair as possible. He could really use his cut-throat razor right about now but this would have to do.

He wasn't going for any Vidal Sassoon 'look', unless that look was beaten up and dragged backwards down the street. He just wanted to change his own look slightly.

He started to walk again. Time to put some distance between him and the coppers. Then he realised his fast walk was too distinctive. So he slowed down a little. Not too much. His long stride was a dead giveaway. He shortened it slightly and added a little discomfort on the left leg.

It may not seem much, but as he thought, all these little things added together. If someone was checking him out from a distance, he would be instantly dismissed as the suspect.

That was the plan. But if anyone got a good close-up look at his face, he was dead. Especially since he'd beaten down two police officers. They never took it kindly when you hurt them, even if they were wrong. And they were wrong, this time.

It was here that he found his second objective. He'd taken this road because of one thing; railings. It was also close to St James's Park. While everyone had gone chasing down Whitehall on foot he was looking for something to make his journey easier.

Cars and buses were gridlocked of course and long since abandoned. Motorbikes and bicycles were the next best bet but he'd seen what happened when a motorbike came roaring passed; everyone attacked it.

If a cycle went around the houses and the crowds he might make good time on the way home. He'd have to avoid as many people as possible, though. They didn't seem to like it if anyone had a better chance of survival than they did, and would do their level best to scupper them.

On his way to St James's Park he saw what he needed at Waterloo Place. To be honest he didn't think he'd find anything but there it was.

There, chained to the railings, was a beautiful mountain bike. His heart almost leapt in his blood stained shirt. It was beautiful because it had been used. All the best things in life had been. It didn't gleam like new. It hadn't been loved with chrome cleaner and hot soapy water. They'd kept the moving parts oiled and working smoothly then proceeded to take it through the dirtiest places on Earth. For all he knew it could have been ridden through every septic tank from Land's End to John O'Groats and he would still look upon it with love and gratitude.

He could see why the bike had been left. Someone had been really paranoid about having their bike stolen. It wasn't just chained to some of the thickest railings he'd ever seen in London, it was one of those chain locks with blue transparent plastic covering the chain. The lock itself looked as if it could hold a truck. He wasn't sure how many people had already tried to remove it but the railings were dented and the bike wasn't standing up straight any more. It looked as if someone had tried to wrestle it off the railings a number of times. Failing that, they'd walked or run away.

Luckily for him, his gift of foresight had prepared him for the possibility of a bike or two abandoned and locked to the railings before he had even arrived. So, on his journey he had been on the lookout for a means to pick the lock. By 'pick' he meant smash it to bits.

Just around the corner he'd spied a bus stop. Not a permanent one. This was one of those temporary ones with a concrete block at the bottom of it. Too heavy to be carried very far but not heavy enough so that it couldn't be lifted high enough to crack the lock off a chained bike.

He'd only noticed it because he was on the alert. The pole looked like it could be a good weapon but the concrete block was not something you could carry around with you and raise over your head to threaten anyone. You'd be lucky if you could get it to shoulder height without soiling yourself in the effort. No, it wouldn't hold up in battle but as a tool to get to something else it was ideal.

Jack approached it and saw another problem. It had been chained up too. What they didn't realise that chaining a concrete block was a little silly. It was like chaining up bolt cutters - you had the very means to liberate the items you wanted to steal.

No matter, Jack bent his knees and grabbed the signpost. He made sure he got a good grip and lifted it using his legs to lift. When it was off the ground and high enough, he sent the edge of the cement base crashing down on its own chain.

"Always lift with the legs," he said realising that he was getting tired of his own internal monologue. What must other people think when he said them out loud? It was like his father was coming back to haunt him with his worn out sayings.

The lock held firm but he didn't expect it to fall apart on his first try. That would be much too easy. Jack lifted the block and dropped the concrete on the chain again. He lifted and dropped again.

"That's the sound of the men working on the chain ga-ang," he sang as he smashed the heavy concrete down like a piledriver.

Whether it was Jack's singing or the block smashing relentlessly, the chain eventually surrendered and fell apart on the pavement in an untidy heap of defeated metal.

Jack stopped for a rest. It wasn't really a warm day but the effort of lifting the concrete block had taken his breath away and sweat had made the shirt cling to his body in a very uncomfortable way. He sat next to the concrete block and looked at the bike chained to the railings down the street.

'Soon, my precious,' he thought as his heart sank.

A man was trying to remove it. If the owner of the bike unlocked it and rode away he would be very disappointed. Happily for Jack, the man wasn't the owner. He had no key and no way to get the bike from the railings. He gave the bike a kick, then the railings, then ran off down the road.

"No patience," Jack said to himself and rolled the round concrete block to the railings and the bike they were holding captive. He would be damned if he was going to lift it and carry it all that way. He stopped for a rest again. He laughed to himself. He might die of a heart attack before anything else.

He placed the padlock on the floor and readied himself for the task of weightlifting his concrete block again. The first lift was a complete shambles. The lock was resting on the pavement but when he dropped the Bus Stop, it merely left a dusty mess on the lock. He'd hit it with the flat part of the concrete. The force had simply been too spread out to cause any damage. The next time he angled the stop so the edge would hit the lock first. The stop crashed down on the lock and separated it from the chain. Every chain had a weak link, it just so happened, the weakest part of any chain with a lock is the bit designed to come apart.

Pulling the bike from the railings and the chain, he got on. It felt strange. There seemed to be no stability to the damn thing. One push and he would be on his arse and being kicked to death by desperate people. He'd spent too much time on an exercise bike which was fixed to the gym floor, but when he began to pedal, everything came back to him and he soon felt much better.

He couldn't remember the last time he'd been on a bike that actually moved. His own was hung up in the hallway. To be quite truthful, most of his exercise routines involved staying in the same place. He rode an exercise bike that was bolted to the floor. He ran on a machine that kept him in the same place. He rowed a machine that wasn't even in spitting distance of water.

He left Regent Street and Waterloo Place in a spin or two of his wheels. He took the stairs in between the Royal Society and the Institute of Contemporary Arts with bone-juddering joy.

Then, he stood on the pedals and motored down Horse Guard Road, St James's Park on his right as he wove in and out of parked cars. He felt free. There wasn't a soul in sight. He passed the other end of Downing Street and he could make out a few military dignitaries all being escorted out of the far end. They didn't seem to be in a rush which meant they either knew something or knew of a good place to hide. Seeing as how Whitehall was just a stone's throw away he bet they were heading to some command post or bunker buried deep beneath the Earth.

Jack had read something about some bunker being built there many years ago. He couldn't swear to it but the cost had run into hundreds of millions so there must be something quite substantial down there. A long way down and far from prying eyes.

He wondered if he should stop and ask if he could come in as well? But he could imagine their reaction. It would either be a firm fast 'no' or he would be shot before he could even get the question out. And he didn't want to be shot. He could avoid gas powered darts but he wasn't Superman - there was no way he was faster than a speeding bullet.

It had been years since he had been in this part of town. The buildings all looked unfamiliar to him. They were typical regency buildings but they all looked the same. Even the doors had a uniformity that must upset the drunk trying to find his way home. If people round here even drank or did anything interesting. They probably stayed home and harrumphed behind their newspapers at the evening news and dreamt of colonialism returning to England. If they went out they took taxis. When they arrived home they were brought by taxi drivers or complimentary limousines. God forbid they should walk.

He wasn't looking around or paying attention to where he was, he was looking at where he wanted to be. He was looking at Big Ben in the distance and sort of heading in that general direction.

After the Imperial War Museum, he could have gone straight down Birdcage Walk but he felt too exposed for some reason. Instead he crossed the road and went down Storey's Gate. Taking the back roads seemed a more sensible thing to do at this point.

Jack nearly fell off his bike a number of times. Because he was looking up, he wasn't really paying close attention to the road, which was a mistake. These weren't the streets of the London he knew anymore. There were cars littered everywhere. He hadn't realised how many cars there actually were, until he saw them all on the road at the same time. Normally, they were parked neatly in two tidy roads at both sides of the road. Now they had all tried to move at the same time and had crashed, mounted pavements and generally just got in the way of one another. Doors were open and cases were abandoned by their open doors. The cars' occupants had tried to take their hastily packed nick-nacks with them. Until, realising they were too heavy to carry and run with them at the same time, they had just dropped them and carried on.

Negotiating a course around all these obstacles and trying to look for the general direction of his escape from the centre was proving just a little bit more difficult than he'd envisaged. He really should focus on one at a time. His ability to navigate and avoid everything in his way was not one of his strengths.

Then, by sheer luck more than anything else he realised he was approaching Parliament Square. The House of Commons was right in front of him and there were no more back streets to hide in. It was main road and Westminster Bridge, or nowhere. No more skulking in the shadows for a little while. He didn't know whether he should be worried or relieved so he decided to be both.

Slowing down he kept both eyes skinned and peeled. In the distance a man shouted something at him and started to head in his direction. He had a 'Boris bike' with him but it had obviously been at the centre of some altercation. The front wheel was buckled and the man looked as if he'd taken a bad tumble judging by the look of his torn suit.

Jack eyed him suspiciously then stepped on the pedals. He didn't like the look of him for some reason. He had one of those secret service looks to him complete with sunglasses. He might reach into his suit at any time pull a gun from his shoulder holster and splatter Jack's brains all over the road. Unless Jack offered a moving target.

There was a shout of some swear word in the distance as Jack rounded the square and started his approach to Westminster Bridge.

In one of his 'possible scenarios' the bridge had been destroyed and he would have to jump over the collapsed section. He couldn't see it happening of course but when you imagine the worst case, you're ready for disappointment.

In that scenario he'd somehow got his hands on a motorbike and was speeding home through walls of flames. He'd accelerated to over 80 mph and managed to jump over with the Thames 'burbling' its disapproval under his wheels.

He wasn't quite sure what top speed he could accomplish on a mountain bike but he guessed it was nowhere in the neighbourhood of 80 mph and if this scenario turned out to be reality he would have to look for another bridge.

18

If he could get across the Thames it would be one of the biggest psychological advantages of his journey. For him, it meant he was well on his way home. This was one of the funnel points he'd imagined, though. This was where more people headed to cross the river. There were no hiding places. It was just a strip of tarmac with water on both sides. Jack stood up on his pedals to get more force behind his legs. If he was going to get through this, he would need a good turn of speed and a fairly straight runway.

Even here, drivers had been trying to use the pavement to get by and had caused accidents. The best place to ride was straight down the centre white line.

It occurred to Jack that the whole work situation was topsy-turvy. People lived North and worked South, lived East and worked West and vice versa. People were criss-crossing London for their work and their life all the time. It just seemed strange. Most people were also set-up to work remotely and still ended up making journeys to work every single day. If he'd been allowed to work from home, he would be there now. Hunkering down, getting himself settled in, maybe cracking open a bottle of water from his store and taking a sedative to calm himself before the world went 'bye-byes'.

Tearing down the centre line he looked in the distance. There were a few cars abandoned but there was a fairly clear path in between. Until he saw the people coming towards him.

They were walking slowly and shambling. They had the look of people who had given up hope. They were the walking dead and they knew it. They just couldn't lie down and admit it to themselves, yet.

At first it looked as though they might step aside to let him pass. There was a little conversation between the individuals when they spotted him approaching. As if they were saying 'let's let him pass, maybe give him a wave and a cheer to help him on his way'. But then they fanned out and plugged the open spaces left by the abandoned cars. They were going to try and stop him.

"Shit," he said with feeling as he unsheathed the kukri with his right hand.

They were linking arms now in a unified attempt to stop him. There were seven of them as far as he could tell and together they blocked every little gap he could make out in the traffic.

"What the fuck are they going to do, all ride on the handlebars? Fucking idiots."

Jack gripped onto the blades handle even more tightly and steered the bike with his left hand. Then he pointed the bike to the place where the human chain had over reached itself. It was too spread out. In the human chain you couldn't tell where the weakest point was but from a distance you could see her. Desperately clinging to her walking friends as if she was clinging to dear life.

Even when they saw the blade the human chain continued to advance. This was the desperate act of a few desperate people. Even if they succeeded in stopping him what would they do then? Draw lots? Or would it be another fight to the death to see who got ownership of the bike.

Jack knew he wouldn't be around at that point, he'd be dead in the gutter. Kicked to death by some brogues, a pair of *Nikes* and some brown sandals. He wasn't going to let that happen to him. If he was going to be kicked to death it would have to be a good solid *Dr Marten* boot worn by someone with a lack of brain cells and a liking for *Northern Soul*.

"Well, you asked for it," Jack said under his breath

He could see their frightened eyes now. Desperate features surrounded them. A look of gaunt horror etched there. They were like ghosts stretched across his path. They knew they weren't going to make it to safety unless there was a miracle. A bike might give them a chance. But not his bike. This was his salvation and he was going to hang on to it. *'You can have my bike when you uncurl my dead toes from its pedals,'* he thought to himself and laughed a little.

The human chain stood firm. They weren't going to part for him. It was their intention to stop him even if it meant they collided, full throttle. Jack aimed for the part of the human chain that looked the weakest. As Jack approached, the two people he was aiming for, closed up and closed their eyes. He swung his blade just before the moment of impact and carved his escape. There was a meaty sound and his blade hit bone. It was the woman, or a girl, he wasn't paying much attention to the sexes at this crucial part in his life. They were in his way and it didn't matter who it was. Forget all that chivalry about women and children first.

Her arm parted from her shoulder. The human chain immediately collapsed into two pieces as her scream rang out across the strange cityscape. Then it went quiet too quickly. He just rode through the gap he had left trying to put as much distance between them and him as he could. The human chain hadn't been expecting him to carry a knife like that. They were expecting a few bruises and scrapes but not this. To be honest he didn't expect to do something like that. It was his own instinct for survival that was kicking in. In moments of crisis it just seemed to do the most violent thing to protect him.

Jack couldn't look back, he heard a few people shouting and then the clatter of feet as a few people tried to give chase but there was no way they were going to catch him. Even with all that adrenaline pumping through their veins they were no match for the adrenaline he was using to power the bike forward at a pace that left them standing.

He didn't slow until he reached the end of the bridge. But he was already figuring out his next move. He needed to find cover again. He was too exposed. He needed to get off the main roads and slip down a side street so he could continue his journey in the relative secrecy of London's back streets. Hopefully there was no CCTV there and all the people would be safely tucked up in their houses.

There was nowhere to go. He was stuck on main roads unless he went by the river and that wouldn't be a wise move. If he put one of his sides to the river it would cut down his options of escape and he wanted to keep them as open as possible. He could head down to Vauxhall or he could head down to Stockwell. Both were fairly open roads. Back streets at either side that could offer cover should he need it.

He stopped and looked at the roads. Left or right? Left would take him down to the relatively straight route but right would take him down more back streets. Ones which he thought he knew a little better.

"Fuck it," he said as he swung the bike to the right and pushed off down the way. "I'll take the scenic route."

19

As soon as he started off, he realised something was different. Cars were moving here. Not many, but a few were heading down the road, slowly, but moving fast enough to get them out of town faster than any walkers.

At the side of the road there were stragglers pleading for lifts. People hitchhiking for their lives and then continuing their journey. Most were limping as if they had fallen foul of the terrified crowd. Picked up and spewed out when they were injured.

They were obviously people who had been caught in the mad crush and sustained an injury or two. They'd picked themselves up and carried on despite their injuries, the instinct for survival pushing them on.

Now they were doing their best to hitchhike home but no one was paying them any attention.

"You on the bike," Jack heard from someone at the roadside. "I'll give you £10 thousand for the bike. Please!"

Jack rode on.

Another pedestrian tried to jump out in front of him on the road but Jack gave him a wide berth. It was a lot better than reaching for his blade and chopping the poor fellow down. If at all possible, he should avoid hacking his way home. It would just attract too much attention.

He was heading towards Vauxhall, he knew that. But he didn't know the name of the roads. He'd walked down this way before during tube strikes. This was when he lived in Clapham Junction of course and London town was just that little bit nearer. He'd been married then and they had owned a one-bedroom flat. He thought it would be great to be married but the lustre had soon worn off. As soon as the wedding ring was on the finger it was as if she turned off.

There were no romantic dinners for two. Instead they hosted dinner parties and went to dinner parties. They were constantly 'visiting'. It was okay once in a while but it seemed like every other night they were with 'friends'.

Then there were the house-guests. Their sofa seemed to be home to all manner of waifs and strays who always needed somewhere to stay in London or had to stay overnight. It was never just 'them' anymore. There was always someone else who had to be looked after. And he had to help do it.

Jack had remembered the oaths they had taken at their wedding. 'Forsaking all others.' The only one being 'forsaken' or taken for granted was him. That's when he stopped rushing home. He'd fight rush hour train traffic to get home only to be greeted by another houseguest or just a wife who would rather watch television than talk to him. What was there to rush home for?

Slowly but surely, Jack started to visit the pub before he went home. It made no odds. The television talked to his wife and she listened. She wouldn't even eat at the table any more. She would take a tray and sit on the settee. For the next few hours everything he had said had been greeted with a, "Huh?" Not even an 'excuse me' or a 'sorry'.

There were also the evenings where they would meet friends in town. They would meet and she would kiss them all on the cheek and when it came to him she did the same. Not a kiss on the mouth, or a hug. Just a kiss on the cheek. Nothing special.

As he rode he contemplated his wife and their divorce. She had said that he never talked to her. He spent too much time at work or in the pub after work. He admitted his culpability but she never admitted that she was partly to blame.

"It takes two to make a divorce," he muttered to himself. In the end he'd accepted the lion's share of the blame and wanted to make a change. But then, she said that they had lost what they had and there was no point. 'Way to work at that marriage.' She wanted out and he let her. No use flogging a dead marriage.

There were fewer cars here. So he wasn't weaving in and out as much. He could get up a good head of steam. It was easier to think of his journey despite the fact that the sights and sounds around him reminded him of a different life.

The MI6 building was in front of him now and on from there was Vauxhall. But it was an even stranger version of itself. There were people in the street. A lot of people. And they seemed to be having a party.

Cautiously Jack reduced speed; there was no need to go speeding into danger. Go slowly, it may hurt less. As he approached the main crossroads at Vauxhall he saw a gallivanting horde of people. They didn't seem aggressive or desperate. They just appeared to be drinking and dancing. And having a good time.

Jack dismounted and walked the bike to the edge of the crowd. Then he just carried on walking. No one was paying him any attention. No one even registered that he had a bike. A car came up behind him slowly and the crowd parted to let it through. A few of the revellers banged on the car's bonnet in time to the music as it went past but they didn't try to rip the driver out of it. They just let it on its way. They were quite happy 'and gay', he couldn't help thinking.

"What's going on?" Jack asked a fairly drunk and semi-naked man dancing in front of him. Whoever said all gay men could dance had not seen this man and his strange shuffling method of moving to the music. He should have his gay license revoked until he learnt how to do it properly.

"It's the end of the world," he slurred in his camp voice. "We're going to party till the world goes 'pop'."

Jack smiled to himself. He watched as more people came out of the Vauxhall Tavern carrying all manner of colourful drinks. No beer or lager, these guys were going to go out with a cocktail in their hands. He didn't have any idea what they called these cocktails but he bet they weren't repeatable in the company of people who read the Daily Mail.

"Pull up a drink, sexy!" the man said in the middle of his strange juddering dance.

Jack was almost tempted to join them. Years of drinking to blot out the nasty part of life had taught him that a drink or twelve made everything seem better. But that wasn't him anymore. And besides, much as he wanted to party this wasn't quite the party he had in mind. They were certainly going for it in every way. A few were also pleasuring one another at the side of the road. Others were sat on the railway bridge facing towards the city. They had the best seats in the house to watch London go 'boom'.

"Thanks, but no. I have places to be," Jack said as he started to push his bike through the crowd.

"Ok hun, but it's your funeral, may as well make it a wake."

Jack just smiled again. "Have one for me."

"Oh I shall, and I'll have one for everybody else I think. Make way, heterosexual coming through," the man shouted and the crowd began to part at the order from the strangely dancing man.

There were a few shouts of, "Hetty," and, "if you need a good ride handsome, I'm right here." But Jack finally made it through the crowd and emerged relatively unmolested on the other side.

A few of the partying people had pinched his bottom as he went through. One had copped a feel of his jeans but he couldn't tell who. He wanted to say that he felt violated but it was just high spirits and these spirits were certainly high.

If you were going to watch your city explode this was a good vantage point. There were better he could imagine, but none that served booze. Or had quite the atmosphere.

If he wanted to watch the town vaporise he would do it from Hampstead, from the Heath. There you could oversee the whole of London. You wouldn't see much. When the first bomb dropped your eyeballs would be ash but then again, so would the rest of you.

Either that or just stay in the centre of London. Trafalgar Square would be a popular choice he thought. Everyone went there for New Year's so why not go there for No More Years?

He was going through all this in his mind when he realised he was now well clear of the crowd and he was still pushing his bike. Shouldn't he be riding it?

A black limousine pulled up at the side of the road and a chauffeur climbed out of the front seat. He opened the back door and pushed a plump middle aged man in a black suit out onto the pavement.

He fell in a panting mess. His face was red with rage and spittle was falling from his slightly blue lips.

"YOU CAN'T DO THIS, I PAY YOUR WAGES YOU UNGRATEFUL SHIT," he yelled.

The chauffeur simply climbed back into the car and floored the accelerator. The car took off down the road with a jump, turned left and vanished down a side road.

The man rose on his knees, face still spitting profanities into the distance as Jack mounted his bike again.

"WHAT THE FUCK DO YOU THINK YOU'RE LOOKING AT?" the man screamed at him as he set off.

"A dead man," Jack said calmly and left him venting his spleen on the pavement.

Looking over his shoulder he saw the man getting to his feet and further back, two police cars were driving into the crowd outside the tavern. He doubted they were there to have a drink or to claim their free 'boys in blue' blow job.

The police cars were swamped, and luckily for Jack, weren't being allowed through. The people of Vauxhall may have had their own axe to grind with the police - something he didn't know about. Or maybe it was just the fact that the bluebottles were the biggest buzz-kills when it came to drinking after hours.

Jack turned back to the road in front of him. There was a sound like a firecracker and then a searing pain across his right thigh. He didn't know what was going on. He thought someone had dropped something at the party. But nothing he knew made a noise like that. Except maybe a gunshot on TV.

"The bastards are shooting at me," he realised as his thigh spurted blood at him. He looked around and there in the distance beside the police car was one of the coppers who he'd beaten up earlier. Taser cop had got a gun.

The cars may be stuck in the dancing revellers but this man had a score to settle and wasn't above shooting an escaping man in the back. Not very chivalrous, but then again most vengeful creatures weren't really known for their manners.

"Fuck this, for a game of soldiers," Jack said and set off as fast as his legs could carry him. He heard another shot and then there was a noise at his feet as something hit the spot where he had been a second ago.

He didn't know the range of this gun but he'd better get out of it as soon as possible. He pedalled as fast as his legs could go and blood seemed to gush like a river from his wounded thigh.

At first he hadn't felt any pain. There was just a gash in his jeans and a sea of red underneath. Then his nerve endings woke up and told him that by no means should he be pedalling at such a furious pace.

He felt hot, his face felt pale. If he didn't stop he was going to pass out. But what about the policemen? If they got out of that crowd, they were going to catch him. They had cars, he had a push bike. A good push bike but it didn't have 120 horsepower behind it, just one copywriter, and a tired and bleeding one at that. He wasn't a match for one horse let alone 120 of the fuckers.

The only thing he had on his side was guile. A rabbit could outrun a cheetah. The cheetah couldn't change directions quickly. The rabbit could. On the straight he would be rabbit stew but throw in a few twists and turns and the cheetah would be left barrelling forward on the turns and would eventually give up.

He took a quick left and rode up the street past two junctions, took a quick left, a right and then hid himself and the bike from view. He checked the road behind him. There was no blood on the road, luckily his jeans were able to soak most of it up and hold it. But that wouldn't last long. There was a large red stain creeping down his leg and if he didn't stop it he was a goner.

Ripping off his shirt sleeve, he quickly tied it around the wound. He tied it tight then wound it around once more and tied the ends together again. Then he ripped the other shirt sleeve off and did the same.

When he was finished he sat down. He was in the garden of a row of terraced houses. He'd picked this particular one because of the high privet hedge at the front. Although he was safe for the moment there was no telling when the police would be back on his trail.

Had they found him? Was it just an accident? It was a little hard to concentrate right now. His head was thumping and so was his leg. It may only be what they called a flesh wound, but a flesh wound hurt like fucking hell. He sat back on the cool black and white mosaic tiling of the footpath. It felt wonderful.

"I'll just catch my breath," he said and then put his head back on the floor. "Just close my eyes for a second."

He never understood how anyone could pass out in the middle of a life-threatening situation. Then he did.

20

He woke up feeling hot and flushed. The feeling in his leg burned but the tightness of the shirt sleeves held in his precious blood. He wasn't sure how much he'd lost but he felt woozy and lightheaded. It was only a feeling. That's all. He should push it aside. Get moving again. If he laid here he might as well make the garden his deathbed. Why not? There were plenty of flowers there?

Propping himself up with his arms he manoeuvred his good leg underneath himself and pushed. He rose slowly and inelegantly but he was up. He hung onto the privet to help him balance while he hopped his body over to his bike.

"It's only a feeling of weakness," he said. "You're as strong as you were, you're just tired."

Jack half-bounced half-wheeled the bike back out onto the street and faced South. If the police were looking for him he hoped they had headed straight down towards Clapham Junction. It was a better thought than the one where they were criss-crossing the side streets scanning the by-ways for any sign of him. If that were the case, there could be quite an unpleasant confrontation. They had guns. They'd gone and armed themselves. And that one policeman was being a little churlish; looking for a bit of payback after the beating he gave him and his partner. It wasn't fair, they beat people up all the time, why couldn't he give them a thorough thrashing now and again?

The upshot of the confrontation was that Jack had to change his plans. He had to head towards Clapham Common. If he could get there without being seen, he could find a parallel road on the other side of the main road and avoid them.

First, he had to find a way through to the Common, he may have lived in London a long time but he didn't know all the rat-runs. This was a case of 'try and find a way home on streets you didn't know'. Interesting but not what he needed right now.

Jack knew the general direction he had to be in, but if you asked him where he was exactly, he would have to reply 'somewhere in South London'. He just had to keep going until he saw a landmark he recognised.

The streets were getting steeper here so he knew he was heading the right way. It was agony on his thigh and his breathing was hoarse in his throat. His chest was beginning to burn too. If he had known he would be doing all this today, he wouldn't have done his usual number of press-ups and sit-ups. He was getting older. Not 'old', just older.

In his youth he had spent whole days riding over hill and dale on his bike. Discovering towns and villages across Yorkshire. He'd ridden over moors in the pouring rain without cause for concern. Nothing bothered him. Now he could barely make it up a hill without nearly passing out. But to be fair, he was 30 years younger then, a couple of stones lighter and didn't have a bullet wound across his thigh that screamed at him every time he stepped on the pedals.

"Always excuses," he smiled to himself. "Man-up, for fuck's sake."

He knew he was going slightly insane now. He talked to himself often, especially during times when he was perplexed or under stress. But now he was extending his repertoire. He was giving himself words of encouragement. Before, he would chastise himself for doing something stupid. Or asking himself where he had put something. Now his imaginary voice was developing a new personality. Before long he would be forming whole conversations with this part of his psyche.

"No I won't."

"Yes, you will."

Since he had left Vauxhall he'd hardly seen anyone. There were a few cars on the main road trying to negotiate the abandoned cars and maybe a few people down side roads but there was hardly anyone around at the moment.

Admittedly, these were backroads and side streets. There should be someone walking around. Having said that when he used to run at night, he was amazed by the Londoners' ability to vanish from sight completely. There were millions of people living in London. But every night the vast majority would vanish into their houses, turn on their televisions and not be seen again until the morning when it was time to go to work, or take the bins out.

It was as if people in London observed some strange kind of curfew when they lived this far out from the centre. If they weren't at home and behind a locked door by 9 o'clock they would be tucked up in a boozer or restaurant not to be seen until throwing out time.

He swung the bike into a road which turned out to be the A3. By chance he'd made it to the road he wanted. This would lead him to Clapham High Street and when he got to Clapham Common he could head East down to Abbeville Road.

When he'd lived in Clapham that was one of his jogging routes. Most people went round and round the park until they were dizzy. He'd tried it at first but there were always dogs who were let off their leashes. It didn't matter if you were minding your own business, the dogs were excitable after a game of fetch. When their owners stopped playing they wanted to carry on. This meant that someone running would get the unwelcome attention of an over playful pooch who may or may not use his jaws to slow him down.

Besides that, there was always the collection of smart arses who wanted to make a comment at your expense. Especially if they were with a group of girls.

'What are you running from?'

'Can't you afford a car?'

'What are those white tapes hanging down from your shorts? Oh, they're your legs.'

Jack found that although running through the streets was a little harder on the knees, you didn't run into as many dogs and smart-arses.

What's a little personal pain compared to the pain of pets and other people?

The pain he was feeling now was a hell of a lot more annoying than a couple of sore knees. Every movement was like someone stabbing his leg. This wasn't going to heal right. He could feel the blood soaked into the jeans drying the material and causing it to stiffen. This aggravated his leg and with the leg in motion most of the time he could feel the edges of the wound sticking together and pulling apart. Not one of the greatest feelings in the world.

Jack passed Stockwell tube station. The gates had been locked but then busted apart. He gave a quick glance inside but couldn't see a living thing. He powered on past the council flats and managed to build up some speed. It was fairly flat here so he didn't have to do too much work. If he remembered correctly there was a short climb to Clapham North, a brief downhill then another up to Clapham Common. It wouldn't kill him but it would slow him down.

Before he knew it the hill was upon him and even though it was an easy climb, it was also a constant one. If his leg had been fine he could have done it seated but he had to stand up on the pedals again. There was less movement on his wound that way and he could shift his weight better onto the pedals to get up more speed on the incline.

The modern blocks of flats were behind him now and here they had turned into a huge mess of Victorian and Edwardian architecture. The stone was almost black in places and would benefit from a good sandblasting. They were going to get a blasting he guessed when half of central London headed this way.

'Nuclear blasting, clears, dust, grime and years of human population away in one single squirt. Kills 99.9% of all humans, even those under the ground.'

He was mixing his sandblasting metaphor with a bleach one but it wasn't as if he was going to be using it in any clever conversations, any time soon.

As he reached the top of the hill he wasn't just greeted by the sight of Clapham South tube station. There was another car jam. It took just one car to do something stupid and everyone else to pile into the back of it.

This time it looked as if a driver had decided that since he couldn't get under the bridge he would try to drive through it. He'd collided with the stone wall and then one by one, drivers coming over the hill, had just ploughed into the back of the jam.

Then the cars had spilled onto the other side of the road causing an instant pile-up on that side too. The result was another roadblock that would take time to circumnavigate. If he was lucky he could climb over it and drag the bike over with him, but he preferred it if he kept moving.

Luckily, he didn't have to do any climbing. The road to the left of the tube station was relatively clear. He thought it was Bedford Road but neglected to look at the sign properly as he swooshed past. One thing he did know was that there was a way through to Abbeville Road, and that was all he needed at the moment. He could still avoid Clapham Common this way. Which was the most important thing. Even though this road always made him feel a little uneasy.

Jack had never liked this road. For him it was creeping too close to Brixton. When he had lived in Clapham Common he'd been warned to stay away from this part. He'd taken the advice and steered clear. Well at night anyway. During the day he assumed it was okay. It was day now so he should be all right. Besides, who in their right mind would be out?

To his right he saw the familiar sight of what must have been a 1960s block of flats against the blue sky. He hadn't really looked at the sky since he'd set off on his grand tour home. It was blue. With only a few tufts of white cloud floating up there like cotton wool. But still no birds. Not a one. They had known; the little bastards and not told anyone.

It was hard to imagine that such a beautiful day could turn bad. But he supposed even World War II had its sunny days. There they were, ripping the life from one another in France. Sun beaming down on them as they sang 'Oh what a lovely war'. English people singing the verses, the Germans and the French resistance joining in on the chorus.

He only thought war looked gloomy because he'd seen so much black and white footage from the old newsreels. When he'd watched every war film from then on they had all seemed grey and miserable because that's how the film had been treated. You couldn't show a sombre and dark thing like war in the bright sunshine. Unless, of course it was a film about Vietnam and then you had to show bright sunny days and miserable rainy nights...

The next thing he knew he was laying on the tarmac of the road and staring straight up at his beautiful blue sky. It was out of focus though. His face hurt. His back hurt, His leg hurt, well, at least he thought it hurt. With so much new pain for his brain to process he wasn't sure what didn't hurt at the moment.

A young man walked into his field of vision carrying a shovel and stared down at him, threateningly.

"What you doing in our manor?" he asked wielding what looked like a garden spade. Which explained his extremely painful face and the blood pouring down his throat from what could only be a busted nose.

"Nothing," Jack burbled, blood clogging his throat. "Just bleeding." He sat up and spat. Fresh blood immediately started to pour down his face - as if there wasn't enough blood covering his body, his nose had to turn into a sprinkler and fill in more of the empty spaces on his clothes. By the time he got home he would just be one complete red 'splotch'.

Jack looked at his attacker. He was holding the spade and Jack realised he was just another young man. Scared and angry about what was going on. Why he was attacking people in the streets just before a nuclear holocaust, was another confusing question? *'Because he can,'* he answered himself. You could get away with pretty much anything when there was no one to answer to. If you wanted to roam the streets belting people with spades, you can. Who is going to stop you?

The kid swung the shovel back as Jack got to his feet and dusted his bloody jeans with his hands, careful not slice his butt cheeks off with the knuckleduster blades.

"What's happening Tubby?" Jack asked as the kid stared at him.

"You're in no position to call no one names," the kid spat.

"Try it, fat arse."

No sooner were the words out of Jack's mouth when the kid started to swing the spade back in his direction.

Jack caught the spade by the handle and pulled. It fell out of the kid's grasp and he almost fell over as it was dragged out of his hands. Steadying himself he stood back and looked at Jack with a new-found fear.

'What was he doing?' he thought to himself. Terrorising a kid. The kid may be all kinds of bat-shit crazy to be out wandering the streets gardening trespassers like this but he was still a kid. And his own sense of morals began to twitch at the back of his skull. This kid had 'shovelled' him. He deserved a good spanking. Or at least a spade in the face like he had received.

Despite the pain the boy had caused, Jack couldn't bring himself to retaliate with the spade. He threw it onto the grass verge beside the road and stepped back.

There was a white van parked at the side of the road and the kid was standing next to it. He must have stepped out from behind it and whacked him. The bike was there on the floor with a few new bright metallic scrapes through its paintwork.

"Get the fuck out of here," Jack said as he started to run his self-diagnostic and assess the damage the kid and the tarmac had done to him.

"That's a very good friend of ours, man," a voice said from behind him. "I don't think you should be talking to him like that."

'Oh fuck, what now?' Jack thought to himself. *'Don't tell me he has a big brother.'* His body should be shutting down for repairs. Making sure everything was functioning. Rerouting essential power supply to main systems. Instead he had another fuckwit to deal with.

"Why are you talking in an American accent?" Jack asked the young white man dressed as a rapper. "And what gives you the right to talk to me like that?"

"Don't backchat us, motherfucker. Can't you count? There's four of us. And just one of you," the youth said as his friends stood shoulder to shoulder with him.

"You think so, huh? What if I've picked up a few friends on the way here? Maybe they're not real friends but I'm sure they can fuck you up very nicely." Jack held up his knuckledustered fists one at a time. "This is Bill and Ben."

The youths took a small but perceptible step back but didn't run. Obviously they still thought they had a chance against the nut-job who had filed his knuckleduster knuckles into blades. Either that, or they were too proud to let one man scare a gang of them off.

Then he pulled the kukri out which had enough dry blood on it now to make it look as if it come out of horror wax museum. "And this is little Weed."

The kids looked at him blankly.

"Before your time, huh? Well, take it from me, you don't want to mess with these motherfuckers. They help me with the gardening. And right about now I'm thinking about doing a bit of pruning, maybe a bit of hedging. Cutting a few things down to size. Making everything a bit neater."

Jack pointed to the biggest youth at the front of the gang. "Weed here is going to prune away some excess growth, like your face. Then Bill here is going to spread a little punishment across your backside," Jack said pointing to the second biggest. "Ben here, is going to turn your guts to mulch," Jack said pointing to the last of the trio.

"Leaving you," Jack pointed back to the pudgy guy who had popped out from behind the van. "I'm going to plant 'Ben' here so far up your fat arse you'll be tasting what you had for dinner last night. Which I'm guessing by the size of you is chips, chips, a side order of chips and a bucket of ice cream to finish."

The youths looked at one another, for a brief moment they were daring one another to make the first move. To put Jack down before he had a chance to carry out his threats. Jack stared back at them with a slow smile building on his face.

He had no idea what he looked like at the moment but the fact that he smiled and he was covered head to toe in blood, mostly his own by now, must have said something about him. Within the space of a few heartbeats. They all turned and ran. Their feet made strange slapping noises on the road and the pavement. All except the fat kid. He seemed to pad delicately down the street, even though his bulk was swinging from side-to-side.

When they were out of sight, Jack slid down the side of the white van gasping. He may have thought his chest was on fire before but now was a completely different story. He may have cracked a couple of ribs when he hit the ground and was now finding it difficult to breathe properly. He grimaced as he looked at the bike. Thankfully they had left it but the thought of riding it now filled him with dread. But with no other means of transport this was the best way of getting home.

"Little cunts," he breathed with feeling. "I hope you're captured by scavengers and made to suck cocks for the rest of your miserable existences."

'That is,' he thought, 'if you survive.'

21

When he was over the bridge at Westminster he thought everything would get better. A straight run home and in bed by tea time. But it seemed events were conspiring against him, big time.

He began to wonder if he had done the wrong thing by waiting for the main bulk of people to get out of the way before he began his journey. He may have been safer in the crowd. Especially when people like 'fatty' and his mates were picking off people who were on their own.

But then he had seen the evidence of people who had been dragged along in the middle of the crowd. Put one foot wrong and they were down and it was all over. Every now and then there were people just laid in the road or on the pavement. They'd been trampled. They'd fallen and everyone had just carried on trampling over them as if they were a piece of litter that no one wanted to pick up.

If he'd fallen, would he have been able to avoid the seething, desperate mass of people? Would he have been stomped into the ground like a discarded piece of chewing gum? Ground into the pavement to become just a red stain?

'Wow,' he must stop thinking like this. Get home and then worry about the mistakes he had made. There would be time for sorrow and thinking of would-a, could-a, should-a, later on. If there were commentators following his progress he imagined they were having a whale of a time analysing his mistakes.

If they were football commentators, they would be counting how many times he had been fouled and how many times he'd fouled someone else. He was sure he was due a red card by now. Or a yellow and a stern warning, at least.

It seemed the further he went on his journey the more damage he did to himself. Well, not him exactly but other people. They were all intent on stopping him for some reason. Surely, they had something better to do? Like burrowing 200 feet straight down and kissing their asses goodbye.

No, they'd rather stand out in the open road and twat people going by on their stolen mountain bikes.

This last injury had really knocked the wind out of him. More of his body was now objecting to his continued forward movement than ever. If all the different parts of his body held a board meeting, they'd be 70-30 in favour of just sitting down and not doing anything for a while - maybe a week or two. But his brain was the chair of the meeting and overruled everyone. It may be the most unstable one at the table, but it was talking the most sense.

Scooping up the bike painfully, he slowly lifted his right wounded leg over the crossbar. It was bleeding again and it told him it was in pain by shooting bullets of information up to his brain and telling him of the fact.

"Yeah, yeah, I'll get to you later. Right now, just do as your fucking told."

He was a mess but his bike was only a little scraped. If he had a chance when all this was over, he would write to the manufacturers and complement them on building a thoroughly sturdy product. It had faced all manner of unexpected attacks a mountain bike wasn't really designed to withstand, but it had kept on going. The bike was keeping it together.

He on the other hand was well and truly fucked. He didn't think any bones were broken. Cracked and bruised perhaps, but his body was taking more punishment than Bruce Willis's character in '*Die Hard*'. And it all added up to one tired and weary fellow.

Luckily, apart from one small hill, it was downhill from here, or on a straight. Which was a blessing he would thank God for later. Thinking about it, that hill could be his salvation. He'd walked down it this morning and thought no more about it. That hill could protect his home from the blast. All he had to do was get over it. If the nuclear devices went off before he got home that hill might protect him. Or so he hoped. He wasn't there yet. But soon. For God's sake, soon.

It didn't last long. The desire to get home was strong but he saw the little gang of people long before they could see him. When he'd learned to drive, his instructor had always said 'look ahead, anticipate what's going to happen, watch the road and watch the pavements - someone is bound to do something stupid and you'll have to react.' It was a statement that had stuck with him through life. He watched people's actions whether they were near or far. He'd seen what could, and what did, happen. The driver who pulled out into traffic just that moment too soon. The man opening his car door on a busy street. The girl so wrapped up in her phone conversation she hadn't seen the lights change. They were all observations where he guessed what was going to happen.

He didn't drive anymore but these were good rules to live by. Other people told him to live in the moment. Worship the 'now'. Fine, but it didn't hurt to look ahead. Especially now. If he didn't do something he could see some bad things happening to what could be a good person.

This situation was pretty clear-cut. They were charging at a door with what looked like a park bench. The wooden kind, that is. They were using it as an improvised battering ram and were smashing it against the door of the house with all the force they could put behind it.

"Open the fucking door, you cunt. There's room for all of us."

There was a muffled shout of something as they stopped bashing at the door then they started ramming the bench again.

"Have it your way, we're coming in whether you want us to or not."

Jack wondered how they knew the occupants had a safe place to hide. It wasn't as if there was a 'vacancy' sign in the window that had been turned off.

Jack slowed the bike, dismounted and hid it behind a bush in one of the gardens down the road. He could have ridden past and no one would have been able to catch him. Unless his leg decided to give way in a moment of panic. But otherwise he could be free and clear but once again, he couldn't help himself. He had to push his bloody nose into someone else's story.

In this story he saw the big bad wolf huffing and puffing and asking to be let in. It was a ridiculous thought, but he couldn't help himself. As befitting the story, the three little pigs would be inside and scared. The big bad wolves in this case weren't huffing and puffing, they had somehow mastered how to use tools and were now using them to get in the brick house at its weakest point - the door.

Fortunately, the door lock didn't break. Like all good Londoners the house probably had locks and bolts running up the inside of the door frame. What had started to break was the door itself. It splintered in the middle. They gave it another few bashes for good measure and the lead wolf put his arm in the hole only to withdraw it quickly and grasp at his fingers. He had obviously been bashed with some heavy, blunt instrument. The other two wolves tried the same only to be beaten back as well, clutching their hands and fingers in pain.

Not to be deterred they picked up the bench again and continued to slam it against the door. If they couldn't get in one way they would get in the other. The other being to pulverise the door to smithereens and then simply walk in.

Jack stood at the garden gate and watched the three wolves in their desperate attempt to get inside the house. He couldn't stop himself. He was going to do it again. Him and his big mouth were going to ask for trouble.

"Hell of a door knocker you've got there," Jack observed with more than just a hint of sarcasm and cockiness.

The wolves stopped immediately and looked at the bedraggled form with the big mouth flapping in the breeze.

"What's it to you?" The bigger, badder wolf asked with a sneer and a nod in his direction.

"Nothing, really. I just think if they wanted to let you in, they would have."

"Fuck off, this doesn't concern you."

"Do you know, I keep telling myself that but I just can't seem to stop myself. Today, I want to stop bad things happening. And you and your friends are a bad thing that is going to happen to those people inside. I can't allow that."

The bigger badder wolf gave a shout and then hurtled down the path at Jack. Legs pounding and arms pumping, he was going to use pure force to knock Jack out of existence. Jack just stepped back from the small gate and prepared himself for 'Wolfie'.

If he wanted to get at him he would have to open the gate or hurdle it. Either way he was at a disadvantage.

In an almost pitiful manoeuvre, he slowed down and climbed over the gate carefully and slowly. Giving Jack the time he needed to unsheathe 'Weed'. The man looked surprised for the rest of his life as Jack swung the blade. He put up his arm to stop it but Weed sliced straight through and embedded her sweet little blade in the man's neck.

If it wasn't for chopping through the man's arm Jack was sure he could have taken his head off with one blow. But this was just as devastating.

Despite what he saw in the movies, very few people survived a sudden dismemberment. Shock would get them, then blood loss and a whole lot of nasty stuff happened too. A missing arm and a 'neck shot' meant 'Wolfie' wouldn't be barking ever again.

Jack pulled the blade out of the man's neck and a fresh pulse of blood arced into the air. More pulses followed as his heart dutifully carried out its job unaware that the man was punctured and was about to go down. He collapsed next to his severed left arm and quivered as his life-force quickly ebbed from his body.

With his dripping blade in his hand, Jack turned his attention to the other wolves. They were paralysed with shock. He had to remember that if you killed the head of a gang there was no one to give orders. The rest of the gang wouldn't know what to do.

On this occasion, Jack thought it best that he take charge. "You can walk away now. It's over. Go home. Hide under the stairs." He pointed in a southerly direction with his kukri and hoped they would take the hint.

The two remaining wolves took a little look at one another then simply walked away from the door. Then they ran, but they didn't run past Jack. They decided to jump over the small fence that divided the front gardens. When they hit the street Jack relaxed and put 'Weed' back in her sheath but not before giving her a wipe.

An image of *'Kill Bill'* came into his head of 'The Bride' carving her way through that house of assassins. Great thought, but if that fight had been real her blade would have been as blunt as the shaft of a sledgehammer.

"Are you all right?" A voice came from the tattered door. "Have they gone?"

"Peachy," Jack replied. "And yes they're gone, leaving a trail of dust in their wake."

"Good, that's good. I thought they would...you know... Would you like to come in?" the voice asked as if he had been politely knocking on the door.

"Sort of defeats the object of all that security doesn't it? Inviting a knife-wielding maniac in off the streets."

"I do not think you are a maniac, I think you are a good man to help us like that. Do you need shelter?"

"I'm heading to it. But thanks for the offer. Been cycling for a while. Thought I'd stop for a breather. Decapitate a nasty man. Be on my way. You know."

"Please come in, you look like you could use a drink. Some water perhaps? It is the least I can do."

Jack thought for moment, a glass of water would be good. Maybe he could also wash some of the blood off his hands and face. Whenever he moved his mouth the dried blood felt stiff on his skin and little flakes cracked off now and again. It wasn't life-threatening, but it was annoying.

"Ok, just for a second. I could use a quick wash. Maybe cool myself down a little."

The door swung open precariously. The wolves had done a pretty good job of blowing his door in, but it had held. God knows for how much longer if he hadn't come along.

Jack shuffled up the path. He didn't realise it but riding the bike had cut off his circulation a little. His left leg was now a little numb. He could feel the prickles of pins and needles as blood flowed back into his empty leg. What with that and his almost useless right leg he must have made a strange picture.

Walking through the doorway and into the hall of the house he felt like he was human again. The house was tastefully decorated. Nice fabrics, delicate colours, patterns that didn't overpower anything. It was a home that had had a lot of thought and love put into it. He saw into the living room of the little pigs. Funnily enough there were three of them; mummy, daddy and the little one hiding in his mummy's arms.

"Hi," Jack said. "Sorry about the appearance, I'm travelling South and some people didn't like it."

Jack wiped his feet on the mat inside the door just to make sure he didn't track any blood onto their expensive looking hallway carpet. It was another habit he had when entering someone else's home. It all wouldn't matter when...yada-yada...bomb...apocalypse and all that. He was getting tired of reminding himself that it was the end of the world but if he kept doing stupid things like stopping...well, end of.

"Please come through to the kitchen, wash, I will get you some water." The man set off down the hallway and Jack followed slowly, careful not to get any gore on the immaculate walls.

"Thanks, I think you're the kindest person I've met today. Everyone else seems to be intent on killing me," Jack said even though warning bells were going off in his head again. *'What was there to be afraid of?'* he thought. *'The man was afraid, and a man who is afraid could do anything.'*

"You have made enemies today?" the man said pouring some water into a glass from the kitchen tap as Jack walked into the busy but extremely tidy kitchen.

"Nothing I can't handle. Thank you," Jack said as he took the glass of water from the man's outstretched and nervous hand.

He was about to drink when he asked himself a question. *'Why is this man nervous? Adrenaline? Why is he still holding the hammer which he must have used to repel the wolves as they reached in to unlock the door? Why is he looking at the glass so intently?'*

There wasn't much. Just a few white particles floating around the bottom of the glass. Something that hadn't quite dissolved yet. If he hadn't been looking, he wouldn't have noticed but there was something definitely in the water and it certainly wasn't a certain hardness which you would expect from this area.

"What line of work are you in?" Jack asked pretending to take a sip from the glass but barely wetting his lips. He pretended to swallow even though he wanted to quaff the water down, it was better he didn't. There could be anything in there.

"Oh that hardly matters now does it? It's not as if I will be going to work tomorrow," the main piglet said looking uneasily at Jack and his drink.

"Humour me," Jack said wetting his lips a second time and watching some of the blood from his face dissolve into the water.

"I am a doctor," he replied. "A General Practitioner."

"Always good to have a doctor in the family. Bet you can get your hands on the right medications when you need them."

"Yes, that is true. Very fortunate when the little man is sick."

"Bet you can get him some stuff to help him sleep when he's up all night too, huh?" Jack looked at the glass and then at the doctor. His face fell further than a coal-miner's on Monday morning.

"I'm sorry?"

Jack motioned to the glass as he swirled it around. "Something hasn't quite dissolved yet."

The Doctor turned pale and took a step back. He'd seen what had happened to the big bad wolf and was now certain that the same fate awaited him.

"Please, I am only protecting my family. I don't know you and what you did to that man… I am sorry." He backed against the kitchen wall and budged the door shut. He didn't want his family to see what might happen to him.

"Don't worry, everyone else is trying to kill me with knives, guns, Tasers, shovels and fists, first time today someone's tried to poison me."

"It is only a sedative. It would have put you to sleep. That is all."

"And then you'd go and lock yourself in the cellar and leave me up here to be cremated."

"You would have felt nothing. It would have been a peaceful end."

"Well, I'm not quite finished yet, Doctor. You won't need the hammer, I'm leaving. You get yourself and your family in your cellar and good luck."

"I am so very sorry. Good luck to you, too. I hope you make it home."

Jack smiled a little, poured the water down the sink and rinsed the glass out. He didn't want anyone else drinking out of it by mistake and suddenly taking an unexpected long nap. He bent down and took a mouthful of water straight from the tap and swallowed it.

"See you later," Jack said as he walked down the short hall and walked through the shattered remains of the door. He didn't hear a reply. Just the sound of another door closing and bolts being drawn.

In a matter of minutes, the family would probably in the cellar. Cosy and warm and safe from harm.

Which is where he should be. Home in his own cellar. Putting his head between his legs and kissing his arse goodbye.

Where was he now? Three miles from the centre of London? Would that be enough? Obviously not out in the open street. The flash from the bomb or bombs would turn him to ash before he knew it.

Was it Hiroshima or Nagasaki where they had found all those shadows on the walls? People caught in the blast. Their shadows burned into the walls like photos on film.

Jack shivered. It wasn't how he wanted to go. He wanted to go in his sleep at the age of 90 not on the street in a blinding flash of light at the age of 45.

He picked the bike out of the hedge and mounted it again.

"Were you lonely without me, Bessie?" he asked the bike as he set off again. He may be worried about dying in the blast but he was now getting increasingly worried about his mental state.

He was never quite the 'full shilling' before he started butchering people with 'Bill and Ben and little Weeeed', now he was naming his weapons and his bike and talking to them. He was even talking to his wounded leg as if it had a personality. What would his psychiatrist make of that? He would of course ask her if he ever bumped into her again. Which was highly unlikely.

Then he had another strange thought. If he didn't see his psychiatrist again, how would he get his anti-depressants? Ok when the bombs wipe everything out there might be a few pharmacies left standing.

But then what? There wasn't an infinite supply of anti-depressants, or water, or food. So he wouldn't just be thirsty and hungry, he would be depressed as well.

Didn't bode well for the rest of the world if he was wandering around in a bad mood. Especially with no laws to stop him. He now knew what he was capable of.

He'd always suspected he was slightly psychopathic. Or sociopathic. Or something like that. He'd had right and wrong drummed into him when he was a kid. But his father's betrayal of his mother was wrong. Yet he did it anyway. So if he took his father as an example, it was okay to do the wrong thing just so long as you weren't caught? Was that the lesson?

He knew it was wrong. He knew a lot of things were wrong, but people did them anyway. The world was full of people, Governments and companies doing despicable things for money. And on the whole they were getting away with it.

What use was the law when powerful people could flout it and go unpunished. This declaration of war was about boundaries. The law of the land said you couldn't trespass on this land but they had. Planes went into no-fly zones. They were testing. 'Shows of strength'. But they were no better than children who were told not to walk on the grass. They could read the sign, they knew it was wrong but if no one was watching, they'd do it.

Jack smirked to himself. *'If they can get away with it, they'll do it.'*

The only crime in the world is getting caught.

He remembered some quote from Jack Nicholson: 'You don't see Tom Hanks, out drinking, whoring and partying every night. That's what I like about Tom Hanks, he doesn't get caught."

22

He turned off Bedford Road and headed down the A2217 - or so the sign said - but it was only for a few hundred metres. It turned into Abbeville Road where it met Clapham Park Road and then it was a straight down to the South Circular from there.

One thing he always found amusing about any journey he took when he had a car was the route conversation. First it was 'did you have a good journey?' Second was, 'how long did it take you?' Finally, it was 'which way did you come?' More often than not the people asking the questions always knew a better route and mentioned that you could see the 'whatever-it-was' if you had gone the way they suggested.

There wasn't much to see around here, except a few ghosts of his past. The young man he was - full of hope and eagerness for life. Someone who hadn't been beaten down by distrust and cynicism.

This way he passed Northbourne Road. One of the many places he'd lived in London. Come to think about it. He'd lived in so many different parts of London he could barely remember their addresses anymore. He remembered little bits of existence. Little 'quirks' of the places that he couldn't get out of his mind, no matter how hard he tried.

Before he was married, Jack and his girlfriend lived in 'the bedsit'. As a single man he'd lived in bedsits before and that was fine. It wasn't a palatial sort of existence but when you're single, it's fine. When you're a young couple it's completely different. There was nowhere to go to get away from one another. But in those days they were young and in love. They worked together, went home together, cooked together and when it was time to go to bed, the sofa magically turned into a bed and they slept the night together.

Funnily enough, it was only when they moved into a house together that the cracks started to appear. When they had a little more room to move. It was quite telling that the more space they had the easier it was to move apart.

And move apart they did. He remembered her saying 'she needed some space' and 'it wasn't him, it was her.' Which was funny in a way. Why did women always use clichés to break up with their husbands or boyfriends? It was as if there was a book of go-to excuses for leaving. 'Wait a minute, let me just get the book out, yes, here it is, I still love you but I feel we've just grown apart.'

Why couldn't they just say, 'I have grown to hate you and I must leave before I slip a knife between your ribs while you sleep.' That would be the more honest approach.

This little bike ride down memory lane was all well and good but it wasn't getting him home any quicker. He couldn't pedal any faster at the moment. He was tired. Almost to the point of exhaustion. He didn't realise how much the gunshot wound had taken out of him until now. It was painful, true. But he had ridden through the pain barrier many times and had come out the other side with a kind of euphoria - a high, almost. This pain was constant and gnawing away at his resolve. Maybe if he got some fluids inside him. Some *Coke* or some *Red Bull* or something, he might be able to keep going.

He'd never had *Red Bull*, or any of those taurine and caffeine drinks that promised to give you wings or energy. Right now he would try anything. If it kept him going that was enough. He could rest later. Then a Bon Jovi song went through his head, something about 'sleep when I'm dead'. Things must be bad if he had earworms about Bon Jovi. Sure enough, there it was. Creeping through his brain, then he started humming. As Abbeville Road went past him house by house he was singing *'I'll Sleep When I'm Dead'*.

He didn't mind Bon Jovi in his younger days but when they went 'cowboy' he decided that there were better things in life. Like music. Even the song *'I'll Sleep When I'm Dead'* was annoying to him these days. What a load of tripe. You don't sleep when you're dead, you're dead when you're dead. But he hardly wanted to get involved in some philosophical debate with a big haired Italian from New Jersey.

Jack passed the *Pizza Hut* and wondered if they had some *Red Bull* in there. *'Doubt it,'* he thought, although a *Coke* might be a good substitute, caffeine, sugar, could do the trick, but he couldn't remember if they served *Coke* or *Pepsi* so he carried on. He wasn't all that keen on *Pepsi*, he liked his sugar delivered the good old-fashioned *Coca Cola* way.

As he hit the South Circular and did a hasty right turn he realised there was a *Tesco* just by Clapham South tube station. A big one. One that must surely have some fizzy liquid complete with sugar, taurine and all the additives that could make a child run in giddy circles for hours.

The South Circular was empty. It was one of the few roads where crashes had been minimal. It was one of the few arteries of London still capable of pumping cars along it, but there wasn't even a flicker of movement. A few bodies lying by the road, but nothing too drastic. He was getting used to the sight of dead people now. They were as normal and as frequent as discarded *Starbucks* coffee cups.

In the distance he could see the green of Clapham Common, the tip of the south east side. He'd managed to avoid the common completely taking this circuitous route and that was a good thing, he thought. It was too open. It was one of the few places in London where you could see for a great distance. And if anyone was looking for a bloodied bloke on a bike he would stand out like a frost-bitten thumb on a hand of clean white fingers.

Even though there was no sign of life he creeped left around the corner. Hugging the wall and the pavement as he went. He'd learned his lesson about appearing round corners with the van and 'shovel boy'. He was sure he couldn't take another spade to the face. His poor nose was a mess as it was. Another shot could make it drive itself up into his brain and that wouldn't be good.

He'd heard that the old 'driving your nose bone up into your brain' was a bit of hokum. But he wasn't about to experiment with the idea unless he was driving the nose bone up into the brains of someone who was attacking him. Yeah he might give that a try. If it didn't kill them at least it would stop them for a few seconds while they got their bearings back.

Martial arts taught practitioners how to strike the weak points. Disorient. Unbalance. Keep going so that your assailant loses the will to fight. It was all defensive. If he wanted to kill someone there were ways and means much quicker than concentrating on tapping weak points. He didn't want to use them.

Christ, what was he thinking? How many people had he killed already and he was getting high and mighty about using martial arts to kill someone? In his mind though. Martial arts had a code. If he was in a street fight, use the rules of the street - no rules.

If he was in a fight with someone who had skills, well that was a different matter entirely. He would have to shoot them if he had a gun, head butt them if he didn't. But otherwise fight the way they fought you.

The entrance to the *Tesco* was in the middle of the building. Sliding doors that had shut fast on some trailing piece of wrapping that blew like a streamer in the breeze. Outside there was packaging from other products swirling around. A pack of toilet rolls had burst open releasing waves of toilet tissue into the air.

"Oh, this isn't right," Jack said to the open air. "This has got to be an ambush."

He stowed the bike at the side of the building and walked up to the front door. It was still working and swooshed open as soon as it detected him. The doors may be working but the lights inside definitely weren't. The only thing he could see were the lights of the fridges at the back of the store, and they seemed too far away. If his drink was anywhere, it was going to be over there.

Realising he was a silhouette against the door he quickly stepped to the side of the door that gave him more darkness to play with. The second he stood aside something cracked through the door where he had just been.

He ducked down and scanned the immediate area of the floor. There was a thin sliver of something across the entrance. Thin strands of wire that stretched across the doorway. Just far enough inside so the light from outside didn't light them up. If he had carried on walking, he would be a tangled mess on the floor and someone would be standing over him with another strange weapon. A pricing gun perhaps and he was about to be marked down in price and put on the end of an aisle.

Whatever had hit the door had not been a pricing gun however. Looking around on the floor he saw the weapon. A Sabatier knife. Small, but thrown with enough force to crack the door a little. If it had hit him blade side, he might not be feeling all that cocky.

He took the knife and cut the wires that were blocking his path. He hoped they weren't attached to explosives.

He laughed to himself, '*Where would they get explosives from?*'

'Same place you did,' he answered himself and then gulped.

Nothing exploded. Which made him feel a little more confident. He started to crawl forwards and away from the door. If they were coming for him, he had better make sure they didn't know exactly where he was. He did it as quietly as possible, so they couldn't get a fix on his position. Now though, he was leaving a bloody trail. His leg had opened up again and a fresh gush of blood was leaving his leg-print everywhere. If his assailants followed the red trail they would find him in seconds. He had to move quickly and quietly.

He scuttled in the general direction of the fridges, checking every corner and every aisle before he moved. While checking behind so no one could get the jump on him.

Then he saw one of the ambushers, halfway down the next aisle. From his position on the floor he could see under the shelf units and could just make out the boots of someone hiding halfway down. He would have to backtrack. Which meant going away from the drinks, those lovely cold drinks. He turned tail and scuttled down the previous aisle. That one had been empty. As he reached the halfway point he checked for signs of any other attackers. No one else was in sight so he crept closer. As he stood he took a tin of peas off the shelf and smashed it down on the man's head.

His hand hurt like hell afterwards but he had achieved his objective, there was an unconscious bushwhacker at his feet. He ducked down to floor level again and watched under the shelves. If there had been a noise, other people may have heard and already be heading in his direction.

Luckily, there was nothing. Not a sausage. Or a strip of bacon. Or a sausage McMuffin for that matter. He crawled to the fridges at the back checking every aisle and every corner. This was an ambush after all and at some point whoever had set it would pull it shut with him in its jaws. But not yet. They were going to wait until he was well inside with no chance of escape.

He had reached the fridge by now and gently opened it. There it was, the full-fat *Coke* he had dreamed of for the last 10 minutes. And joy of joys, it was cold. He removed it from the fridge as quickly as he could and twisted the cap off. It was one of the small bottles, but it was heaven in plastic to him. He gulped at the liquid and felt it bubble down his throat. To a thirsty man *Coca Cola* was nectar. Even if the sugar was bad for you and caused all sorts of bodily dysfunctions it was delicious and just the kick he needed. He immediately felt better. He stopped drinking when he felt the first uncomfortable build-up of bubbles in his stomach. That was the problem with fizzy drinks. They made you belch and now he could feel one of the bigger ones building up inside him ready to explode like a geyser of carbon dioxide.

Jack held off but his stomach was telling him that if he didn't get rid of the gases soon he was going to be in trouble. He put his hand over his mouth and tried to expel the gases silently. The gases had a different idea. They were coming out like they were being shot out of a cannon. Using his hand like a silencer was not going to stop this belch. It came out from his stomach, travelled up his throat and came via his mouth out through his fingers like a geyser. Anyone in this quiet space could have heard it.

"Pardon you," said a voice somewhere to his left followed by a little snigger.

"More tea, Vicar?" came another voice from his right.

"Better out, than in," a third came from somewhere else on the right.

'Oh fuck,' Jack thought to himself. *'Ambushers with a sense of humour. What could be worse?'*

For a moment he tried to mentally fix their positions. If he was right, they were all around him and moving in. They had drawn him into the trap and were now drawing the noose tight. Why hadn't he seen their feet, when he had checked under the shelves? Unless they had been standing on the shelves. Clever. Very clever.

As soon as he was inside and past the point of no return they closed up his exit and started moving in for the kill. Stupid, stupid, stupid.

His thirst had made him take a risk. He knew it was an ambush. He knew someone would be here to separate him from his senses or his life but his own hubris had said 'yup, you go right on in, it's not safe, but you can handle it.'

Jack sat with his back against the fridges, he was lit up like a Christmas tree and they were approaching in the dark. Time to change that.

First action; get out of the headlights. Across from the upright fridges were the long open-topped freezers. Whoever had left the supermarket had covered what was left of the food with grey thermal sheets to keep the cold in. There was very little food left but they must have pulled them over by force of habit.

As quietly as possible Jack climbed into the freezer and pulled the grey sheet over himself. After what he'd been through so far today, it felt lovely. If he could stay in here for a couple of hours he would be fine.

Trying to keep any noise to a minimum he crawled under the sheet until his body was hidden from view then he stared out of the edge to check the lay of the land. From where he was positioned he could see the heads of his attackers heading round the edge of the freezer. They weren't being as quiet as they should be now. They had their quarry cornered, and would make him pay for raiding their larder.

As soon as he saw that all three had passed the side of the freezer, Jack quietly slipped onto the floor, skittered across it and climbed into the next freezer.

He heard their voices as they realised he had gone. They were confused and more than a little angry.

"How did he get past?"

"Don't know, we were watching both ways, he couldn't have slipped out before we got to him could he?"

"Not without us seeing him."

"Then he's still here somewhere. Spread out."

"Why don't we turn the lights on, it'll be easier to spot him?"

"Ok, you go and do it, we'll start looking."

Jack wasn't as keen on the idea of turning the lights on as these guys were. With one flick of a switch they could cut down the cover of darkness that was keeping him out of their clutches. Every light on meant fewer shadows to hide in.

He crawled to the end of the freezer that was nearer to the door. The guy who was tasked with turning on the lights had to go this way. He heard the footfalls approaching and readied himself for a full-on assault. For some reason they had completely abandoned their stealthy approach. Was there any need for it? He was in here somewhere and they were going to kill him for drinking their *Coca Cola*. Why tip-toe around when they had him?

'Well, for one reason,' Jack thought as he appeared behind the ambusher, *'you give away your position to someone who is about to do something desperate.'*

Jack got his left arm around the man's throat and used his right to hold it so he could squeeze. It was a choke hold which he'd never really tried before. The ambushers hands went to his arm but couldn't wrest it from around his throat. Jack kept squeezing. If he held on too long, he would kill him. He just needed to hold on long enough so he passed out. It looked simple in the films but he hadn't counted on the strength of a man who was as strong as a panicking gorilla and trying to breathe.

In his terror he lifted Jack completely out of the freezer with a violent jerk. The extra weight of Jack on his throat made the choke-hold even tighter. In his panic the ambusher had given Jack a better way of killing him.

Long guttural noises brayed around the dark supermarket. Jack was turned and twirled around in the man's desperate plight to eject his passenger and his legs slammed into the edge of the freezer. His wounded leg started pumping fresh agony around his body.

It was only when Jack was being twirled around like a bad version of 'airplane' that he realised how big his ambusher was. Jack was 6 feet 2 inches and a solid 15 stone but just hanging onto this guy's neck was giving him vertigo. He was also twirling him around as if he was a kid on someone's shoulders at the Lord Mayor's Parade.

If this guy decided to run backwards and ram him against a wall, their combined weight would turn him into mincemeat. Or there would be a 'clean-up on aisle 4'.

Jack hung on in desperation more than anything else. If he was bucked off he was dead. He might be dead if he hung on, but there was a better chance he could choke him into unconsciousness.

The beast of a man just kept on swinging. This was a man who was used to heavy weights. This was a man who worked-out. This man didn't spend hours on the running machine trying to lose weight. This was a man who power-lifted. And Jack was the dumbbell who had just picked a fight with him.

The beast shook him left then shook him right, but Jack hung on. Then the Beast decided to bend and shake at the same time. Which was to be his undoing. He stood up straight and shook Jack to his left. There was a cracking noise from the Beast's neck.

The Beast timbered to the floor and hit it face first. Jack rolled forwards over the Beast's head to try and ride the momentum but instead propelled himself into a metal bin containing reduced price mops.

"Not my best landing but any one you can walk away from is a good one," he said as the other two ambushers appeared from out of the gloom of the supermarket.

They were almost upon him when Jack grabbed one of wooden handled mops. It wasn't a pugilist stick but it would have to do. After tackling their hulk-like partner he wasn't ready for another hand-to-hand fight.

"Sticks and stones, will break your bones," Jack said as he drove the handle straight into the first man's stomach.

The man doubled up and collapsed immediately to the floor. The mop wasn't heavy enough to swing as a club but as something to poke it was perfect. Some people always thought swinging a baseball bat at an enemy was the best way to go. In a confined space, it was impossible to swing, but use the bat to poke or punch. Then it was possible to really do some damage.

The second man was on a mission and it just didn't register that his friend had been taken out of the game with just one jab. He was going to show this prey who was the boss. He was going to put him back in his place no matter what happened.

Jack poked the mop handle straight into the man's right eye and he screamed. He tottered back a few steps as he cupped his eye. Then he stood up straight and charged again. This time the handle struck him straight in the teeth.

He reeled backwards barely managing to keep his feet on the tiled floor. He swayed a little then stood up straight and stared at Jack holding the handle pointed at him like a spear.

Two attacks and he'd been sent back both times. He held his face as blood started streaming between his fingers. He looked at the man on the floor clutching his stomach and the beast staring wide eyed into the darkness and stopped.

He had a choice; continue and get fucked up like his friends or stand back and live to fight another day. He made the right choice. Live. He stared at Jack and simply backed away holding his poor broken mouth. His eye was a mess but better to have one eye than no eyes. He held up his hands in surrender.

"Go," he said through his broken mouth, his one good eye watching for any move that would signify another attack.

Jack held the mop ready for any 'funny stuff' but when he saw the surrender in the man. He lowered his weapon. He looked around briefly and saw what he wanted. There was a case of *'Relentless'*, another energy drink, he imagined. He picked up a box with '6 cans' written on the side and then slowly backed his way to the door. He glanced around as he went making sure there were no other ambushers. Or the one he'd clobbered had woken up and was ready to gut him in some ingenious way. When he reached the doors, they swooshed open and let him out into the sunlight.

Jack dropped the mop and went to retrieve his bike. He was expecting a bullet in the back as he turned away from the shop and was almost hoping it would happen for a moment. If they shot him, at least it would be over quick. No more of this running around going nowhere. Instead, the supermarket doors closed and he heard a 'click'. They were counting their losses and shutting up shop. No more ambushes. They'd had enough. Time to batten down the hatches and ride out the storm.

23

Jack opened the box and popped open a can of the *'Relentless'*, it was warm, sticky and gassy, but he didn't care. He took a long swig and belched loud again. This time, he let it out without worrying if anyone was going to kill him. He emptied the can in his second swig and popped another open. If there was a warning about drinking too much of the stuff he would deal with it later. He needed a boost and this was the thing to do it. If he had any Pro-Plus he would also swallow a handful of those as well and to hell with the consequences.

He belched again and swigged long and hard. This time he emptied the can in one draught and gave a side belch from the corner of his mouth. It wasn't as powerful as his first but it would still embarrass a vicar at Sunday afternoon tea.

This time he heard laughter. It was strange. In the last hour he can't recall anyone having anything to laugh about. The comments from the Three Stooges inside were funny but they had more of a malevolent quality about them. They certainly weren't laughing *with* him.

As Jack retrieved his bike with one hand and carried the remaining cans with the other, he scanned the immediate area with a careful eye. Everything was normal, or as normal as a deserted Clapham South could be just before a nuclear war. There was one incongruity, however. Most people had run for their lives. Or driven for their lives. There on the bench opposite were a couple of old folks sitting there as if they were out for an afternoon stroll and had decided to take a breather.

What was even odder was that they were smiling at him.

"You ok, son?" the old man said.

"Son?" Jack said feeling an unfamiliar chuckle rise in his throat. "I think you ought to get your glasses checked, I'm looking at 40 in the rear view mirror and it's so far behind it's gone over the horizon."

"You're a 'son' to me and the missus, 40 was 35 years ago for the both of us."

Jack wheeled his bike over the road to where they were sitting. And offered them a *'Relentless'*.

"No, thank you. It'll keep us up all night," the man laughed.

"What are you two doing out here?" Jack asked squinting across the expanse of green and making sure no one was running towards them with a gun and a squad of police cars.

"Having a rest," The old woman said kindly. "It looks like you've been in the wars, young man. Do you need to sit down?" She patted the seat next to her and smiled up at him with her crinkled face. She had on some light make-up. Not enough to hide her features, but enough to add a more youthful glow to her old face. She was a woman who had grown old gracefully and only decided a little make-up was good enough these days.

"Hah, if I sit down, I'm not sure I could get up again," Jack replied. A statement not so far removed from the truth.

"Where are our manners?" the old lady said. "I'm Margaret, and this is Vincent."

They offered their hands and Jack shook Vincent's hand first: a firm and confident handshake that didn't try to stay holding for too long. Margaret's handshake was one of a lady. If you so wished, you could lean down and kiss the back of her hand. He didn't but it was refreshing to see that some women gave you the option. Formal, yet feminine.

"Hi, I'm Jack, what are you two doing out here, if I may be so bold to ask?"

"Taking the air, as we've done ever since we retired," Vincent said looking up and down the road. "It was busy earlier on so we decided to sit and watch the madness go by. But it's quietened down now. We might start off again in a few minutes. There's no rush."

"Are you sure there's no rush?" Jack asked a little worried for his new, aged friends. "Things could be…"

"We spent 50 years running around in this world before we retired. Ever since then we've been enjoying the world at our own pace. We're not about to change now," Margaret said.

"But…"

"Yes we know," Vincent interrupted. "It's fine."

"But, you should be heading for cover," Jack told them as if he was telling a young child it was about to start raining.

"We are, but these days, we do it at our speed. What happens, happens. If we get home, good. If we don't, then that's what's meant to be."

"I can't believe you're both so calm about all this."

"I'm not, I'm shitting my pants, but there's not a lot we can do about it."

"Vincent, there's no need for that," Margaret chastised, giving him a playful punch on the shoulder. "There's no excuse for bad manners or bad language," she continued.

"Yes, sorry about the belch earlier. 'Pardon me'," Jack added as if he was apologising to his mother.

"Don't worry about it," Vincent waved his liver spotted hand at him. "The old girl is always having a go at me about my manners. I can't help it. After so many years together you'd think she'd be used to it by now."

"I am," Margaret confided. "It's the other people who I feel sorry for when you start yourself off."

Jack had to laugh at this lovely old couple. Their lives were over and yet they were still riffing off one another. It made him think about all his relationships that had died for one reason or another. Somehow they had stayed together, through thick and thin, rough and smooth. They'd vowed to take one another for better or worse, and had stuck to their promises.

It made him think of a similar promise he'd made in front of a church full of people.

"Where are you going?" Vincent asked pulling him back from the abyss of his thoughts.

"Mitcham," Jack replied.

"Wife and kids waiting for you?" Vincent asked.

"No, no one. Just me."

"That's a shame," Margaret replied. "Children may be a constant worry but they are a blessing. We wouldn't have had such an eventful life if it wasn't for our two."

"Maggie, I don't think this boy wants to hear too much about our life. Looks like he has a place to be," Vincent said softly.

"Of course. Jack, you get on your way. Get yourself home. Whether we all live or die today it's always best to do it in your own bed."

"Are you guys heading off as well?" Jack asked, concerned.

"Yes, just a few more minutes while we get our breaths back. We'll get home. Don't worry."

They shook hands again. Margaret in that same endearing feminine way and Vincent with a warm shake that said 'I'm a good man'.

Jack ditched the rest of the *Relentless* and set off on the bike. He couldn't resist a quick look back to make sure they were on their way. They were getting to their feet, slowly and carefully. They weren't as steady as he imagined they once were but at least they were moving again. They faced North and tottered off on their walking sticks.

He didn't want to say anything while he was talking to them but he had seen Vincent's hand in his jacket pocket while he had been talking. What sort of gun he was pointing at Jack he couldn't make out, but there was something in his jacket pocket and it wasn't a packet of *Werther's Originals*. Vincent and Margaret may be old but they certainly weren't stupid. His guess was that one sudden move and he would be carrying a bullet in his gut. Vincent's hands may be old and shaky but he bet he could hit a big and bloody target like him with relative ease.

He always wondered what would have happened if he'd stayed married. What if they'd lived together for 50 years and then one of them died? Would the other have slowly wasted away? Missed the other one so much that they had died too? Vincent and Margaret would probably die together. One wouldn't end up missing the other. There was something quite poetic in that. Only death separating them.

He rode past the Majestic Wine Warehouse. That had been ransacked as well. Made sense. If you were going to loot, may as well do it bulk. Saves a looting trip later on.

When he'd lived in this area, he never went there. He never took booze home unless he was with someone else. Strange that he could spend most nights in a pub but could never bring himself to take a tray of beer home and sit and watch television while shouting at the screen. He just couldn't do it.

Also when he lived here, the *Tesco's* wasn't a superstore. It was a derelict building. A massive eyesore. Underneath it all there was a beautiful building if you could see past the broken grimy windows and the netting placed over them to stop pigeons nesting there.

In one of his 'If I was a rich man' dreams, where he won the lottery and had more money than sense, he would restore it to its natural beauty. He would turn it into a hospital. Put money in trust so that it could operate without having to rely on the National Health Service. His hospital would look after everyone. The homeless, the poor, anyone who needed it. There would also be a part where the homeless could stay until they got themselves back on their own two feet.

Another feature of his hospital would be a service where, if they wanted, they could use the hospital as an address. They could get unemployment benefit until they got their own place and start afresh. If they wanted to. He knew some people wanted to get away from society and so had chosen a life on the street.

It was all a benevolent dream he had now and again. It was more than some cities did for the homeless. He knew that in the past New York actually gave homeless people one-way tickets out of the city. The homeless were sent to rural communities where it became 'their problem'.

He thought his idea was better. Or at least more human. In London these days their answer to the homeless was to treat them like pigeons.

Wherever pigeons could settle they placed wires, or protruding nails so that they couldn't settle. It was the same with the homeless, they put revolving seats in bus shelters or protruding metal 'bumps' in doorways to stop them lying down as they sheltered from the elements.

There wasn't so much as an outcry about this practice, more of an 'exclamation' and a 'what is this world coming to?' but nothing more drastic than that. Londoners had more pressing things to worry about. Like, what was dinner tonight? Or that presentation they had to do tomorrow.

If Jack had managed to win the lottery and build his Homeless Hospital he knew what would happen. The locals of Clapham would be up in arms moaning that it encouraged the wrong 'element' to move in next door. They would be writing to their MPs and protesting outside. They wouldn't do anything to help the homeless but they would be doing everything to help themselves and stop their house prices going down.

The milk of human kindness had passed its sell-by date around here.

Oh yes he liked that one. Shame he couldn't tell it to anyone.

24

He coasted down the hill and narrowly avoided a body that was stretched out over the road. There were two gruesome indentations in the body that looked as if something really heavy had been rolled over him.

The man had been run over and then left in the middle of the road. All the other bodies were pulled to the side so that vehicles had been able to get by, but this looked recent. Blood was still weeping out of the poor man's mouth as if he was talking to Jack.

He was really starting to lose his grip on the reality of the situation. Another twinge from his leg and a fresh rivulet of blood escaped from his bindings. The pain was keeping him sane. But he really should at least attempt to dress it in some way. Anything would be better than bloody jeans tied with shirt sleeves.

As he reached the bottom of the hill he saw the road towards Balham and there looked to be another problem to add to his 'incredible journey'. A queue of cars. And each one still had a driver and passengers.

And they were crawling slowly up the road. And they all looked normal.

It was enough to make him start to apply the brakes. As he approached the back of the queue he noticed in the distance some sort of barricade. They were stopping the cars one by one then allowing them through. Or at least it appeared that way. A car went roaring through the barrier and the people left behind closed it behind the departing vehicle.

"Weird," he said to himself and moved slowly through the orderly line of traffic. It was the first time he'd seen a line of traffic since he'd set off. Today, they were all at angles and crashed and weeping petrol onto the roads. But here was order again. A typical English traffic jam. All lined up and slowly trying to go somewhere.

It took him back to his family holidays. All sitting in a car. Each one wishing they were wherever they were supposed to be, rather than sitting in a stifling hot car, with an overheating father and an almost tearful mother, trying to find a way round the jam, on an out of date map.

On the right, just ahead, he spotted a *Boots* chemists. Fortune had smiled upon him. If he was going to do something about his dripping leg he could nip in there, sort himself out and get back into traffic without facing some nutter who was trying to kill him. It looked like civilisation hadn't quite left Balham just yet.

He walked the mountain bike to the front of the *Boots*. Like a few stores the metal shutters had been left unlocked and the doors left open. The lights were still on and he didn't get any warnings from his 'sixth sense'. He couldn't make out anyone hiding or any movement. But that didn't stop him from hesitating and having a quick internal dialogue.

'Was it safe to go in?'

'Why are you asking me? I got here the same time as you.'

After *Tesco's* he was reluctant to set foot inside another shop again. His last 'shopping experience' was not something he would recommend to friends. On a scale of 1 to 10 he was giving it a '10' in very unsatisfactory.

Slowly he walked into the shop and dragged his bike with him this time. He left it by the checkout and hobbled over to the 'first aid' section.

Like all the other shops it had been raided but by a more civilised group of people. Some shelves were empty while others were still half empty with their products standing in orderly lines.

Who would have thought it; when the world was ending the centre of London turned to crap and civilisation began again at Balham.

Here, people had taken what they needed and left the rest. Luckily they had left a few bandages, some antiseptic spray and cotton wool balls. He even found some scissors so he could cut the cardboard stiff part of his jeans open without ripping them down his legs.

He collected everything he needed then sat down in the first aid aisle. First he cut the shirt sleeves off his strangely coloured jeans and then the jeans themselves, revealing a mess of blood, half-formed scab and the strange looking furrow in his flesh.

The bullet had cut through the thigh all right. Right through the skin, and the layer of fat that supported it. It looked worse than it was but everything on him at the moment looked worse than it was. He really should have stitches on the graze but he wasn't sure he had what it takes to stitch up his own leg. Putting a needle and thread through his own skin was something Rambo could do and he was no Rambo.

He poured some antiseptic on the wound and sincerely wished he hadn't. He sucked in so much air through his teeth he was in danger of hyperventilating. Or at least sucking his teeth down the back of his throat. There were also some very colourful swear words. Some he didn't know that he knew. He poured some more antiseptic over the wound just to make sure and nearly screamed the front windows out.

Picking up wads of cotton wool he managed to clean around the wound. He cleared up the worst of it getting off as much of the mess as possible leaving wisps of cotton wool sticking here and there. It wasn't the neatest clean-up job but it would have to do, for now.

Next came the medical tape. He attached strips to one side of the wound then gradually pulled it closed with more tape on top of that. They weren't butterfly stitches but he thought he did all right. He didn't care if it scarred, he just wanted to make sure it wasn't a yawning chasm of a wound that would take ages to heal and would increase the possibility of infections along the healing process.

He then tied a big wadge of bandage around his leg and finished that off with medical tape too. He wound it around his leg a couple of times, to make sure it didn't come loose, and gave it a once over to make sure he'd covered all the leaky bits. Pleased with his efforts he hauled himself back to his feet and tested the leg. Where the bandage appeared loose he fixed it down with tape. He bent his leg to 90 degrees and where the bandage came free, he taped it back up. As a field dressing it wasn't half bad. The leg felt okay for the moment except for a slight sting from the antiseptic.

He was ready to set off again. There was only one more thing to do. One jean leg was cut off mid thigh and the other one flapped around the top of his blood-soaked trainers. That just looked plain stupid.

Bending down to pick up the scissors he began work on the left leg of the jeans with the precision of a drunk surgeon. Within seconds it fell to the ground revealing a white leg that showed just how bad the right one looked. If he could find some spray tan that might make both legs a little closer in colour, he wouldn't look like some bloodied harlequin but he shouldn't be concerning himself with aesthetics now. He kicked his little makeshift 'surgery' under the shelf in an attempt to keep the place looking a little bit tidy and hobbled back to his bike. If he could have found a bin in the middle of *Boots* he would have used it but the store planners hadn't seen fit to include one so the underside of the shelves would have to hide his untidiness.

On his journey back to the door he spotted a special offer on *Coca Cola*. He picked up a can, popped it and drank the contents greedily. He wasn't about to pass up a chance to get a bit more sugar into his system.

He stood for a second and let loose another belch. The smell of antiseptic confused his senses a little but it was still that thick *Coke* taste he loved. Normally, he'd go for a diet *Coke* but he was sure his body needed the sugar.

Now, he had to see what was going on up ahead. It looked like they were searching the cars from a distance. What was it, passport control?

25

With his bike in hand he walked past the queue of cars to the front. The people inside watched him as he hobbled by them. He expected someone to lean out and shout, 'There's a queue here, you know?' But no one did. So he walked brazenly by ignoring the people waiting patiently in line.

There looked to be trouble up ahead. People were running around and barricading the road with wrecked cars. It all looked as if they were fortifying themselves for a battle.

Puzzled, he headed towards the man who looked to be pointing the most; these were generally the people who were giving the orders. They pointed a lot, talked too much and did very little. He looked every inch the military man. He had the bearing of a man who was used to the military but not someone who was used to command. Jack's guess was that he was in the army but maybe a cook or someone from the offices. He'd had the training but never the opportunity to use it. Until today.

Now, he was throwing orders around and people were obeying without question. When he pointed, his army followed his directions. They were building their barricade. It was obvious now. There was something on the road ahead that was attacking them and they were standing their ground here.

They were between a rock and a hard place. In front of them God knows what? And behind? A few megatons of explosives about to take the skin off their backs and their skeletons.

This didn't fit into Jack's plans at all. That was 'his' road home. As far as he saw it he had two forces to beat here. The ones building the barricade and the ones who were on the other side. He wasn't for taking sides but you can bet the people on the other side weren't as friendly as the people on this side. And looking at some of the people on this side they weren't cuddly teddy bears, either.

They looked desperate. It was a look he'd seen a lot today. These people were used to riding a desk or a shopping trolley. They weren't made for this. Come to think of it, neither was he. But he wasn't going to allow any of them to get in his way.

Jack walked slowly up behind the man in charge and cleared his throat to draw his attention. He didn't want to get too close in case his fright got the better of him and he turned and stabbed Jack with whatever weapon he was carrying.

The man covered in sweat and dirt, turned around with wide eyes. He looked confused at the figure who stood before him.

"Shit, what happened to you?" the man said a little too harshly. "You look awful."

It was like one of those situations where you felt a bit under the weather, then someone points out that you look like shit and you may die at any moment. This in turn makes you feel worse and you want to curl up in a hole and sleep it off.

"I'm having a bad hair day," Jack replied dryly.

The man laughed a little at the absurd comment and relaxed. If he was expecting Jack to attack him, this comment completely disarmed him.

"Looks like you can handle a fight," the man said.

"No choice in the matter sometimes, what's the situation?"

The man looked him up and down for a little while. Naturally he was wary of someone walking up behind him covered in blood, but since Jack wasn't waving a machete and shouting 'death to Balham' he looked safe enough to confide in.

"Hijackers," the man said. "Every car that goes through they stop. Pull the people out and then drive off with the car."

"Can't they just put their foot down?" Jack asked.

"First few did, then they tied chains across the road to lampposts. Made a mess of the next car. Made a mess of the people too."

"How many are there?"

"Don't know, they're hiding at the sides of the road so we can't count them properly. My best guess would be about 20 or so."

"Any other way round? Down the side streets?"

"All blocked, they've been pretty thorough. Burning cars, blocking us off at every turn. This is the only way through. Unless we backtrack into town and no one wants to do that."

"Got any guns and people who can shoot?"

"Some, but not many. Every time we shoot they just go back into hiding. Think they're trying to get us to use up our bullets so they can rush us later. They're clever. Don't really show themselves except when they stop a car and by then we've got another dead family lying in the road."

"Show me," Jack said with an air of authority that the military man ought to recognise and respect. Say something with enough confidence and you could get away with murder or suicide if you were ordering them into battle.

"Follow me up on our 'gate', you can see better from up there," he said with a certain amount of hope that this dishevelled man could be the answer to their prayers.

Jack scanned the street with weary, but sharp eyes. Could he head down a side-road and sneak up behind them? Could he drive pell mell down the middle of the road? Judging by the piles of bodies lying by the roadside and down the side roads they'd already exhausted these options. There were bodies everywhere. Ripped out of their cars, killed and then cast aside.

"Have *they* got guns?" Jack asked wondering if the hijackers were holding all the cards.

"They shot a few people at the beginning, but then they just spread chains across the road. That stopped the cars, then they just pulled them out and... well, you can see."

"How long since you heard a shot from them?"

"About half an hour, that's when they went into hiding. We're assuming they've either run out of bullets or the first hijackers took the guns when they drove off."

"Makes sense. The leaders would have wanted to keep the guns for themselves, and they would make sure they got the first cars too."

Jack's eyes raked the scene for any more clues. It would help if he had a better idea of numbers. Or if he had a clue where they were hiding, but there really wasn't much to see. There was a slight movement behind a wall but that could have been anything. He thought for a moment, if they didn't have guns, they were just playing a waiting game. As soon as someone this side got desperate enough they would set off in their car and then they would spring their trap.

Looking back at the line of cars, he could see the looks of desperation staring from every windscreen. It wouldn't be long before someone threw the barriers back and the whole kit and caboodle of them would throw themselves on the trap.

Facing the road south again he checked out the lamppost where the chain was fastened, he checked further down the road and saw another chain. That too was fastened around a lamppost just high enough to chop through any car attempting to speed out of there.

"They've got a back-up, just in case the first chain doesn't hold," Jack muttered.

"Yes, it's not a great position for us. We may have some guns but not enough bullets to take them all down. Even if we could see them."

Jack thought for a moment or two. This could last for ages and they were running out of time. It was a bit of a Mexican standoff in Balham. They needed to draw the hijackers from cover so the people on the barricades could shoot them. He wasn't about to ask where they got the guns from. If you really wanted a gun in London, there were always ways and means. Not legal means but someone would know someone and if the price was right they suddenly came to the surface.

"I have a plan," Jack sighed reluctantly, immediately regretting what he was about to suggest. He couldn't stay here, and if he wanted to get through he would have to carve a path. Little 'Weed' was going to have to do some pruning again.

"If you've got a way out of this mess, I'm all ears," the man said. "What have you got in mind?"

"Get the people with the guns on the barricades and get them to back up my play. I'm going to do something either very heroic or very stupid. If it works, we're heading out of here. If it doesn't, well, we'll get to that if it comes to it."

"You sure about this?"

"Course not, get your shooters on the barricades and get me a hammer and chisel."

The man gave a call to someone who jumped at the mention of his name. Like a flash he hopped over to 'the General'. He wasn't a General but if Jack called him that he was sure it would flatter him and make him more eager to help.

"He's going to sort it out," the General said. "Anything else you need?"

"Got a bulletproof vest?" Jack asked.

"No," the General smiled. "But I imagine one look at you and those men out there are going to think twice about shooting you. You look as if you're already dead."

"What makes you say that?"

"Just looking at you. That isn't all your blood is it?"

"Well, I had a few disagreements on the way here. Not all of them pleasant."

"I'll bet," the General said as his second-in-command ran up behind them.

"Everything's in place, Jim. Ready when you are…" he left the sentence unfinished, he wanted to know his name. Not that it mattered of course. When all this was over he'd either be dead or riding away on his bike. They weren't about to start going down the pub together and thinking wistfully about the day they fought together behind the barricades.

"Jack," he said.

"Jack. Good luck."

"Hmmmm." Jack took the hammer and chisel from the man and stuffed them into the waistband of his jeans. In a practiced movement he took 'Weed' out of its leather sheath. The blade wasn't all that bright anymore and had a few 'chips' on its edge but that's what you get when you chop through bones. He tested the edge and gave himself a slight cut on his thumb, yes it would still be lethal enough for his purposes.

Of course he was royally screwed if they had guns. He was even more screwed if they all attacked at once. Or, if one of them even had a samurai sword. Or a spear. Nail clippers he could handle, but anything else and he might be in serious trouble.

He had to stop thinking like this. He remembered one of his phrases; paralysis by analysis. If he went on like this, he would stop himself and run away shouting 'mummy'.

He began walking a little unsteadily at first as the cars that functioned as gates parted before him. There was a terrible feeling of vulnerability as he walked past them and stepped out into the open space. He heard the cars bang together as he went on his way and the noises of feet on car bonnets and roofs behind him.

A glance over his shoulder and he saw two gunmen on top of the cars. They looked like the sort of people who really shouldn't own guns. Only in the fact that they had the look of people who would rather shoot at you rather than look at you. But maybe that was the type he needed watching his back right now. As long as they didn't hit him by mistake, he was as happy as he could be.

He also saw a little crowd of spectators behind the gunmen. For them this was better than Monday afternoon television. They were too afraid to do anything but were quite happy to watch someone die in an effort to do something for them.

Jack smiled to himself. There were people who were smart to hide and there were others who were stupid enough to poke their heads over the parapet. And he had just poked his whole body over it. For now, he had to concentrate on the job in hand.

The first chain was a good 20 yards away. He imagined it was 20 yards but he wasn't all that good on distances. In a nutshell, it was too far for a lonely walk out into no-man's land even if you had the gruesome twosome behind him watching for any flicker of movement by the roadside.

He walked with as much confidence as his leg allowed, which wasn't much. He stared straight ahead and didn't even look from side to side. If they had guns and bullets he was dead anyway. If they didn't, they would attempt to stop him when they saw what he was going to do. He also had 'Weed' in his good, left hand and Bill and Ben waiting to join the fray if it came to it.

The best he could hope for was that he could take as many of the hijackers with him as possible. Their numbers had dwindled with every car they had jacked. The strong ones had taken the first cars, these were the dregs. The followers. They weren't as assertive as their leaders and so he was at a bit more of an advantage. Not much, but enough to make them think twice when a cocky son-of-a-bitch with a kukri walked down the street looking like he had just hacked his way through a male voice choir. He didn't know why he thought of a male voice choir, he just had this amusing image of a Welsh Choir singing tunefully and beautifully and him chopping them down one by one.

He was only 10 feet from the chain now and he veered to the right hand side of the road where the chain was fastened at one end. Realisation must be starting to hit the hijackers' brains by now. They would have to make their move.

They were late. He was now standing at the chain wrapped around the lamppost. It was tied around a few times then secured with a padlock. It wasn't as formidable as the bike lock he had smashed to smithereens earlier but it was obvious it could take the roof off a car and any unsuspecting heads that were poking up at the time.

Jack put 'Weed' in between his teeth and took out the hammer and chisel. Then all hell broke loose. Two 'jackers broke cover and came at him spitting anger in his direction. A bullet from the barricades took out the first one in a messy way. Thumping into his ribs and dropping him on the spot. The second one however kept coming in his direction. Jack Dropped the hammer and chisel and took "Weed' from his teeth.

The jacker had a small blade in his right hand and was eager to put it between his ribs. Jack caught his arm with his right hand and pushed it aside twisting his back into the charge. It left him a clear path to the attacker's stomach. With some force Jack pushed it straight into soft flesh and angled the blade upwards under his ribs. If there was a heart in there his blade would find it.

He didn't see the horror and anguish in the man's face as he went limp. He removed the blade and heard the sigh of breath that escaped his lips. As he dropped the body next to his fallen comrade another 'jacker' appeared. He was probably hoping that the first two had finished the loony covered in blood but got there just in time to see their failure. He launched himself at Jack, only to be greeted by the hard metallic blade of Ben slicing across his throat. The blade cut deep across his larynx and slashed across the delicate arteries in the neck.

Jack stood back as the man tried to say something and hold his throat together. There was nothing he could do. He fell to the floor holding his throat then fell forward. A pool of blood began to form under the man's face as another shot rang out from the barricades.

Crossing the road from the left side were three more men. The middle one collapsed when his knee exploded in a flower of red, but the other two carried on. Jack greeted the first one with a punch to the belly from Ben. The man, not realising what had happened, tried to stab him with what looked like a kitchen knife. Jack caught the blade with his gloved hand and twisted the blade from the man's hand.

"Look down," Jack said. "You're dead."

The attacker did and saw the waterfall of blood that was pouring from his stomach and the ripped t-shirt he was wearing. In his shock he turned away from Jack and 'Weed' chopped across the back of his neck with ruthless efficiency. It didn't decapitate him, but there was no way he'd be head banging again.

The last of the three walked forward smiling. He was a little more sure of himself Jack thought. He was looking for weak points.

He seemed to be paying more attention to Jack's bandaged right leg than anything else.

"Want to dance?" the jacker asked as a bullet whizzed through the air missing him completely.

"I'm not a very good dancer," Jack replied waiting for the man's attack. The jacker had two blades, one in each hand and the intelligence and patience not to throw himself at the dangerous man with the big blade. Two small blades didn't equal one big mother fucker of a pig sticker. He was going to wait for Jack to lunge, throw himself off balance then play 'pincushion with Jack's stomach and chest. Or head.

"I.." he didn't finish his sentence. Jack threw the kukri straight at the 'jacker' and it embedded itself in his chest with a sound that reminded him of a butcher's cleaver slamming into a slab of meat on the block.

"Not interested," Jack said as the jacker fell backwards onto the street. It felt appropriate. He fell into a pile of bodies that had been dragged from their cars. It looked 'tidier' than falling anywhere else. It was only right that he died in the middle of his handiwork.

Jack walked over and pulled the kukri from the man's chest. He was going to wipe it on his jeans leg but remembered he'd cut the jeans' legs off. Instead he bent down and wiped the blade on the 'jackers' jeans. Then walked back to where he'd dropped the hammer and chisel.

A few hard strikes and the padlock gave way. The real strength of the chain had been in how many times it had been wrapped around the post. The padlock was just there to stop anyone unwrapping it.

Clattering to the road the chain also fell across a few wayward arms and leg and he heard a short but clearly audible cheer from his audience back at the barricades.

Checking the road he'd just walked down, the two shooters were moving up slowly behind him. They were looking in doorways behind bushes and down alleyways. When they were convinced there was no one going to jump out they moved on.

Then the gates parted and the motorcade inched its way down the road at a snail's pace. He could almost make out a few smiles in the front car. God knows how long they'd been waiting but as with any traffic jam, as soon as there's movement, there is a moment of hope as you crawl along at 2 miles an hour hoping you'll get up to 5 miles per hour, then freedom.

Jack really didn't share their hope. There was another chain a hundred yards or so, further down the road. This was the last block to the open road. If he was a 'jacker' the first chain would be where he would keep the people who were attacking and taking the cars. The rear chain would be where reinforcements were waiting.

'General Jim' had said there were about 20 and he wasn't about to call the man a liar. He looked the type to give you accurate intelligence. If all that was true, there were another 14 or more 'jackers' in hiding ready to murder them in the street.

Jack held his hand up and made a fist. He'd seen that move in the movies. He thought it was the hand signal for 'stop'. If it wasn't he was going to look foolish. If it was the hand signal for 'spray my back with bullets' he was going to look even stupider. Luckily for him the motorcade stopped.

Heading to the centre of the road again, Jack continued his confident walk. He was signalling to the jackers that he was going to do exactly the same again. Giving them the choice of 'fucking off' or fighting. And they had seen for themselves what happened to the last people who had chosen the 'fight' option.

To add a little more cockiness to his attitude he started to swing 'Weed' a little. Like he was swinging an umbrella after the nuisance of a little downpour. Gone and forgotten. But ready if there was another cloud ready to start another one.

This time, they didn't wait for him to reach the next post. The jackers had seen what had happened at the first chain. They all decided to attack at once.

From every side they seemed to pour out of the woodwork. Contrary to General Jim's estimate there were more than 14. He would have to have a word with him about that.

As the two guns started firing behind him and picking off the front ranks. Jack almost turned on his heels and ran. It's what every fibre of his body wanted to do. His mind told him that he was either going to shit himself and run or stand and fight. Jack made a decision. He put down the hammer and chisel and raised his blade.

26

Dropping in a crouch Jack swung the kukri and took out someone's leg. A short step to the side and he pulled the blade upwards across another man's chest. There was no rhyme or reason to his defensive strategy he just pulled the blade across each attacker as they came forward. He didn't raise his arm to chop or pull back to swipe, he just pulled the blade where it needed to go. When it met resistance he just pulled harder.

It was a great economy of effort. Most people tended to lift and chop but he'd watched a flick knife fight once and seen how fluid the motions were. They didn't leave themselves open to attack. Each move flowed from one to the next. Even with knives so small and lethal it was a beautiful thing to watch.

He had the advantage of reach with the kukri. Only by about six inches but it was enough to stop the majority of the gang getting close enough to use their blades. It made them hesitate, it made them think. It gave him the seconds he needed to calculate the next attack.

While the kukri swung on the left, his right knuckleduster blade did its own damage, not as much, but enough to give pause to anyone attacking his flank.

Behind him the two sharp-shooters had decided to join the hand-to-hand fight. They had left the relative safety of the barriers and walked out with knives in their hands. Their bullets had gone but they had wreaked enough havoc to remove some numbers from the opposing force.

There were wounded and dying everywhere now. Planting his feet in an empty spot on the ground he waited for the battle to come to him. The attackers would have to climb over the dead and dying to even get a chance of cutting him to ribbons but that meant watching where they put their feet. One topple and they were within the reach of his blade. Let everyone else lose their footing. He was going to stand firm and take them all. One-by-one if necessary.

One of the sharp-shooters fell with a knife sticking out of his abdomen and Jack swung his blade up and removed the arm that had delivered the blow cleanly at the elbow. There were screams and curses from every angle as he continued under this barrage of ramshackle human flesh and bone. But he cleaved through it inflicting more screams that cut through the quiet afternoon air.

The blade of his kukri was now caked with blood. Every cut he made was less lethal. There was a reason you always wiped your blade after a fight. Caked blood blunted the blade. It built up all over the keen edge. Soon it would be like trying to kill people with a rounders' bat. And in this fight he needed a one stroke kill or he would be overcome by the greater numbers of people.

His last swing barely cut the t-shirt of the next attacker. He was as surprised as Jack was and decided to keep heading forward. This was the time for Bill and Ben to take up the fight. Weed had done enough. She'd decimated their forces and now needed to rest. She needed cleaning, sharpening and maybe just a little oil to remove anything microscopic adhering to her surface. In short, she needed a spa day, with a facial to have her shining with health again.

While 'Weed' rested, Bill and Ben swung into action. They didn't quite have her 'reach' but they were more dangerous in close-quarter hand-to-hand combat. Each punch punctured flesh and scraped muscle. The inch-long blades ripped stomachs and lacerated necks and faces. Even if you didn't die from the punch, you knew you had been hit. Jack kept on punching the 'jackers' every time they came too near. At some point, he took a knife to the fleshy part of his waist and it hurt to high heaven but two retaliatory punches to his attacker's stomach almost disembowelled him.

There were more people on the floor dead and bleeding now than there were standing. Jack's stance was winning the battle. The remaining jackers would have to climb a wall of bodies just to get to him. There were only four of them now. And one of him. The second sharp shooter had fallen to a knife to the throat.

Although Jack hadn't known them he felt a sharp wave of sorrow sweep over him. They hadn't asked to join this fight. Neither had he for that matter but they lay dead and he stood living. Their sacrifice would ultimately be forgotten. They were heroes and their names and deeds would die with them.

Jack stood fists clenched with his gloves and Bill and Ben ready to take on the next attacker. But without the weight of numbers behind them the few survivors weren't all that keen to attack any more. Two of them were already visibly backing off. While the other two just dropped their knives. Defeated, they resigned themselves to their fate. They turned one by one and began to walk away, knowing that they were dead.

Jack watched them go. It was over. He relaxed and fell backwards onto a small pile of bodies behind him. Too tired to realise what he was doing he just sat on the pile of dead men as if they were a sofa on which he could rest his weary bones.

A groan escaped one of the men lying on his left and Jack forced 'Weed' through his skull with pure force. The blade was dull but there still enough point at the end to focus the force of his arm.

General Jim approached slowly from behind. He was checking the dead. The last thing they needed was someone to get up and start the battle again.

"That was one of the most amazing things, I've ever seen," the General said.

Jack was breathless. His chest was complaining at him again. And his leg. And his face. And now his waist was bleeding all over him.

"I hope you caught it on your *iPhone* camera, because I'm not going to do it again."

The General gave a chuckle that seemed out of place on this Balham battlefield. He gestured to the people in the lead cars. The doors opened and three men started dragging bodies to the side of the road so the motorcade could get through.

"And another thing," Jack said breathlessly, "you can't count."

"Sorry about that, but it was my best guess." The General offered his hand and Jack held on for dear life. He pulled himself up carefully, trying not to stand on any bodies.

"Who were they?" Jack asked nodding towards the two gunmen who had kept his back clean and then joined the fight when it was needed.

"Don't really know," the General replied. "I just know them to nod at in the street. Couple of ne'er do wells, who finally did well, I suppose."

"Brave men," Jack said. "Make sure you say a prayer for them."

"You a religious man?" the General asked. "Didn't have you pegged as a bible-basher."

"No, I'm not religious, but it can't hurt to remember a brave or good person, once in a while. If a prayer helps do it, I'm all for that."

"You're a brave man too. Should I say a prayer for you?"

"No point. The things I've done today have been pretty bad. Worse thing is, I'm not really sorry about any of them."

"Only the penitent man can enter heaven?" the General said.

"Now who's being religious?"

The General chuckled a little as the last of the bodies were being dragged off the road. Even the two 'heroes' were simply put on the pavement. The ultimate sacrifice and their bodies would be cremated in the streets of Balham.

"How did it come to this?" the General asked no one in particular. "Today will go down as a sad day in history."

"Who's going to be left to write about it? They say history is written by the winners. There are no winners, here."

"Someone will survive."

"Old story, probably an apocryphal one," Jack said. "'Nothing important happened today'."

"What do you mean by that?"

"'There's a story that when the Declaration of Independence was signed, England's King George III wrote in his diary, 'Nothing of importance happened today.'"

"Trouble is, George never even kept a diary. The real quote came from King Louis XVI of France in 1789. The French Revolution."

"What's your point?"

"Even if it's written down, even if it's passed down by word of mouth; someone's going to tell it wrong. Even what's happened here today will be lost. Misquoted. Your story, my story."

The General nodded in agreement. "But you'll remember and I'll remember surely that counts for something."

"I'm medicated. Every day is a battle with my own thoughts. Sometimes, I can't even tell what's real."

"Wow! You are messed up," the General said.

"Wouldn't have it any other way," Jack said offering his hand.

The General took it and shook it. Even though there was more blood covering Jack than ever.

"Want a lift?" the General asked as a car stopped behind him that was packed to the gills with children.

"Just need my bike and a clear road."

The General walked behind the car and took the mountain bike out of the back of the car that seemed to be overloaded with supplies. Wise considering the amount of children that were crammed into the seats. The General had indeed been fruitful and multiplied.

He walked it round to Jack, passed the handlebars over to him as though he was performing some military ceremony, then saluted him.

"Bon chance," the General said.

Jack returned the salute in a thoroughly sloppy manner and managed to deposit more blood on his forehead, if that was humanly possible.

"Good luck," Jack said and watched as the General climbed into his car and drove over the chain that had been unlocked from the second lamppost. He was leading his motorcade to safety. The cars all followed their General, there were a few smiles now that they were on the move again, but on the whole most still wore the grim mask of fatality that they weren't going to survive this day.

A few cars peeped their horns at Jack as they went by. Kids in the backs waved at him. Some looked at him with terror in their eyes. He may have just saved them, but he had done some bad things and he must have appeared like the bogeyman to them.

'If you don't behave, the man with knives for hands will come for you and snip off your nose.'

Jack thought back, wasn't that Struwelpeter or Edward Scissorhands? Looking around on the floor he found 'Weed' lying in the road. She wasn't looking well. She looked like a big red and brown stick, thick with blood. She needed that spa day he promised her.

When we get home my precious I shall lavish you with attention and praise.' He picked her up and placed her awkwardly in the leather sheath that was her home.

"Put on a few pounds lately my love."

The explosion was something he hadn't expected. Hadn't even thought about. Hadn't even guessed possible. A blast of hot air knocked him off his feet and back onto the road. He wasn't in the main blast area but the shock made his ears ring and blew his damaged body a good three feet backwards.

For a few moments he lay on the ground and checked himself. He was too tired to lift himself up. He rolled over onto his stomach and slowly moved into a kneeling position and then used his nearby bike as a climbing frame.

Turning around he looked down the road at the motorcade. The last few cars seemed fine. But the front few were ablaze. There was someone running at the side of the cars on fire while other people tried to put them out.

From the look of things there was little hope that the General had survived or his wife, or his kids. Or the kids in the second and third cars.

The flames belched out of the cars and the sky filled with a black smoke. The remaining cars turned off the road and tried other avenues of escape. Maybe they would make it if they struck out on their own. The drivers were panicking, trying to get away without any thought or plan.

'No matter what you do, they will all die. You can't save anyone.'

There was that voice again. His inner voice. No matter what he said or what he tried to believe, it never lied to him. It told him the painful truth. No, he couldn't help anyone. They were all doomed to die and he couldn't stop anything.

The fates had banded together and decided that on this day. No one was going to get out of here alive. He didn't understand. They had a fighting chance to get away, why not kill them in the firestorm? Why here? Why in front of him?

That was the real horror. They were dying in front of his eyes. If he made it home and got in his cellar he couldn't hear the screams of the dying. Couldn't feel their anguish as their lives were brought to a full-stop.

God or some other divine jester was dangling hope in front of him. For him, for everyone, then yanking it away as soon as he reached out to grasp it.

In a few minutes, the living had driven off and left the dead to burn. There was nothing they could do. They had scarpered and saved their own miserable necks. No, that was unfair. He couldn't blame them. They had a chance to live and they had taken it.

Jack walked the bike to the pavement and stood on the footpath. He began to walk up behind what was left of the motorcade. They hadn't got too far. But far enough that it took a good few minutes for him to reach the last car standing. It looked to be relatively unscathed until he got to the front. It was an incinerated mess with shards of metal ploughing massive furrows up the bonnet. The windshield was shattered too. There was blood on the front two seats. The driver and the front seat passenger hadn't been lucky at all. By the looks of it they were wounded, maybe alive, but bleeding to death in one of the other cars.

That was a story with an unhappy ending waiting to happen. If they were bleeding to death they couldn't go to a hospital. They would just exsanguinate slowly in a friend's car. And what of the kids in the back seat? They would watch as their parents died slowly, only to be left on the side of the road.

It didn't bear thinking about the sorrow that they were going to feel or were feeling now. He was telling stories in his head. None were positive.

Jack reached the front car and stared in at the flames that were licking around the roof of the car. It was only just a few minutes ago filled with supplies and people who had just been given a slender glimpse of hope.

Checking in front of the car his eyes darted around looking for the cause of the explosion. Land mine? What the fuck could have caused this? Had the 'jackers' tied another trip wire across the road?

There was glass all over the road. Not windscreen glass. This glass was too curved. It was black from being burnt. It was all around the first two cars. The third car was the one that was only wrecked at the front and that one only had a few pieces of windshield glass around the sides.

The curved glass looked like it had come from a bottle. It wasn't an explosive after all. The evidence suggested Molotov cocktails. Bottles full of petrol or other combustible solutions, lit with a cloth 'wick' then thrown at the cars.

Basically, they were crude incendiary bombs. They wouldn't have caused an explosion unless the flames had got to the petrol tank. Or what if the flames had ignited a spare petrol canister that the escapers had hidden in the backs of their cars?

Either way, big boom.

Was this retribution for the battle that had just taken place? If it was and they had seen the remaining cars split off down the back roads, they would be after them now. There was no telling how far they had got or even where they were. They had split off in too many directions to follow.

After the bridge at Balham there were more back streets, rabbit-holes and rat runs than ever before. They were gone.

All that was left was him and his lonely journey back home.

27

Balham and the bombed vehicles vanished behind him. He was back on the bike and his pedals seemed to move slower than before. It wasn't just the physical fatigue that slowed his pedal, the mental anguish was chipping away at his determination. Every incident felt like he was leaving another part of his soul behind him. Losing himself to every piece of madness that turned up on his journey.

Would there be anything left of him by the end of the day? Was this part of dying? Losing your will to live bit by bit until when the time came you were an empty shell? Something that wanted, even welcomed, the sweet release of death.

He'd seen that look in some old people before. There were some whose bodies had betrayed them. Young minds locked in bodies that didn't have the strength to take themselves to the bathroom unaided. There were others whose minds had given up on them. They didn't know where or when they were.

They had moments of lucidity but they became fewer and farther between.

Sometimes you saw an old person in good mental and physical health. Their bodies and their minds weren't as good as they were in their forties or fifties but somehow they had maintained a good outlook on life too.

Then there were the curmudgeons, miserable and twisted, nothing to live for, but living anyway just out of spite. Spreading their misery around like a bad smell. Probably one which they created themselves. They seemed to live forever. They would have the worst house in the street with the biggest garden and if your ball went onto their property they would either keep it or prang it with a garden fork.

Kids would run past after school shouting names at the closed curtains and on Hallowe'en his was the house that always got egged.

As a kid he'd done things like that. He'd regretted it as he got older and tried to imagine the curmudgeon as a human being who had thoughts and feelings. Then the old bastard would do something that got on his nerves and he'd be right back with the kids in spirit, throwing eggs, playing knock and run on the old bastard's front door, or shovelling dog poop through his letterbox.

Jack imagined that after the bombs dropped these would be the characters still left alive. The rest of the country would be burnt to a cinder except for the properties owned by the most miserable gits in the Universe. And whenever and in what direction you kicked a football it would always end up in their garden which had been left untouched. Nuclear missiles had missed but every other projectile was in their front garden ready to be stamped on or smashed with a walking-stick.

It didn't matter about radiation or lack of food either, they'd still look the same and come out in their dressing gowns, waving their wrinkled, liver-spotted fists in the air shouting profanities at the 'little bastards' and threatening to tell their parents.

He wondered if Keith Richards was like that? He was grandfather age wasn't he? Would he come out with his *Fender Telecaster*, a blunt sticking out of his mouth complaining about the kids. Or would he come out and invite them in if he had some good 'Mary-Jane' for them all to share.

Jack liked to think that 'Keef' would be the latter. Of course, he would have words of wisdom; 'Now kids, don't do the bad drugs, but these are sweeeeet.'

That was an image he smiled to himself about. Mainly because it took his mind off the faces of the kids in the back of General Jim's people carrier.

28

The road was clear again and his bike rolled slowly over the ground. He was on the move but his heart lay heavy in his chest. There was a sick feeling in his stomach and tears ran down his face. He should have been crying for himself and his situation but the tears weren't just for the kids who were dead and dying today but for what he believed.

Despite his single existence and his desperate attempts to leave humanity alone, he occasionally saw how utterly inhuman humanity had become. Beneath the trappings of society and all the talk of goodwill to all men, he knew man's savagery could never be removed completely from any situation. It would be sitting there under the surface ready to reassert itself if someone got in someone's way, someone was a different colour, or someone believed in a different God.

Living alone, Jack could lock it away. Or more accurately, lock it outdoors. Staying indoors he could believe there were places that were free of such horror. But that place had the population of 1; and he was not likely to start aggressive actions against himself in there. Or would he? There was no telling what his strange mind was capable of. His mind was a strange and wonderful animal but it wasn't quite normal. But then normal wasn't always 'good'.

He didn't understand people. Never understood their selfishness, their greed, their desire to own everything. He understood one emotion at the moment; anger. He was angry. The tears weren't really sorrow or sadness.

He realised he had taken his pills this morning. But they were only a dose that kept him functioning under normal situations. His real emotions were creeping out due to the abnormal happenings of the day. One by one he was reacquainting himself with the 'nut-job' within. So far he had been cold, distanced, measured. You wouldn't think it to look at the destruction in his wake. But he knew he could be much worse.

As a young man he suffered from the red mist; it was a family trait. He'd gone for a beer after his part-time job. Money was tight back in those days and if he wanted an education he would have to pay for it himself.

Normally he was a jovial character, footloose and fancy-free, then a pub fight had broken out and the next thing he knew he was standing in a war zone. After the fight there were people lying on the floor and two of his friends had come up and asked him how he was?

"Fine," Jack had said. "What happened?"

Ian looked at him as though he was insane. "You don't remember?"

"No, why?"

Ian told the story how they had walked in and someone who Jack knew had threatened him. Jack had simply lashed out and creamed the guy. It would have been fine but he had friends who didn't like what he had done. It turned into a full-blown stand-up, knock-down fight. Then the bouncer, a beast of a man ran over with his philosophy of 'hit the big one first'. He did. Jack had simply turned around after getting a full-on haymaker in the face and then smacked the bouncer so hard they heard his fillings clang together in Budapest.

That was red mist. That was real out of control and he had spent his life suppressing that anger. Now that civilisation was coming to an end maybe his mask of civilised behaviour should drop. Celebrate the anger within.

He wouldn't have to pretend to be interested in meetings anymore. If someone gave him stress he would give it straight back. No holds barred.

On the footpath in the distance Jack saw movement. A figure strolling down the road. From here it looked like one of the men who had left the fight at the end. He remembered that t-shirt; one of those grey *Lonsdale* ones with capped sleeves. This boy liked showing his muscles. They were a warning not to mess with him or they'd be for it.

While his friends had taken side-streets and back roads to escape, this guy had the balls to stick to the main road. Even after the explosion he had carried on in full view of the world. Maybe he was the one responsible for the Molotov Cocktail?

'That would be just perfect,' Jack thought as he stepped on the pedals with renewed vigour. He was about to get a 'piece of his mind'. The piece that was seething with rage and illogical thoughts.

The bike closed easily on the man. He was sort of jog/walking. Not walking but not running either. He was moving fast though, he had somewhere to be and was going to get there.

What surprised Jack was, he wasn't looking around. He obviously thought he was blameless in all this. He hadn't been holding up a road full of innocent people so he could car jack them and then drive away in their vehicles. Murdering them to do it. And he was walking, but hurrying down the road as if he was late for watching *'Eastenders'*.

He wasn't the only one to blame but there was a big dollop of blame sat on his doorstep. He may not have been the ring leader but he was in with them. And because of him, innocent people had died. Jack had to redress the cosmic balance. Put a few things in order. Starting with him.

He was closing, just a hundred yards or more now and he would have him. Like always he was already planning what to do. He couldn't draw the kukri and behead him as he went past, the blade was covered in human sludge and wouldn't do the necessary damage. He could ride by and hit him with 'Ben' but by the time he got close the thug would hear the tires on the road and he would be able to avoid his swinging fists easily. He could drop the bike and go after him on foot. No, his leg wasn't fit for anything that strenuous yet. In a couple of days maybe, but right now, he was better in the saddle. Jack decided his best course of action and smiled to himself. Different. He slowed down enough so that as soon as Mr *Lonsdale* saw him he could put the plan into action. If this worked it was going to be good. If it didn't he was going to look like an idiot. But seeing as how no one else was watching, it was worth a shot, or a throw, at least.

Lonsdale's head started to turn as he heard the bike approaching, there was very little background noise now. No cars came past, no noise in the distance, no trains shuffling along metal tracks, any sound travelled a lot further without being overpowered by something else.

Jack stepped off the bike letting it travel forwards as he hung onto the handlebars. His feet hit the ground and he swung the bike in an arc around his body. He let go when it was aimed directly at Lonsdale and it flew through the air like a missile.

Lonsdale was shocked to see Jack. He must have assumed he had either been blown to kingdom come or had scarpered in one of the remaining cars. He was also shocked to see the mountain bike launch itself. He had only time to turn his head to look for escape when the bike hit him in the back.

Mountain bike and Lonsdale hit the pavement together in a tangled mess. There were a brief few moments where he literally didn't know what hit him until he saw the bike sitting on top of him. Then he saw Jack limping over to him. And the colour drained from his face.

"It wasn't me," he said holding his hands up to the vengeful face that stuck itself in his field of vision.

"It wasn't you who what?" Jack asked.

"Whatever man, I didn't do nothing. I got to get home."

"So, you weren't the kid who came at me with a knife when I was fighting the rest of your buddies? Funny, I remember you were one of those who were sneaking around the sides. Hoping to stick me while I wasn't looking."

"Wasn't me, I'm just minding my own business man. I never seen you before in my life."

Jack leant over the youth and sniffed. He smelled of petrol. Reeked of it. Must have got it on him while he was filling his Molotov Cocktails. Circumstantial evidence. Wouldn't hold up in a court of law. Jack had an eye witness though. He had definitely seen him and that t-shirt at the fight. He'd run away to pick up his 'bombs'. It wasn't cowardice. He was getting his weapons.

Jack drew back his good leg and kicked the youth across the face. It didn't feel in anyway honourable to resort to such tactics but right now he didn't feel honourable.

Jack moved the bike off the youth and towered over him. He wanted to kill him but that would be over too soon. Instead, he wanted him to suffer. Leaning over Lonsdale's leg he punched just under the kneecap. Letting 'Ben's' inch long blade slip into the cartilage that held it in place.

A scream rent the air as Lonsdale clutched helplessly at his now useless knee.

"Please stop. I ain't done nothin'."

Jack's answer was to punch 'Ben' into the side of the youth's other knee and twist slightly to create more damage.

Another scream cut through the air like scissors through ribbon. The youth cried and begged holding both of his legs now. There was no way he would be able to walk properly. But then all the people in those cars wouldn't walk again and Jack clenched his teeth. There was more work to be done before he left this murderer alone. Strong young fella like him could probably walk on his hands. He could still crawl to safety.

Jack looked at the *Lonsdale* t-shirt. It was usually worn by people who followed boxing. A noble and skilful sport. But then again it also attracted a minority who liked violence. This guy probably liked hitting people weaker than him. There was nothing of the noble pugilist about him.

There was that thing about boxing, wasn't there? You punched them in the shoulders, right on the muscles up there. After a while, it weakened the shoulders and the arms, made the opponent drop their gloves so you could go for the body and the face.

Drawing back his arm, Jack mercilessly punched the blades into the muscles of Lonsdale's left shoulder and then right in a quick one-two. Then he stood back and assessed his handiwork. The youth was screaming and crying in turn.

"Please, don't kill me," he begged as the blood ran from his wounds. "Don't hurt me anymore, please."

"No," Jack said quietly. "No I won't."

Jack turned away and picked up the mountain bike. Despite being used as a missile it was still in full working order. Jack still had that note to the manufacturer he had to write. It was going to be full of praise and words like 'hardy', 'strong' and 'dependable'. In his head, Jack had already moved on. He was thinking of things he had to do next.

"You're not going to leave me here?" Lonsdale asked from his spot on the road.

Jack looked at him with cold, uncaring eyes. He didn't see a human being in distress anymore. He saw a murderer. A cold-blooded killer who burned children alive.

"Stop, please. You gotta help me."

He rode off with the screams of the young man in his ears. He didn't look back.

All these years he'd watched as bad people had done bad things and gotten away with it. Politicians, businessmen, bankers, young people beating up old people in their homes and raping them. Old people casting aside the young, throwing them on the scrapheap before they even had a chance.

For too many years he had read the newspapers, watched the television and felt powerless to do anything about it. Today was the day things were going to change. It's time for a clean slate. Wipe off all the past grievances and all the past inactivity. From now on, he would do something about it.

And no he wasn't going to sign petitions and write to his MP or go on endless marches that no one paid attention to. He was going to act. He was going to use his own moral judgement. And punish the people who did wrong. The liars, the cheats, the bullies, the thieves and the rapists.

If there was a God this nuclear war was His next flood. A flood of radiation and explosive power that would wipe the earth clean of wrongdoers so they could start again.

'That can't be right,' Jack thought. Some of the most conniving people in the world would be sitting in their bomb shelters now. Thanking their lucky stars that they'd been saved from the end of the world.

Jack felt the anger rising in his chest again. This wasn't fair. The people who controlled the fate of the world were hiding in their bunkers while everyone else had to take their chances upstairs.

If there was real justice, they would be at 'ground zero' while everyone else hid in the bunkers. There was no real courage in pushing the button if you weren't up here to face the consequences.

Lost in his own thoughts he barely saw the little girl wandering by the crashed car. She was crying with tears falling down her grimy face. A lost little girl in an empty world.

Hearing her voice Jack slowed his bike and looked up and down the road. There was no one in sight. No one alive, anyway. He was blocking out the sight of the dead bodies in the few cars that were strewn about the place.

He could ride by and forget about her. Obviously her mother or father would be looking for and… and… He couldn't do it. He jammed on the brakes and stopped right by her at the edge of the road.

It was one thing to punish the bad people but to not help the good people?! That was a crime too. He had to do the right thing. Leaving an innocent little girl alone on a deserted street was like leaving her to die. The best thing he could do was take her with him. But was it? If her family were looking for her they might be scouring the area now and if he took her, they would probably be still looking when the bombs hit.

Damn. Seeing both sides of a situation wasn't all that great. He thought about it for a little while and looked up and down the street. Nothing. And she was a little girl. She couldn't have wandered far. But if there was no one on the street they could be one of the dead people in the nearby cars.

He made a decision. If he couldn't find her family on his way, he would take her home. She would be safe there. Although he hadn't stocked up on baby food.

With the hand that meted out punishment and violence and was home to 'Bill' he tenderly picked up the little girl and sat her on the cross bar of the mountain bike. Her tears falling on what had been her white dress.

"Where's your mummy and daddy?" Jack asked as softly as he could manage.

Puzzled by a face that was dirtier than her own. The little girl stopped crying and stared up at him. She used her fingers to wipe her eyes then looked around at the landscape. She stopped crying and looked at Jack.

"Too-too-tay," she said.

Jack smiled at her little face and her dirty, white dress. He had no clue what she was saying.

"Great, hold tight to my waist, sweetheart, I'll get you to safety."

Her little dirty face looked up at him as she put her arms around his bloody shirt. Jack could tell she didn't quite know what to make of him.

"We're going for a little ride."

With one hand on the handlebars and the other supporting the little girl, he pedalled slowly. She quieted now there was someone holding her. How she trusted him Jack had no idea. Maybe it was a survival thing. When there is no one else around, trust the first adult who comes along. The burning question was what to do with her? He was fine with punching people or chopping them to bits but it had been so long since he had someone to look after, he didn't quite know the next move.

He continued his slow journey now past Tooting Bec station and looked forward to the next part. It was downhill all the way to Tooting Broadway and he could afford to give the pedalling a miss for the next few minutes.

These were the bits he loved. Every year he took a week off to get lost. He'd get his own bike off the wall in his flat, pack a bag of essentials and set off in any direction he fancied. Sometimes he would catch a train to get him to somewhere outside the M25 and start from there, but in general he headed south.

He loved this country, the little villages hidden from view the fields of crops and the strange and tangled woods that ran wild. Unsullied by human hands.

It was then that Jack applied the brakes, slowly. His little burden didn't need any sudden movements to upset her, she was upset enough. He looked back up the road to Tooting Bec Station.

"Too-Too-Tay?" Jack asked the little girl pointing to the tube station. He expected her to say 'talk like an adult for fuck's sake' but she just smiled and pointed to the station sign.

"Too-too-tay," she replied.

It had been stupidly obvious. He would have kicked himself if the saddle wasn't in the way. *Too-ting Bec Taytion'* he said to his child-like brain.

He set down the bike and held onto the girl as tenderly and firmly as he could without crushing her.

Walking back up to the tube station he pulled out 'Weed' again with his free hand. She may not be as sharp and as dangerous as she usually was, but if anyone had the idea of attacking him the sight of her would put the fear of decapitation in them.

Tooting Bec station like a few others was a problem for Jack. It had 4 entrances and exits. All on the four points of a road junction. Whenever he had left the tube here he became confused. The arrows pointed to names of roads and south and north and west and east. It was one of those stations where he could never figure out where he was supposed to go. He would ask the attendant and they would look at him as if he was mad. They would point to the appropriate sign and he would go that way, embarrassed that a fully grown man didn't know his east from his west.

Jack went into the nearest entrance that led down to the ticket hall. The lights were on and though he wasn't expecting a trap, he was ready for one. Walking into the brightly lit hall there was an underground attendant staring at him from the top of the escalator.

"Anybody lost a kid?" Jack asked the man.

He'd forgotten that he looked like shit. The little girl in the nice white dress now had smears of blood on her clean-ish clothes and had already smeared a little on her tear streaked face.

"Yes, thank God," he replied finding his voice hidden behind his tonsils. "They've been looking for her, she must have wandered off. We've been searching the platforms and the tunnels. We had no idea she managed to get up here."

"Well, here she is all's well that ends well," Jack said trying to hand the little girl to the man behind the closed barriers. She was reluctant to be handed off to someone else but with a few kind words she gave up her grip on her bloody friend.

"You should get down here yourself..." the attendant began.

"I can't, I have a place I should be," Jack replied.

The attendant simply nodded. "God speed."

"I might need it," Jack replied giving a little wave to the little girl as he backed away to the exit. He'd made a mental note of which one to head to if this went well. He didn't want to be standing at the signs again trying to figure the way out.

He turned and bounded up the stairs. He had done a good thing. He hadn't killed anyone and the little girl was safe underground where she would die of thirst or starvation. Yes, well done Jack.

He shuffled back to his bike and then let himself freewheel down the road. If this was God speed, it didn't feel very fast.

29

He rode past what was left of Tooting Market. He had freewheeled down to here but now he was back on the flat and had to pedal again. It was frustrating but he knew it was better than walking.

Looking at Tooting Market the edifice was white and classical in nature except for the shutters which were grey and filled with 'tags'. The people who had stalls in the market had obviously tried to shut it down for the coming apocalypse. They'd pulled down the metal shutters and locked them from the inside somehow, but they hadn't counted on the ingenuity of the people trying to get in. Desperation had given them 'smarts' and the viciousness to do the unthinkable.

Somehow the invaders had commandeered a 219 bus and driven it straight into the shutters. It could even have been a bus driver looking for supplies. Then they'd simply backed the damaged bus away and streamed in to grab whatever they could.

It looked as if the inhabitants of Tooting Market had put up a brave resistance. The 'brave' lay dead on the ground all around the entrance. They obviously hoped to hole up here until after the big one and live on the fruit and veg and food stalls inside.

That is until someone decided they shouldn't have all that food to themselves and should share it with everyone else. Now there were bodies all over the place. The young and the old had been battered to death in the assault and left exactly where they had fallen. It was barbaric. But that was people for you. Welcome to the human race.

He rode past keeping his eyes peeled for anyone who posed a threat. That hadn't helped him at all last time. But he had been daydreaming when he had ridden too close to the van. It was just one van surely it wouldn't matter. Well, yes it did. Now he had a flat face and some very iffy ribs.

Tooting Broadway station greeted him with its familiar facade. The gates had been broken open and he could see people still pushing and shoving to get down the stairs.

How many people were down in the tubes now? Millions? Lining the platforms? Hiding in the tunnels? More importantly, would it save them?

Hell, he didn't know if he'd survive, let alone anyone else who may be seeking refuge down the tube.

Every tube station he'd been able to look down into seemed to be full to overflowing with humanity. He couldn't speak for the tube stations in the centre of London as they would be no shelter from the power of the blast, but the ones on the outskirts were the only hope for most Londoners. He wondered how many people had actually escaped. And what had they escaped to?

Years ago he'd seen a TV series called 'Jericho'. It was a small town in the middle of nowhere and all the big cities had been nuked. It only lasted two series but they had fallen back on a rural existence and were always at war with neighbouring towns.

Tooting Broadway Station was different to the other stations he had seen. All the others had this 'come one, come all' policy. Tooting Broadway had two tube employees standing outside. Big guys. And they were carrying buckets of cash and what looked like watches. It seemed free enterprise was rife even now. What would they do with the cash afterwards though? Jack was sure the Bank of England wouldn't be promising to pay the bearer anything from now on. The currency of the future would be water and food. Paid for with bullets.

Jack rode on. Most people round here had managed to get out of London before the big crunch. The few cars that were left were probably owned by the people huddling in the tube station below. They probably thought that after the explosion they could simply climb into them and drive off safely.

Even at this distance a big chunk of central London could fly over destroying anything in its path. What people didn't consider that after the blast, Big Ben, the Houses of Parliament, the Millennium Wheel and Trafalgar Square would be nothing more than gigantic pieces of flying shrapnel, if they weren't vaporised.

If you came out of the tube to a world that hadn't been levelled by the force of the blast, it would have been seriously bombed by flying masonry.

He'd always noticed the houses they'd built after the bombings of World War II. There would be a crescent of beautiful Victorian houses and in the middle would stand four brick built abominations that just didn't fit with the surrounding architecture. Some buildings had been restored to their previous stone glory but where money was tight the bricks would come out.

Stepping on the pedals he passed the *Sainsbury's* which had more obvious signs of looting. Broken doors. Broken windows. A smattering of dropped items on the threshold. He wondered if the looters had managed to collect their Nectar points and then turned away. His mind was making light of the situation again. It should be punished.

To the right he saw the main building of St George's Hospital looming over the houses and wondered if the patients had been evacuated. What was he going to do, go and check? Why was he behaving like he had been recruited by the apocalypse police anyway? He took another dip in the road and decided to build up a good turn of speed that would take him through the traffic lights at the bottom of this hill. He wasn't going to stop if they were red - even if every one of his far too many driving lessons told him to stop.

Besides he would need it to get over the bridge that separated Tooting from home.

In the distance he saw the monolith and his heart

began to sing a little. It stood against the sky like a beacon of hope. Even if it did look horrible.

30

He was starting to panic. It seemed like everyone had reached some sort of cover now except him and here he was pedalling through the middle of Colliers Wood. Wasn't it only a few hours ago that he had walked up to the tube station and thought nothing of what the day might bring?

On the one hand he'd got a little exercise, on the other he had murdered a few people. Make no bones about it, this was not the best Monday he'd ever had. But he imagined the worst was yet to come for a lot of people.

Even here he could see people still heading down the tube. But he knew that it wouldn't amount to much in the long run. You may be down the tube safe and sound right now but what happens afterwards?

This wasn't World War II and this wasn't the blitz. There weren't any doodlebugs flying overhead and when the bombing raid was done there wouldn't be debris left. In the centre of London there probably wouldn't be much left. A few fucking big holes and a nasty case of radiation just to put the tin hat on everything.

Even if they survived the bombs what were the people going to eat and drink while they were down there? Worse still, where were all those people going to shit and piss? They might last a few days without water but that number of people sitting in their own filth was going to cause disease. And because they would be sitting in close-quarters it would be easy to transmit it from one to another. If they came out too soon the radiation would get them.

It was a hopeless situation. If they stayed down in the tube, starvation, disease, death, if they came to the top, starvation, radiation, death.

They were only delaying the inevitable.

They were all going to die. You could last a month without food. You would start to digest your own body but you would survive, sort of. But without water they would be dead within a matter of days. Some may have taken water down with them. The looted shops all around were evidence that they had grabbed a handful of supplies. But he bet there wasn't enough to go around.

What would be going on underground after a few days was anybody's guess. He'd put a wager on that there would be fighting, stealing. Hell, if things got bad maybe some cannibalism.

Was he going to be much different from these poor souls sheltering from impending doom? Well, yes he was. Truth was, he had prepared for this. He had been preparing for this for years. It wasn't as if this had suddenly appeared out of the blue. World powers had been butting heads for decades. Minor wars, skirmishes, border incursions, air space invasions...they had all been testing the strength of their future combatants resolve.

Now they had gone past the point of no return. They now had to prove they were willing to go through with the biggest mistake in human history, even if it meant their annihilation.

No one was going to lose face. Their fingers were hovering over the button. Probably some had already been pressed. Some may be even checking that all their facts are true before they even consider pushing it. Some, may even refuse to do it.

It must now be a matter of minutes.

What an irony it would be if he was obliterated now. He was so close to home. He rode up the hill to the main crossroads by the Tandem centre and coasted down the hill at the other side. He couldn't remember Colliers Wood being so quiet. The roads here were empty. Anyone who could get out by car had gone. There were a few car smashes but someone had had the foresight to roll the cars out of the road so that others could get by.

There was a thoroughfare or a gauntlet of cars all showing their rears to the centre line in a defiant yet defeated attitude. Cars of every make and model lay broken and ripped. Metal bodies torn asunder. Their windshields, headlights and tail lights, jagged open wounds.

Glass and shards of plastic were peppered across the surface of the road forming a carpet of blades for his bikes vulnerable tyres to dance across.

This road covering was the one thing that finally put paid to the tenacity of his poor bike. He felt the tyres wobble slightly under his weight, then he felt the rims of the wheels crunch across the fragments of glass.

He coasted to the bottom of the little hill before he realised that continuing this way was more work than it was worth.

"Fuck," he shouted and got off the bike. There wasn't anything he could do. He wasn't about to try and repair the puncture. It would take too long. Besides, his sanctuary was just a hop, skip and a jump away. He placed his fallen comrade gently on the ground and silently thanked 'Bessie' for her service. He had to do the final stretch without her. He started to move.

The adrenaline wouldn't allow him to walk. He was too 'excited'. He would have to run the last half mile even though he was ready to drop. The adrenaline would keep him going, though his lungs were desperately dragging in air.

Jack started to jog and then to run. His ribs hurt from the jarring his body was taking. He slowed down a little, he would have to take it carefully. The last thing he wanted to do now was fall and knock himself out. Or worse, fall and do more damage to himself that would leave him helpless on the floor.

"One. Step. At. A. Time," he encouraged himself. "One. Foot. In. Front. Of. The. Other."

It wasn't so much as a run. They used to say that walking or running was a controlled falling. This was an almost out of control falling motion that only saved itself at the last moment by a strong desire to survive. His right leg wasn't responding to the signals from his brain properly. While his left leg was doing its best to run flat out. If he carried on like this, he would be running in a circle.

This was impossible. Running was out of the question. He settled into a kind of lollop that was a cross between limp and a small jump. Ungainly as it may have looked, it got him moving again.

"Let's talk about style, later," he gasped. An old term he'd picked up from football. One of his teammates had somehow managed to feebly wobble a ball over the goal line. As they rushed back to the centre spot for the 'kick-off', Jack had gone up to him.

"Bit of a mess that one, don't you think?"

"Let's talk about style, later."

Damn, was his life flashing before his eyes? That was a great moment in his life. Did that mean he was about to witness all his other moments in a quick succession then be burnt to a crisp?

"No," he said out loud. "Not today."

He struggled onwards. Slowly the ground between him and home began to shorten. It wasn't much, but he couldn't think like that. He had to believe he would make it. After being on the bike, which ate up the miles, his limping speed just wasn't satisfying in any way.

Step by agonising step he moved and he wanted to cry, he wanted someone to help him. He wanted to sit down. He wanted to fall down. He wanted it to be over. Just sit down and let it all happen. But he had come all this way. Now was not the time to give up. Keep going.

Every bump in the ground seemed to be rising up to stop him. He scuffed the soles of his trainers on the ground every time he misjudged a step and nearly tumbled. but again he seemed to catch himself.

The trees that he passed this morning were different now. This morning they were green and the leaves rustled slightly as a gust of wind caught them.

Now they sang to him. "You won't make it. You'll die with us. Come and rest in our shade, we'll look after you. Rest here, you did your best, now it's time to rest."

Stumbling and reeling he almost took them up on the offer. Instead, he stopped for a second and took a breather. Hands on his knees he looked off into the distance.

The turn off to his road was just ahead and then it was a short distance to his flat. He almost sighed with relief. Straightening up he started to walk and stumble again.

The trees were tutting at him in the background. 'So close and yet so dead. Such a shame, I've known him for so long. Used to walk past here every day. Now deader than a doornail.'

He couldn't believe he was imagining trees were talking to him now. They'd never done that before even in his most drunken moments. Of course the only thing going through his mind back then was, 'got to get to the toilet'.

In his drinking days he would walk home from the pub. And it didn't matter if he went to the toilet before he left the pub, by this phase of the journey he was desperate to go again. If he tried to run or jog the uncomfortable feeling in his bladder would grow stronger and uncontrollable. But if he walked, he might not make it in time.

Pissing was the last thing on his mind right now. It just felt like he'd been down this road so many times and in so many different states. This one was a doozy. Half-broken and beaten with minutes or seconds before the world was blown to bits? This was a first. And a last.

Jack turned the corner triumphantly. He expected to see the gates to the flats. One of the last barriers to his salvation. He could be through that in seconds and safe. Safe from all the bad people and all the nasty bombs. Safe to rest and heal from the damage of the day. Safe to sleep. His chest sank and thoughts of sanctuary dissipated in his poor, tired mind.

"Oh come on," he cried. "Give me a break."

There in front of the gates was one of the policeman who he had knocked out. The one who had shot him at Vauxhall. The one who was now pointing a gun at him and now had a shit-eating grin plastered across his face from ear to ear.

"Good afternoon, Sir. We have reason to believe you have been involved in an altercation."

Beside him was an officer who looked far more serious. He was also much bigger and looked more determined than the previous officer who had accompanied him. He had no grin on his face. He had a gun in a holster but had not removed it. Instead he read from a small card in his hand.

"Mr Walker, you are under arrest for murder. You have the right to remain silent. If you give up that right, anything you say will be taken down in evidence and can be used against you in a court of law."

In his breathless and forlorn state, he almost said something amusing. Something that said he was bad-ass. Something to mark the moment. Then he thought better of it. 'Pistol Pete' just needed one excuse to pull the trigger and his brain cells would be flying out of his ears in a spectacular attempt to get away from the bullet crashing through his forehead.

There was no escape. He was too tired and in too much pain to do anything anymore. He leant against the wall and put his hands up. Hopefully they would take him to a prison cell nearby that could take the pounding of nuclear warheads seven? Eight? Miles away.

"How did you find me?" Jack asked quietly.

"Ever heard of CCTV?" the grinning policeman said triumphantly. Not shifting his gaze or aim for a second. "We've been following you. Even did a facial recognition search. Got your identity, your address, your taste in music, right down to your subscription for 'How it Works', everything. Everything you touch, we know about."

Truth was, Jack guessed that's what they'd done. He knew there had been a danger of that but he'd hoped against hope that there was too much going on for anyone to single him out. It wasn't just NCIS that had all that gear, even London's bobbies had all the fancy technology these days.

Why wouldn't they? With all the terrorist fears and such he wasn't surprised that they hadn't had the whole population of London tagged by now. Some sort of chip that was connected to their bank cards. That's how he'd do it.

That was another theory of his. The chip in your debit card wasn't just for security, it was for tracking you. If they could track mobile phones by where their signals 'pinged' off towers why not be able to track your Credit Card? Simple really.

"We've had our eye on you since Westminster Bridge, Walker. Nasty. Poor girl lost her arm. Died. We nearly caught you at Vauxhall but you made a few friends down there. Wouldn't let us through.

"Then there was Dr Kapur's house. Admirable work there saving his family but butchering that poor local boy. Then *Tesco's*. And Balham. You're a regular one-man army aren't you?"

"I'm just trying to get home," Jack replied.

"Murdering your way home, Mr Walker."

"They would have killed me, given the chance."

"One thing, Walker. It's against the law. Your journey is one long line of incidents that leads right back here."

"Leave it Greg, let's get him back to the station. No point in rubbing it in. We've got other things to be doing," the other officer broke in, matter of factly.

"Ok, just one more thing. I owe him a beating."

Before Jack could move or the other officer could protest, 'Greg' stepped forward and slammed the butt of his pistol across Jack's face.

Jack fell back with spots of white light exploding in his eyes. His jaw and lips were numb. Pain flared in his face again. His nose felt blocked and his teeth felt as if they crunched together and came apart in his mouth. It only exacerbated the pain he was still feeling from his spade face attack.

"Lay down on the floor!" the policeman shouted.

Jack had been hit before. Many times in fact. But never with the butt of a gun. He wasn't shocked or surprised. It was just the sort of thing he expected. If they couldn't shoot him with a gun they would hit him with it. If they couldn't punch him they would trip him. Always expect the worst and when it happens you won't be surprised.

He was back at school again, in the playground. He was being picked on because he was the smallest of his group. The big kid had just smacked him in the face and was going to do it again. We'll not this time fat boy.

Then he was back at home, his father was punching him. He'd gotten in between his mother and father while his father was in one of his rages. One of the rages that used to send him scuttling to his bedroom terrified when he was young. Then he'd grown-up. The scared young boy was gone. There was a man standing in his place and he wasn't about to go scuttling anywhere.

Jack stood up straight and faced the two policemen. Blood was dripping from the corners of his mouth and his tongue felt too big inside it. His teeth felt broken. But his face was an expression of determination again. Single mindedness. No bully was going to hit him again. And if he did he was going to get his punches in as well. 'Don't let the bully see you cry - punch the fucker in the eye'.

The officer tried to point the gun at Jack again but he couldn't, Jack was in the way. Jack put his body as close to the officer as he could without getting intimate with him. At close quarters he wasn't able to point his gun at Jack but he wasn't about to let it go.

On the other hand, Jack was in the ideal position to use his strength for a little close-quarters hand wrestling.

Jack grabbed 'Greg's' arm with one hand and grabbed the gun with the other. With two arms against his one, the officer couldn't stop Jack pointing the gun barrel at the other officer.

"No," the officer said as if he was scolding a bad puppy. "Don't let him…"

Jack kept the barrel pointed at him and then simply squeezed the officer's finger which was resting on the trigger.

The gun barked and the other officer looked at them both with a mix of surprise and shock. He had been aiming his gun at the wrestling men but had decided not to shoot. There was every chance he would hit his fellow officer. He didn't expect this. He didn't expect to be shot like this. To die from a bullet from another officer's gun.

The second officer crumpled to the floor without uttering a word. He just fell. It appeared as if he may put his hands out to stop his fall but he didn't. He fell until the ground stopped him. And then he lay still.

The policeman's hard face twisted with the horror at what he had just done. No, not him. It was his finger on the trigger, but Jack had killed his partner. Jack had guided his hand and his gun to make him a murderer. This was the devil guiding his hand to do wrong and now he understood all those sermons on Sunday. The devil made you do all the wrong things. It wasn't him. He was good. He was doing good work.

Despite the policeman's denial, Jack hadn't finished. His strength hadn't deserted him. He had found more determination. He had one last job. And he wasn't going to let anything stop him. Jack bent the man's gun arm at the elbow and then forced the gun to officer's chest. His gun hand was now lost to him completely. It belonged to the murderer. He tried to beat the back of Jack's head with his fist but each blow accomplished nothing. He tried to prise his body away from him, turn him so he could regain control of his hand and his gun but nothing would move him. The officer felt the heat of the recently fired gun under his chin.

"Don't," the police officer said, more of an order than a request for mercy. He stared defiantly straight into Jack's eyes and tried to wrestle the gun away from his face again. But one hand on the gun wasn't enough, his other hand beat again on Jack's back. He tried to push Jack away again, tried to use his feet to drag Jack's legs from under him but there was nothing he could do to shift the unmoving weight that had control of him.

The gun barked again and the police officer that was 'Greg' became a dead weight in his arms. He let him fall to the floor and stood back. He felt weak again. He hadn't wanted to kill them, but somehow his survival instinct had kicked in again. Adrenaline and 'red mist' - a lethal combination.

"I was going to surrender, you moron," Jack cried. "You'd still be alive if you hadn't done that," he shouted at the corpse on the floor. Why he was shouting at something that was unable to hear anymore, he didn't know. He just felt better doing it. Trying to reason with dead men was up there with flogging a dead horse.

Jack started to cry. He wasn't sure if it was exhaustion, pain or sorrow, he just needed to cry for a moment. Just a moment. The officers deserved his tears for a second or two.

Jack sniffed back the mucus that was collecting in his nose. He was going to wipe his eyes with his arm but there didn't appear to be a patch of arm that was free of blood now. Even his leg which was white in Balham was splattered with blood and gore. He needed a shower. He wondered if the water was still on.

From where he was standing he heard the radio before he saw it. That unmistakeable squawk that said there were other officers somewhere, whiskey, tango, foxtrotting.

Looking around he saw the police phone on the floor by the other constable. He'd been phoning in the capture while Pistol Pete was whipping him with the gun. It was on and someone was talking. What had they been talking about when the gun went off twice he didn't know, but if they had heard the shots they would be on their way. This didn't really bode well for him. He hop/crawled over to the device and put his bloodied ear to the device. It was a crackly mess but he could still manage to un-mangle the words.

"...no response. Gunshots fired. Officers are not responding. Converge on suspect's house. Repeat, officers may be in need of assistance.'

Jack threw down the phone like it was red hot and looked to the security gate. It would take them a few minutes to get through that. Then, the door, then the inside door. It may be enough time.

He tapped the code into the gate. It chirruped at him and he fell against it. It opened and he almost fell to the floor. Blood was dripping from his bullet wound again, his fight must have reopened the gash in his leg. He staggered slowly to the door of the flats and opened it. He was inside but he didn't go up the stairs to his flat and his rosewood neck guitars.

The place where he lived was on the second floor, or so he would have everyone believe. But that was a front. Where his mail arrived. Where everyone believed he lived. But that wasn't where he intended to spend the last minutes of his previous life.

A nuclear blast would destroy everything above ground level. Every stick of wood, every brick building would be destroyed, blown to bits. That wasn't going to be his fate.

He unlocked the mortice lock on the ground floor flat and pushed the door open. He was ready to drop. Ready to give in. Every muscle ached and screamed at him. His breath clung to his lungs. His face felt white and bloodless but he wouldn't stop.

Drawing the dead bolts across the door he stepped into the lead lined box that was flat 2. Then turned another handle and a loud 'clunk' secured the door completely.

All this had started with his apocalypse pack and sort of gotten out of hand from there. Yes, he had the apocalypse pack for the fight, but what about the bombs?

In the days of 'buy to let' he had bought the downstairs flat when it had gone on the market. For a London flat it was cheap - just like his flat on the second floor.

The difference was the second floor flat had a loft. The ground floor flat had a basement. One that he could 'modify' in secret.

He'd applied his 'apocalypse thinking' to a series of 'What ifs?'

What if there was a nuclear war? What if there was no water and electricity? What if there was no food? What if there was radiation? What if the air was poisonous? What if he had to stay underground for a year? What if someone tried to get in? What if they did get in? What if, what if?

He'd listened to all his own questions and over the years built his own private shelter with a metal hatch on top. Truth was, it wasn't all that little. He'd built a living space, for one. With everything he needed to survive.

He'd also had the foresight to booby-trap his little atrium. The flat was an unwelcome little place as it was, but if someone did manage to get in he wanted to make sure they didn't get out. The first wave of attackers would serve as a deadly example to anyone else who tried the same stupid manoeuvre.

For this he'd set up a series of explosive charges attached to a series of switches down in his bunker. Four separate explosive charges in the four corners of the room. If he blew them all at once it could destroy the floor and destroy the hatch - allowing him to escape if the building fell on his doorway. Blow them one at a time and he could wipe out anyone trying to get in.

For the moment, he had to concentrate on getting into his little bunker first. The switches were under the rug and through the hatch. If anyone got a bullet into him now, his defences meant nothing. He threw aside the rug and dropped to his knees before the big metal hatch. He slung it open and eased his broken body into the dark narrow space, his tired feet trying to catch the top rung of the ladder he knew was down there somewhere. It wasn't as easy as it had been on all the other times he'd lowered himself down. His body wasn't really up to obeying all his orders. Fatigue was telling him he really needed to have a rest now, please.

His feet refused to step on the ladder properly. It was as if they weren't his legs anymore but belonged to a young baby refusing to get into its romper suit. It took precious seconds to get his head below ground level and then he had to persuade his arm to reach up and pull the hatch back down.

After several weak attempts the hatch dropped and clanged shut. He turned the lever which locked it shut with a great amount of difficulty then dropped the six feet to the floor of his hidey-hole.

As he landed he felt his ankle give way and he tumbled to the floor.

"Come on!' he yelled. "Is there any part of my body you're going to leave working?"

He didn't know who he was shouting at but obviously they weren't paying attention, his ankle began to throb painfully.

Finally, he was safe, or so he thought. He nearly said 'safe as houses' to himself but then stopped. No houses were safe anymore. His bunker was safer than houses but was it safe enough for the cataclysm that was approaching?

He heard people shouting outside. Trying to force the door of the flat open. But there was no way they would get in there without a battering ram. There weren't just deadbolts on there. The lock of the door operated sliding metal slats that fitted neatly into a metal frame built into the wall.

They would have to take the wall down to get in that way. Then he heard something hit the front window of the flat. "No, not that way either, bullet-resistant glass in a metal frame, built into the wall."

Even if they did get through the window, or the door, all they would find was a hatch that wouldn't look out of place on a submarine and was even more secure than the windows and doors.

Not all of Jack's precautions would survive the coming blast but they would certainly delay a few interlopers with sledgehammers and a couple of hours to spare.

If they had a tank they could easily blast through his line of defences but they didn't. They may have one of those little battering rams to get through the flat door but even that would take time. Time that the world had just sadly run out of.

There was a strange sound. One he had never heard before. It was the sound of a 'wipe', a wave of something. And then silence. It was like he'd gone deaf but he could still hear his own breathing. He crawled quickly from the entry passageway into the main bunker and pushed the heavy metal door closed with his good foot. Even down here he felt the sudden heat permeating the earth around his bunker.

Barely able to reach the door handle from his position on the floor, he closed it as best he could. This was his main fortified room. The passageway wasn't as strong. He'd built it to collapse in a certain way should he need to escape in a hurry, or the hatch had been fused shut. Another 'What if…?'

From upstairs, the passageway was virtually impenetrable unless you had the aforesaid sledgehammers and time. But from down here he could pull a few supporting lintels out of place and the whole thing could fall apart like jenga. Hopefully not crushing him in the process.

The silence was now amazing. When he'd built the place he hadn't sound-proofed it. Another job on his 'to do' list. He could always hear the thunder of traffic from outside. Now something far more ominous was happening.

It started as a tremor. A distant shaking like a truck approaching on the road but it grew louder. It seemed to be coming from everywhere. At first he thought it was just one roll of thunder, but more joined the sound. Like an orchestra beginning to tune up. A cacophony of cataclysm.

His 'What ifs...?' hadn't prepared him for this. It was like the planet was being ripped out of its orbit by a giant hand and shaken like a rattle. This wasn't the sound of beads rolling around in plastic. This was the sound of thunderclaps being slammed together. He covered his ears as dust from the reinforced concrete exploded from newly formed cracks as the earth shifted.

Was he about to be buried alive in the very thing he thought would protect him? Fear had fixed him to floor as if he had been bolted there. If he could move there was nowhere to go. The panic which usually drove him to action, held him down and wouldn't allow him to move.

The sounds and shaking began to taper off a little, then a little more. He could physically hear the sounds receding into the distance. The wave that carried phenomenal destructive power had come and gone. Carrying on with its destruction elsewhere. But what had it left in its wake?

It sure wasn't going to be Disneyland out there.

When he realised it was safe to move. He did. And every single injury reminded him that moving was for people who hadn't spent their last few hours getting hit, shot, tripped and pistol-whipped.

The dark of his hidey-hole really wasn't much of a comfort, either. In fact, it was pitch dark. There could be monsters hiding down here.

"It would help if you turn the lights on, moron," he said to himself and heard the voice bounce off the concrete walls.

His own voice somehow felt unusual to him. His throat was sore. Had he been screaming? Attempting to stand, his ankle reminded him that it wasn't one of his best ideas especially since his gun-shot wound was moaning at him for putting too much weight on his right leg again. His ankle was all kinds of a mess but his other held him up long enough so his hands could find the makeshift light switch.

It wasn't easy. It was a switch on a sort of lamp that was attached by a hook to the wall. Every time he swished his arms to grab the switch, the lamp shifted so he lost it. Finally, he grabbed the damn thing with both hands.

He could barely hear the click as the lights flared into life and then the whole bunker lit up. He looked around at what would be his home for the next month or so.

"Hi Honey, I'm home," he shouted.

"Good day at the office, dear?" he asked himself in a high falsetto.

"Oh the usual," he replied. "Client misbehaving, nuclear apocalypse. You know?"

He fell exhausted to his knees. The adrenaline smashing through his veins had really done a number on him. Every trial had pushed him to the limit and now it had stopped, the adrenaline had gone leaving him a shambles of a human being.

He bent over and placed his bloody gloves on the ground. Breathing hard and staring at the floor he lowered his pain wracked body slowly to the dusty floor as if he was about to do a press-up. Feeling the cool hardness of the concrete on his hot flesh he sighed. It felt good. So good. No more pedalling. No more running. And especially no more hacking people to bits just because they were in his way.

The downside of it all was that there may not be anymore 'upstairs' either. He heard the Geiger-Muller tube in the hatchway entrance clicking like crazy even through the metal door. Thankfully, the tube in here was clicking at a steady safe rate. No danger. He'd done it. He could go to sleep.

The last thing he thought before he closed his eyes was, *'Damn, I left my alarm clock upstairs.'*